MEANDER

Wooing Ms. Maudie

For Tom & Joan Buell —
Friends from long ago wonderfully
renewed.

   With affection and great admiration
for their gifts and tireless determination
to make the world a better place.

Blayney Colmore

July 2010

A Novel

Blayney Colmore

Library of Congress Control Number:		2010908924
ISBN:	Hardcover	978-1-4535-2368-1
	Softcover	978-1-4535-2367-4
	Ebook	978-1-4535-2369-8

This book was printed in the United States of America.

To order additional copies of this book, contact:
Xlibris Corporation
1-888-795-4274
www.Xlibris.com
Orders@Xlibris.com
82873

MEANDER

CONTENTS

For Richard and Mo Davy who took us in as if we were kin and taught us that we *are* kin—to each other and to our mother earth.

PREFACE

In 1984 my wife and I and two of our five children spent 7 months in Chiredzi, Zimbabwe. Our other three children joined us for the final two months. I had been given a sabbatical after a decade as rector of an Episcopal parish in suburban Boston. The Diocese of Massachusetts had a companion relationship with three Anglican dioceses in Zimbabwe.

I had an experience akin to the old circuit riders, driving through remote bush to Anglican congregations—African and European—gathered in small groups in huts and colonial houses scattered over a vast area.

We lived in Chiredzi, a town in the southeastern Lowveld of the country, a hot, arid region inhabited almost solely by wild game until a river was dammed to the north and water diverted for growing sugar cane. Before the collapse of Zimbabwe's economy after 2000 the Lowveld was a busy farming and commercial region of some 10,000 people. It was no one's homeland and the people were a mix of tribes and nationalities.

As it does so many white westerners, Africa got under our skin and remains there. Our children have been back. We still count some of those we knew there among our dearest friends.

Richard and Mo Davy—who took us into their lives as if we were family—have visited us several times in the States. Richard is a doctor who ran a clinic caring for most of the Lowveld. He delivered babies, treated myriad cases of malaria, did brain surgery sometimes on a kitchen table. Mo is a nurse with the dazzling omni-competence found only in the remote places remaining in the world. They became our guides, our friends, mentors.

As I write this I have just read an email from Mo saying that Richard's cancer seems to be spreading.

It is tempting to be angry or despairing that Richard Davy has cancer. But if I learned anything from Richard and Mo it is that we are not in charge and we need not be in charge. Because God (reality)—no matter what it may serve up—is utterly trustworthy. I often wondered how they could meet some of the challenges of living close to the bush in a profoundly dysfunctional country with such humor and optimism. Now that I have had more opportunity to experience nearly equal dysfunction in my own country, my admiration for their Zen attitude has grown even greater.

Though the novel contains a few historical characters, it is a book of fiction, entirely my fancy. My two remarkably skilled sister-editors gave themselves to the task of cleaning up my sloppiness with diligence and love. Without them whatever messes you may find would have been infinitely worse. And you would be enduring another 10,000 superfluous commas.

My long suffering wife Lacey deserves a medal for enduring my multi-year obsession with this book.

It may be that our species will turn out to have been a brief experiment in the history of our planet. To have spent time where our kind is thought to have first emerged is to have gained a glimpse of what it must have been like—and what it just might be again—when we understood ourselves as a part of and partner to our mother earth.

Lacey is never happier than when she is up to her elbows in dirt, enduring black flies as she plants vegetables around our place in rural Vermont. Despite having grown up in the sophistication of Fairfield, Connecticut, she never seemed more at home and in her element than in Chiredzi, Zimbabwe.

I had an international, but more urban, upbringing. Thanks to Lacey and those months in Zimbabwe—and now in Vermont—I have been introduced to the earthy parts of my being.

The novel's title, **Meander** refers to the rivers in Zimbabwe that flood and dry up with the changing seasons. They determine when one can travel where. We got our old Peugeot wagon mired in a few. And like the lives of Maudie and Oscar they meander, cutting new channels in unexpected places that require major changes in the plans of people near them.

Fascinated by how the shrinking of the planet is making so many old assumptions obsolete—in gender, race, nationality, commerce, politics—I have tried weaving some of those changes into a story set in Zimbabwe. You can decide whether it stretches imagination too far.

I confess I have fallen in love with Oscar and Maudie and their story. I hope you might also. Let me know: *blayneyc@earthlink.net*. And I keep a blog at *www.bloglayney.blogspot.com*.

PHILADELPHIA. MAY 21ˢᵀ, 2022

By the authority vested in me . . . Oscar's mind wandered as the Dean's mesmerizing voice droned on, granting MBA's to Oscar and the other 836 people who had come to the Wharton School of Business and Finance at the University of Pennsylvania a year ago last September, and survived the hazing that he'd found business school mostly about. He looked around for Maudie. Two years ago he didn't know there was a Maudie. Nor could he have found Zimbabwe on a map. Less than two years since that day in Dr. Rubenstein's class when Oscar slumped low in his chair, praying—along with every other student in the lecture hall—he wouldn't get called on.

Mr. Anderson!

Oscar's face turned red as Professor Rubenstein looked up from his seating chart. Rubenstein smiled. [*How different these eager kids look from their pictures in the view book.*] All eyes turned toward Oscar as the professor asked the first question of their MBA career in a newly introduced course, International E-Marketing. It was about an equation Oscar had wrestled with for most of the previous sleepless night. He had found it impenetrable.

Mr. Anderson, would you be kind enough to explain to us the working pieces of the equation that quantifies the relationship between frequency of hits on an internet site and expected advertising revenues?

[*How the hell,*] Oscar wondered, [*if I can't understand the first equation in the first course, can I hope to slog my way through this miserable school?*]

Oscar jerked his 6'5" frame upright in his chair to what he hoped might seem a more dignified position. He wished he hadn't worn his stained Exeter Academy tee shirt and torn jeans. Even more—at this sweaty moment—he wished he hadn't been so arrogant, thinking he could easily jump from Late 18th Century Transcendental Poets as a Harvard undergrad into the flesh-eating world of The Wharton School of Business and Finance.

* * *

OSCAR'S BOOK

Oscar, his father had asked him, *are you sure you really want to inject yourself into that take-no-prisoners, bottom-line world? It's not much like what you've been doing up to now. Seems like you ought to have a mighty good reason to pass up a Fulbright.*

Twenty-two-year old Oscar Anderson had been going to school, writing papers, bullshitting with friends, whatever came up. None of it offered him useful clues. [*What I've been doing? I have no idea what I've been doing up until now.*] Seemingly his father, whose question sounded more than a little insulting, did. For just a moment Oscar thought about asking what exactly it was. The problem, of course, was that his father's opinions—he always had one—though well meaning, were usually not to be trusted. Still, it unnerved him to think his father might know him better than he knew himself.

I know it's not exactly what you meant, Dad, but you've put your finger precisely on why I want to do this. I've spent my whole life thinking your thoughts. I'm a bleeding heart, liberal-arts junkie, just like you. I could spend my life vaguely pissed that more than half the people in the world have been left to suck hind teat. I've always admired the way you speak up for the underdog. But I'd like to do more than just be on their side. I'd like to try actually learning a practical skill that might give me a shot at somehow being a part of their climbing a couple of rungs up the ladder. Maybe it's a pipe dream, but I don't think I can live with myself if I don't at least give it a try.

Oscar hoped his father didn't take that as a rebuke. He didn't mean it to be. He loved his idealistic clergyman father. And he respected him more than any other man he knew. But he didn't have the kind of faith—if that's what it was—that simply caring and trusting in God's love ever actually moved the world closer to the economic justice that so often was the focus of dinner conversation at their family table.

* * *

Professor Rubenstein—Oscar found his voice, but only for an embarrassing squeak—*I couldn't make heads nor tails of the equation.* A deflating moment for Oscar, Summa cum Laude, Phi Beta Kappa, darling of the Harvard English Department. He'd turned down a Fulbright at Oxford to come to Wharton. He wasn't used to facing defeat in the classroom.

Mr. Anderson—Oscar heard scorn in Rubenstein's voice: [*My business school career might end right here*]—*you have a great future in business. Truth is, no one understands that equation, but most students would pretend to. Most CEOs pretend they do. The first rule of good management is to admit, without apology, when you don't know. Bankruptcy court is cluttered with the ruins of pin-striped poseurs who have tried to bluff their way out of owning up to not knowing something. First rule of good management: you don't have to know everything. And when you don't, admit it.*

It took a moment for Oscar to realize he was being praised. He didn't hear the nervous laughter around the lecture hall. A drop of sweat rolled down his cheek and onto his laptop, still waiting for his first keystroke.

From across the room Maudie Mugabe took no pleasure in watching Oscar fidget. She was relieved that Rubenstein hadn't called on her. She had thought she understood the equation and would probably have confidently ventured an answer. After a year at The London School of Economics she felt ahead of the game at Wharton. Now she worried that her confidence might not be justified. Maudie's mind drifted back to the argument she and her father, President of Zimbabwe, had when she spoke to him about leaving London for Philadelphia and Wharton.

* * *

Maudie's Book

Zimbabwe is a socialist country, Maudie, her father had insisted, *and I am a committed Marxist. All that American nonsense about a free-market economy is merely cover for their guilty conscience for plundering the world. I'm afraid it could poison your mind, ruin your for the crucial role in our nation for which I have been preparing you.*

Father, anyone who intends to play a role in global affairs in the next 20 years is going to have to become intimate with cyber space and e-commerce, no matter what their political or economic philosophy. And for the moment the United States is where you go for that. I can learn what I need from them without getting contaminated by their eccentric economic beliefs. Besides, my mother would have been thrilled to know that I was going to spend time in the States. She may have disagreed with their politics, but she loved the people, and she loved visiting, especially Philadelphia. You know, the city slogan is "Cradle of Liberty."

Her father's eyes rolled to the sky.

Your mother, rest her soul, tough and smart as she was, was a dreamer, and a shopper. She loved Philadelphia because her favorite personal shopper was at Wannamaker's Department Store. She was not preparing to run a struggling socialist country. You are.

Maudie bristled but kept silent. She hadn't missed that he'd left God off of *rest her soul.* Maudie didn't believe in God. She was pretty sure her father didn't either, but she knew he would never have left God out of that liturgical formula when her mother was still alive. In these moments when she sensed the waning of her mother's softening influence on him she missed her terribly. Her father had an earned degree from the London School of Economics, honorary degrees from countless universities around the world. He had fought as a guerilla liberator in the bush against Ian Smith's white regime, and spent many years in their prisons. To Maudie he was a hero, brilliant, fascinating, compelling. She adored him equally as much as she admired him. And he was also Shona, a son of Africa, and his arrogance and chauvinism sometimes galled his daughter, as she knew it had her mother.

Maudie had learned from watching her mother negotiate with her father that it worked better not to openly challenge his prejudices. In many ways her mother, who was half Swedish, half African Shona, was a more subtle and effective politician than her father. She had done the unthinkable—introducing feminism to a traditional African culture. She sponsored family spacing (birth control) clinics, legal rights for wives in domestic disputes, and she persuaded her husband to support universal education for girls as well as boys. Because of the respect she enjoyed among progressive women around the world, the once-a-decade international women's meeting had been held in Harare two years before she died.

*   *   *

FIRST (AND LAST) ASSESSMENT FROM A DISTANCE

Maudie studied this fresh-faced American boy who had just admitted in front of the entire first year class that he didn't understand the formula in the first night's reading. [*I would never have admitted that.*] She wondered, was it naïveté or arrogance, this boyish American owning up to his ignorance, seemingly without shame? She knew for certain that if she, an African woman, had admitted that she didn't understand, she would have confirmed the prejudices of everyone in the room.

She looked him over: [*My, he is very attractive. Even in those sloppy American college-boy clothes, even with a complexion that looks like he lives under a rock, he's quite an elegant man.*]

Maudie understood that Oscar's Exeter Academy tee shirt was a clue to the source of his courage. It made Maudie uneasy that, just looking at the photos in the online view book before classes began she found herself drawn to some subtle sophisticated look she picked out in a few, whom she would learn were "preppies." Her father was right, American claims to being an egalitarian society were more propaganda than reality.

Maudie had a royal bearing. At 5'8", she was a head taller than most Shona women. Her tan complexion was a passport to places of power in Africa. This racial privilege offended her, strengthened her determination to use her access for improving life for Africans of every hue. But she couldn't pretend that she didn't enjoy its benefits. She knew she was beautiful, her father had told her so all her life. Men of every race and nationality behaved self-consciously, around her. Her deep brown eyes were deep-set above high, polished cheekbones. Her jet-black, closely cropped, Afro hair accentuated her sharp features. She had about her an air of intensity she had discovered intimidated men. Her loose, casual, American style clothes didn't conceal the graceful curves of her body. Nor her strong, shapely legs.

Despite her sophistication, Maudie could assume the traditional Shona woman's role her mother had when it suited the moment. Comfortable exercising her keen intellect, among African men she often remained in the background, not challenging traditional male primacy. Her father was elected President of Zimbabwe before she was born. Growing up in the presidential palace (once the residence of the Rhodesian Prime Minister) with access to international travel and shopping, Maudie was a member of the international power elite. She shared her mother's love for beautiful clothes and fine things, enjoyed dressing in high style for formal events, watching heads turn as she entered a room. Despite embracing the perks of money and power, Maudie never fully made peace with the contrast between her family's lavish life and the poverty of most Zimbabweans.

Her fellow Wharton students nor American business leaders she met seemed to Maudie much concerned about economic inequality. But in addition to becoming conversant with fast changing cyber markets, Maudie hoped perhaps this American university in Philadelphia, where Americans first met to throw off the yoke of servitude, might provide some practical tools for empowering her fellow Zimbabweans—particularly women.

Maudie lost the thread of Professor Rubenstein's lecture as she stared across the room at the pale preppie who had just openly displayed his ignorance. The first, but hardly the last, intrusion into the careful plans she had made for these two years at Wharton.

Maudie would have scoffed at the suggestion that she and Oscar came to Wharton with similar motives. And Oscar would have found it mortifying that a bright, beautiful African woman could so dazzle him that it might divert him from the dedication to justice he was determined would shape his life. Neither of them could imagine how the two years would weave their contrasting histories into a single complex fabric,. Or that by the graduation they would have so thoroughly altered the fabric of each other's futures.

* * *

An Inauspicious Start.
September 9, 2020

Hi, I'm Oscar.

Maudie hadn't seen him standing behind her in the cafeteria lunch line.

Maudie, she responded, ignoring his outstretched hand. [*Americans think surnames are superfluous, if not pretentious.*] When she'd watched him slouching in his seat in the lecture hall she had no idea he was so tall. In Africa, at least among the Shona, she was used to looking men straight in the eye; more often they had to look up to her. Only the Ndebele, the Shona's tribal rival, were tall enough to look down at her. Her height had proved useful in power relationships and, appealing as she thought he was, Maudie didn't like giving away nearly nine inches to this baby-face Anglo. And she feared he'd probably caught her staring at him earlier.

Nice to meet you, Maudie, he replied cheerfully, reaching down and grasping her hand, despite her not having offered it, pumping it vigorously. [*This is why I promised myself I'd never get involved with an American man. Their comical enthusiasm, endless adolescence.*] In Africa his dress would have marked him as a day laborer, perhaps a field worker, certainly no MBA candidate at a world-class business school. Maudie had learned to dress down like young people the world over, but she never forgot that she represented emerging African womanhood and that she was being groomed for the highest places in her nation's government. Her khaki trousers and denim shirt from Nordstrom resembled what most in the class wore, although decidedly more upscale. Her hand-tooled Italian loafers had belonged to her mother. She wore them as a way to keep alive her connection to her mother whom she had adored, and because she thought they were classy, ageless.

It took a lot of courage to admit that you didn't understand that equation. Years of diplomatic receptions had taught Maudie the art of putting strangers quickly at ease, making them feel special. She was 15 when her mother died and she became her father's official hostess.

Oh, you're in that class, too? Maudie was sure he'd noticed her, men always noticed her. *Well the truth is,* Oscar continued, his voice rising excitedly, *that I'd sat and stared at that frigging equation for two hours last night, determined to figure it out, and I never did. For some reason it jumped off the page and became the symbol for my coming to Wharton, as if I had to be able to understand it or I could kiss off the next two years. So I thought I may as well own up to it, face the music right off. I thought I might be on my way out of here by this afternoon.*

I see. Maudie was nonplussed by his confession, this outpouring of unsolicited information from a stranger. She wondered what it was going to be like to spend two years with these American men, overgrown boys wearing their hearts on their sleeves. *Well it certainly turned out well for you. Rubenstein made you look like Bill Gates.*

I'm intrigued by your accent, Maudie. I'm trying to make out where you're from, Oscar said, deflecting what he wasn't sure was making fun of, or complimenting him. He often spent his best energy scrambling to claim some smidge of dignity. *I hear some, maybe, Africa, and some Europe, and, of course, a little American TV, in your accent. I guess everyone on earth has some of that these days. But I must say, the way you speak is much more pleasing to the ear than you usually hear anywhere these days.* Maudie made herself another mental note about what might be required to adjust to this drop-all-barriers culture. [*We haven't even gotten our soup, and this guy's coming on to me.*] She felt cautious. Was this subtle American racism? Was he toying with her? She decided to play it straight.

I was born in Zimbabwe and have lived there my whole life. Maudie was annoyed at his suggestion that she had TV-American in her accent, though she supposed she probably did. She was determined not to respond to whatever foxy agenda she suspected Oscar was laying out for her. *I went to school in Switzerland for what you people call high school, then did a degree at Oxford, and spent a year at the London School of Economics.*

Wow! Oscar exclaimed. [*I'm quite certain I've never heard an adult African—or European man—say "wow".*] Maudie thought. *I guess I've been living with too many antiquated stereotypes of African women. Like they don't usually do Oxford degrees, or the London School of Economics. Apologies for what I know must be my ignorance, but am I right that you're pretty unusual? London School of Economics and everything?*

This was all moving way too fast for Maudie. Either this guy was a hopeless chauvinist and racist, or he was the most out-in-the-open, up-front person she'd ever met. Determined to retake the initiative, she responded with a loaded question of her own.

You ever hear of Sally Mugabe?

Oscar didn't appear as uncomfortable with the question as Maudie had hoped. She'd meant to put him off balance, slow him down, but he seemed to be studying her question as earnestly as he had the equation in Professor Rubenstein's assignment, and, she hoped with no greater success. She couldn't have known that Oscar's father was a player in international politics, and his mother an active feminist, and they followed with particular interest the role of women in the developing world.

Sally Mugabe, he repeated, looking thoughtfully into space, *I know that name. Isn't she a big African feminist? Maybe convened some international women's conference in your country? Wasn't she married to the President? And didn't she die a few years ago?*

Now Maudie who was off balance, unprepared for the emotional tidal wave his unexpected response triggered, sweeping over her. She felt her eyes fill. She was grateful her swarthy complexion largely hid the rush of blood to her face. She was proud of her African upbringing that taught her the discipline to control her emotions.

She was my mother.

Maudie saw she had finally stunned him into silence. The effort cost her every ounce of energy she had stored up to navigate her way through her first day in this strange new place. She was drained, feeling vulnerable, and despite tight rein on her feelings, she worried he could see through to her emotional exhaustion.

Oh God, I'm so sorry, Maudie. I had no idea. I really didn't mean to pry. I'm so rude sometimes, so thoughtless, and I really don't mean to be. God, I'm such a klutz.

Maudie felt caught between compassion for this curious man's sensitivity and fury that she might now be obligated to set aside her own emotional burden and tend to his embarrassment. His unguarded air, his empathy—evoking old grief with an intensity she wanted to believe she was finished with—made her want to fall into his arms. She was once again glad for Shona discipline, keeping her impulses in check.

It's perfectly all right, she said coldly. They both knew it wasn't. *You had no way of knowing. Everyone came here with a story of their own.* She wasn't about to ask him for his. [*If I ask him for his story, there goes the rest of my energy, and the afternoon.*]

I've really got to run, she said, *Nice chatting with you, but I've got an appointment with the Director of Housing just now.*

But what about your lunch? Oscar asked. *You've got to eat. Would you like me to save you something so you could eat it later. I could bring it to you at the library?*

That's kind of you, Maudie answered, *but I really don't have much of an appetite.* Another unwelcome, unguarded moment for Maudie, increasing her discomfort, making her feel even more vulnerable. She was aware of his eyes on her back as she hurried off, with strengthened resolve not to get enmeshed with any of these over-eager American men. She'd met many American men, but none who had set off her caution alarm with the upsetting intensity this one just had. She'd thought she'd be much tougher when she came up against what her friends in Switzerland called "American disarmament". *Watch those guys*, they warned her, *they're so charming. Just when you decide they're for real, you'll find them in your pants. They're dangerous, randy boys. And sneaky.*

[*Not what I came here to do*], Maudie thought as she hurried away. [*There's a struggling country back there, desperate for fresh leadership. It'd be a betrayal to let one of these American airheads knock me off course. You're going to keep your guard up for two solid years. You hear me, Maudie Mugabe?*] Her heart raced, her head swam. She hoped all that discipline drummed into her by her parents, and her Shona genes, were up to this. [*For an Anglo, he's one beautiful man! Discipline, Maudie. You're just over—tired.*]

As he stood watching Maudie disappear around the corner, Oscar sensed a seismic shift in the picture he painted himself of the two years at Wharton.

* * *

MAY 21, 2022

COMMENCEMENT COMMENCES

By the authority vested in me by the president and trustees of the University of Pennsylvania, I confer on you all the rights and privileges pursuant to the Degree of Master in Business Administration.

Oscar finally spotted Maudie several rows behind him on the opposite side of the aisle. He tried to catch her eye but she seemed to be concentrating on the Dean's words. Oscar fantasized about where the two of them might be a year from now, doing what. Maudie had remained steadfast in her determination to focus on her vocation. Until recent events rearranged Oscar's plans, neither dreamed that graduation wouldn't mark the end of their relationship. Oscar had finally reconciled himself to letting go of his dreams of spending his life with Maudie. He knew her better than to expect her to weaken, but things were unfolding in pretty fast and crazy ways. [*Who knows how all this may shake out?*] Even as he reminded himself that Maudie had done nothing to make him think anything about their futures was any different now, Oscar allowed himself enjoy a few what-ifs.

Until the past weeks, any possibility that something might extend their relationship beyond the granting of their MBA degrees was on no one's radar.

* * *

FAMILY VALUES:
AN UNLIKELY MIX

Oscar and Maudie were drawn together like the poles of a magnet by seemingly opposite forces. Oscar, an idealist with a fierce belief in equality and justice, was embarrassed at how quickly his libido could trump his idealism. The moment he first saw Maudie that day in the lunch line he was too stirred up to even stand still, shifting from foot to foot like a racehorse in the starting gate, desperate to get her attention.

Maudie, though she was up for some diversion while she filled out her resume, was fiercely focused on her future. Not that she ruled out a fling at some of American student life that her friends in Zimbabwe and in Europe made sport of as childish. [*Why not, so long as I'm here for two years? Some harmless fun.*] But she knew she needed to keep a tight rein on her appetites. Challenging for a young woman with normal desire and far above normal beauty. Focused and disciplined though she was, she still chafed against her father's heavy-handedness in wanting to manage her life. More than she sometimes admitted to herself, it was a struggle to keep a short leash on her desire for at least a taste of the life every young woman wants.

*   *   *

A Battle of African Wills

Father, I am too old to have you trying to control my personal life.

This is hardly about either control, or your so-called personal life, Maudie. You are the daughter of the President of our struggling young nation, the first nation to throw off the yoke of western colonialism. [OK, *Father, no need to make one of your patriotic speeches to me.*] *Every step you take is being closely watched by those who wish us well, and even more closely by those who want to see us fail. You have been my hostess to the world, and my confidante in the years since your dear mother died. Everyone understands you are being readied for succeeding me as president. Unfair as it may seem, your birth as my daughter has ruled out your having a personal life in the way others do.*

Maudie had been through this with her father countless times. In the past it was about less consequential matters,—dress, language, friends—whatever he deemed appropriate to prepare her for the future he envisioned for her.

[*Sometimes I get so tired of this. What I wouldn't give to have just one day all my own, when I could forget about protocol and Zimbabwe, and my future.*]

The planning for Maudie's schooling in Switzerland ignited a fierce argument between them. They clashed over how many and what sort of security people would accompany her.

You will have four CIO agents who will live in your dorm and always be near enough to ensure your safety.

CIO?! Those goons aren't bodyguards, they're spies. Why do I need four spies, except so you can monitor every day of my life even from thousands of miles away? How do you expect me to have any life, with a bunch of your goons spying on me everywhere I go?

They are not goons, Maudie. And they aren't spies. They are among my most trusted security people. Every one of them was with me in the bush during the darkest days of our struggle against the Ian Smith regime. They respect our family and understand the need for the utmost security against the many different groups and people who have an interest in seeing us fail. Or even worse.

They will be protecting you, not spying on you.

[*What's the difference?*]

Maudie knew arguing was futile. She had gradually come to understand what her father and his comrades went through during those years of war. Eleven years in Smith's prisons, most in solitary confinement. Eight years in the bush fighting the dreaded Selous Scouts. Her father had firsthand knowledge—as she did not—of what was required when the stakes were that high. She seldom asked him about those days, though she always felt that if she was to take on what he hoped, she should know more. Her father never spoke about them unless it was politically expedient. Maudie knew that was because of the atrocities they had experienced, those they suffered, and those they perpetrated. You didn't have to read Wilbur Smith (which she had, a little, on the sly) to know the war had been merciless on both sides.

Her father warned her about the assassination plots the CIO had uncovered and thwarted. As she knew she would have to, Maudie relented. The CIO agents went with her, first to Switzerland, then to England and the London School of Economics, and on to Philadelphia when she enrolled at Wharton. But thanks to her wiles, her toughness and charm, Maudie broke down much of the rigid requirements of her keepers, becoming almost friends with them. She gradually persuaded them to cut her more slack so she could enjoy graduate school a little more like some of her fellow students.

Or so she thought, until the afternoon Oscar invited her for a ride on his big BMW motorcycle. It was a couple of weeks after they had met and before they began regular dating

*   *   *

Philadelphia.

September 25, 2020

Sorry, Miss Maudie, but no, she heard someone from behind her say, as she was about to throw her leg over the cycle. She was excited, picturing a thrilling, wind-swept ride behind Oscar, gripping his trim, athletic waist, his head towering above hers while they sped along the expressway to the Main Line on a perfect fall day.

Hearing that voice infuriated her. She hadn't seen him, had no idea he was shadowing her so closely.

This is hardly dangerous, Welcome, Maudie said, making no effort to disguise her anger. Welcome Ncube was her favorite among her CIO handlers. Unlike the others, Welcome didn't rag on her about the dangers of being seduced by the bourgeoisie ideas of the unprincipled Americans. Or the randy, sex-obsessed men. Welcome seemed to understand her need for some normal life. She noticed he even—when he was officially off duty—dressed in jeans and tee shirts, the universal uniform of young people in the States. She knew his fellow agents gave him a hard time and she admired him for not caving. It made her feel close to him. But she worried that his colleagues might tell her father, and Welcome would be replaced.

Motorcycles are simply out of bounds, I'm afraid, Miss Maudie. I'm sure the young man understands.

Oscar felt caught, and even more disappointed than Maudie. He understood why Welcome would stop Maudie from riding with him on his powerful BMW bike. Worse, he understood it was one more reason why this relationship he'd begun to fantasize about was unlikely to get off the ground.

He's right, Maudie. This was a bad idea. Fun, but too reckless. I mean it's not as if you were just some random young woman. (As he heard this come out of his mouth, Oscar hated the sound of it. He knew it was exactly what would reinforce Maudie's conviction that they could never be more than friends.) *No reason we can't take your Mercedes and have just as good a time.* (He knew this was a lame attempt to rehabilitate himself in Welcome's estimation.) [*Get the CIO guys against you and game's over.*]

That's bullshit, Oscar, and you know it. In their conversations over the first weeks, Oscar had never heard Maudie swear, and he'd been uncharacteristically careful to watch his own language. [*She must really be upset.*] *Welcome has thrown cold water on any enthusiasm I had for the afternoon. Don't take it personally, but I'm going to head back to my apartment, get started studying for that Stat exam we're all dreading.*

Oscar took it very personally, scrambling for some way to rehabilitate himself with Welcome without losing face with Maudie.

I feel bad about this, Maudie. Last thing you need during our first week of hour exams, is to alienate Welcome, or your father, over a silly ride on an American honky's motorcycle.

Maudie laughed, a big relief to Oscar who still didn't feel on firm enough ground with her to know if it was OK to make race jokes, even at his own expense. Nor had he any idea yet whether she regarded him merely as a happy diversion from the grind of Wharton, or maybe had a spark of the feelings that were increasingly preoccupying him.

Don't let it worry you, Oscar. My father and I go through this sort of thing frequently. Since my mother died he has shouldered the dual responsibility of being my only parent, and wanting to guard my future on behalf of our nation.

Though there would be more talk between them about her father and what he expected of her for the future, this was the most Maudie had revealed of herself and her unique role since they met. It gave Oscar a small tingle of thrill. Maybe she was beginning to feel connected enough to him to let him in a little. But it also stirred his anxiety—her eerie sense of duty to her father and her country. Didn't exactly compute with what was increasingly on his mind.

I'll see you on Monday at the exam, Oscar. Good luck with your studying.

Oscar wished he could spend the weekend maybe studying with Maudie, but he couldn't muster the courage to suggest it.

You, too, Maudie. If you run up against any stumbling blocks, I'd be happy to try to help you over them.

[*I can't believe I said that. What an asshole.*]. They both knew Maudie had a much stronger background in Statistics, from her year at The London School of Economics, than he had. [*Classics at Harvard, dummy, doesn't make you a likely tutor for a Stat exam.*] He braced himself for her reply.

Sweet of you, Oscar. I actually feel I've got a pretty good grounding in this course. I'm feeling mostly OK about this exam. But I do appreciate your offer.

[*Oh man, how come you didn't ask her for help, numb nut?*]

* * *

PHILADELPHIA.

OCTOBER 10, 2020

When Oscar's parents came for a visit—several weeks after classes began—he had casually mentioned Maudie to them along with several others he had met, cautious not to put too much energy into describing her. He wasn't eager for a lot of cross-examination from his mother who always sensed when he was holding back, somehow getting him to talk about the very things he'd promised himself he wouldn't.

So, Os, I bet Philadelphia's a pretty sweet place to spend the fall, huh?

You have no idea, Mom. After those October deep freezes in Cambridge, this is like living in the tropics.

And I know you can't tell anything by their looks, his mother probed gently, *but something about the students we've seen walking around campus makes me think they're an especially interesting bunch. And, from what I can tell, they're from all over.*

Oscar and his parents had traveled the world. His father's 20 years administering the Episcopal Presiding Bishop's Fund For World Relief had given them access to, and a fascination for other countries. Prizing diversity was a big piece of the family ethic.

You know, Mom, at least 30 percent of the people in my section of Wharton are from outside the U.S. And from some pretty interesting backgrounds. There's even one woman—I've gotten to know her a little—whose father is president of Zimbabwe.

Robert Mugabe's daughter? his father asked, his bushy eyebrows popping up.

Uh huh. Oscar couldn't believe he had so quickly violated his resolution not to call attention to Maudie.

I don't know anything about his daughter, but I know a little something about him. And what I know is not good.

Look, Dad, Maudie and I haven't begun negotiating any treaties yet; we've studied together a few times in the library, and gone to the movies once or twice. [*That was lame. And way too revealing.*]

Maudie. Sweet name. How involved do you think she is in Zimbabwe politics?

[*Cool it, Oscar, the old man's fishing. If he only knew that she's being groomed to succeed her father. And that I'd kill to hook up with her.*]

Who knows? Oscar struggled to sound vague, detached.

Because the word in the State Department is that her father is trying to pave her way to succeeding him.

Is that so? And how do you and the Masters of the Universe at the State Department feel about that? Since they were already into it, Oscar figured he may as well see what he could find out about some of what he would feel uncomfortable asking Maudie.

Well,—his father ignored Oscar's sarcasm—*we* [*what's this we shit? Since when did you join the State Department?*] *all hope she would be an improvement over her father's disastrous regime. Anyone short of Genghis Khan would be. I used to go to Zimbabwe three or four times a year, mainly to help expedite the country's exporting of surplus crops to other southern African nations that hadn't enough to feed themselves. Since Mugabe started confiscating the white farmland, not only are there no more exports, but now, thanks to his corrupt mismanagement, the country can't feed itself. And when I tried to plan a trip there this past summer, I was denied a visa.*

Maybe that's because you refer to the government's land redistribution as confiscation, Dad. You, above all, should know the screwed up politics of land in the history of Africa and western colonialism.

I detect maybe you've spent a little more time with this young lady than just a couple of library visits and a movie.

And maybe you've spent a little too much time over at the State Department. Those guys are nothing but stooges for the IMF and the World Bank. Not to mention the CIA. I thought you were supposed to be independent of all that. Guess maybe they're not the bad guys anymore, now that they've taken you and the Fund into their fold. Maybe you've relaxed your independent judgment since they've made their fat wad of corporate money available to the Fund.

Now Boys—not the first time Oscar's mother had refereed one of their jousting matches—*it's not often anymore that the three of us have a chance to spend a weekend together; let's not wreck it with a battle over politics.*

Sorry, Mom, it's just that it frosts me when Dad mouths the bullshit he hears from those guys who only care about keeping markets open for US plutocrats.

I'm going to honor your mother's wish on this, Oscar, but before you go condemning the work of the Fund in Zimbabwe, you might want to take a look at the stats on grain production and exports before and after 2000, when the land transfers began. And then consider the implications for the average subsistence peasant.

Oscar took note of his father's subtle shift of language, from "confiscate" to "transfer." It was small but they both placed great value on language. In these clashes a small word change could be a significant concession.

You guys still like Irish pubs? Oscar, with that subtle signal that his father had heard him, let it drop. *Because McShea's downtown is one of the best I've been to. You can get a good meal and a pint of Guinness for a decent price.*

I'm sure it will be just as good, and half the price of anything we could find in New York. Oscar was grateful for his father's signal that he accepted Oscar's offer of a temporary truce. He suspected the first shot had been fired in what would be a difficult, complex conflict between them if he should be lucky enough for his relationship with Maudie to ever go anywhere. More worrisome, he couldn't help wondering whether ~~than~~ he wanted to believe in what his father said. [*Maybe I'm more willing than I like to admit, to check my judgment at the door of Maudie's bedroom.*]

* * *

Maudie's Mental Meanders
April 2022

Maudie sometimes wondered why her mother had married her father. To her they seemed as different as chalk and cheese. (Maudie, like many Africans who had lived and gone to school with the old colonialists' children, in Zimbabwe private schools and abroad, sprinkled her talk with expressions borrowed from the people her father had fought against.)

Very different backgrounds, no doubt, but *were* they really so different?

Her father had become a warrior, the only black African leader to win a war against colonialists. But he was Shona, not an Ndebele warrior. Shona—by reputation—fought from necessity, not choice. The fear he inspired even in those close to him had once puzzled and upset her. Why should they fear this Shona patriot who had spent years in prison and risked his life for the freedom they now finally enjoyed? [*He's stern, but not scary. Not to me.*]

As she grew older and became aware of how intimidating she herself could be to those who envied and feared her power, she understood better.

Maudie's grandmother was Swedish, her grandfather a Shona. Her mother was born and lived her whole life in Zimbabwe. Maudie's tan skin favored her mother more than it did her father's deep black complexion. As she matured Maudie wondered whether she was more like her mother or her father. But now that he had begun to consult her in important matters, Maudie could see that her parents were more partners in governing that she had realized. Her father could quickly lose his patience and threaten to use his power to bully. Maudie remembered how her mother could quietly cajole him, slow him down until his temper cooled. She tried, with some success, to play a similar role.

[*What would he be like now if Mother had lived? She was the only one who could tease and cajole him when he had one of his paranoid tantrums.*]

Despite the beating he took in the international press for abuses of power, Maudie knew him as the brilliant, innovative hero who won his country's independence when no one in the world thought it possible.

[*And then magnanimously agreed to allow that snake, Ian Smith, to run for, and be seated in Parliament. Elected by the same thugs who had murdered the freedom fighters. Which of his critics in the west would have been so forgiving?*

[*Father has these two sides in him, battling with each other. He cares deeply about our young country and wants our people to succeed. He also loves the good life, the perks that go with his office. Why shouldn't he? He earned them.*

[*I hate this fucking double-mindedness. Sometimes I wish I'd never gone abroad, been exposed to the western racism that makes Europeans so scared of Africans gaining real power. Sometimes when I see Father throwing his weight around or boasting about his wine cellar I get edgy, thinking about how I know that plays in the west.*

[*Look at that—fucking. I didn't even know that word when I went off to school in Switzerland. Now it's become one of my favorite swears. Thanks a lot, Oscar! If Father ever heard me use it he would blush so hard it would even show through his beautiful black skin. Maybe Father was right, maybe my whole way of thinking has been corrupted, like my language.*

[*Could all that schooling in the west really have gotten to me? Those fatuous slogans—unfettered free markets, globalization—the IMF forcing struggling economies to adopt their so-called open markets. But Father did a degree at the London School; it didn't ruin him. It was my going to America and Wharton that put him over the edge.*

[*Oh get real Maudie. When he was in London he was steeling himself to lead a bloody revolution. Ermine academic hood or not, he graduated to war and the bush. Not exactly your agenda. He keeps warning me it could become my agenda too, if this mess we're in goes off the rails. Am I tough enough to lead our nation in war if I ever have to?*

[*And what about this Oscar guy? What's with that? You're enjoying amusing yourself with a rich, white American boyfriend? Interesting how fast Father picked him out from all the others I told him about. Father reads me better than Oscar does. I don't think Oscar has any idea how taken I am with him. I hope he doesn't. I need to keep my exits open. Father has seemed better about it than I expected. Hm. Oh Lord, you don't suppose Father's got some ulterior motive? Well of course he does, Maudie. He always does. Always calculating, figuring the odds. Oh shit! Wonder what he sees in Oscar that he thinks might prove useful? Wonder what I do?*

[*No need to obsess, Maudie, Father knows it's only a for-the-moment thing. Just for Wharton. Or does he perhaps have something more in mind for Oscar? I'm pretty sure it isn't Oscar's good looks, which is what first attracted me. He sure is good looking! And quite a wonderful man. Different. Well, it's a fun diversion for two otherwise tedious years of this American business nonsense.*

[*Is it, Maudie? You think Oscar's in it for a diversion? You think you can just walk away when we graduate? En garde, Maudie! And if Father is cooking up some use for him? He doesn't often consult you before he sets things up in your life that he has in mind for you; you'll be the last to know. But what possible use could an innocent like Oscar be? You ready for what that might look like?*]

*　　*　　*

AND OSCAR'S TAKE?

PHILADELPHIA, OCTOBER 2020

Oscar had been happily relieved to find the work at Wharton more interesting than he anticipated. Even the dreaded Statistics—that washed out most of the other humanities do-gooders like him—seemed to him a challenge, full of fascinating, useful information.

[*Business school is like shifting to Sushi after a steady diet of Burger King. This exotic food is tasty, no doubt more nourishing and better for you, but pretty soon after I eat it, I'm hungry again, never satisfied. No emotional highs like there were in Romantic Poets. How do you nourish your famished soul at Business School?*]

It wasn't long after he arrived at Wharton that Oscar found the answer to his question. It wasn't in Statistics.

* * *

PHILADELPHIA. NOVEMBER 2020. DID YOU FEEL THE EARTH MOVE?

Oscar often revisited that night their first year at Wharton when their courtship became a love affair. Although he suspected it was quite different for Maudie, its intensity, undiminished in his memory years later, made Oscar understand it was then he began to hope that he and Maudie might forge a lifelong bond.

Oscar was embarrassed bringing Maudie to his apartment, a studio, with a bed, a table, two chairs, TV, couch, a tiny bathroom and Pullman kitchen. He figured Maudie, having grown up in the Presidential Palace in Harare, must be used to living in splendor.

[*Thank God I made the bed this morning. Would have been nice if I'd washed a few dishes. My God, heart's pounding, light headed. Look at that grubby bedspread, the floor needs a rug. Good Lord, dots of tooth paste, goobers from flossing, all over the bathroom mirror. Maudie's gonna take one look around this place and flee.*]

So this is where you live? Her smile didn't reassure him. **How long does it take you to get to school in the morning**?

[*Jesus, you're beautiful! I must be dreaming. You're so sophisticated. Breathe, Oscar; try not to act like a jerk.*]

Oscar, Maudie was unperturbed that he seemed not to have heard her question. It had been a throwaway question, meant to calm Oscar. He looked tense, as if he might burst into tears or run away. **You've been with a woman before, yes**?

[Christ, do I look that whacked out?] **Sure, of course, yeah, I have, I mean not a lot, but this isn't my first time.** *[Christ, Oscar, you're hopeless. Calm down.]* **But the others have all been . . .**

Maudie laughed. **White American girls; yes, Oscar?"**

[Shit, my face must've just turned beet red, my dick just went limp, this is going to be a disaster. How embarrassing.]

Maudie laughed again. **It's OK, Oscar. I know you're all tied up in knots trying so hard not say the wrong thing. Relax, Sweetheart, I came here because I wanted to. And you don't need to freak out about sleeping with a black African. I'm only three-quarters black African, remember? My mother was half Swedish.** She laughed again, harder.

Christ, Maudie, what can I say? I'm just an over-privileged, uptight, fucked-up, middle class white boy from suburban America. I never even felt up a girl until I was in college, and we were both so drunk we may as well not have bothered. I didn't mean anything about black or white. I was talking about the others *[others, Oscar? Both of them?]* **not meaning to me anything even remotely like what you do.**

Maudie sat on the edge of the bed and patted the place beside her, gesturing to Oscar to sit too. When he did, she put her hand lightly on his thigh and turned toward him, their faces so close, as she spoke her words brushed his face with gentle breath.

Oscar, even though my father is president, I had a pretty traditional Shona upbringing. My mother was half Swedish, but she grew up in Zimbabwe. And when she married my father she adapted to his ways, probably because she understood that his ambitions would be squelched if she didn't. And he is an African man, so it just wouldn't have worked any other way.

But I was sent to boarding school in Switzerland when I was 16, took my degree at Oxford, finished a year at the London School of Economics before I came to Wharton. I haven't exactly led a sheltered life.

Oscar was grateful for Maudie's sensitivity, trying to reassure him. His pulse began to slow down.

Maudie, Do you think your father understands that you've become pretty different from the daughter he thought he was bringing up? Oscar hoped to buy a little time, maybe relax a little, maybe not wilt when it counted.

I think my father, once he knew he wasn't going to have a son, which was soon after I was born and my mother first got sick, gave up whatever

he might have once thought about my being a traditional daughter. And when he began to consider me as his political heir, I think he also pretty much put away any lingering issues he may have had about my gender. He probably just chooses not to think about personal moments like our being together like this. He remains focused only on whether I'm being properly groomed for what I will need to come back and help him run the country.

Oscar was suddenly overcome by emotion. *Maudie, you know I really am drawn to you so powerfully. I can hardly think about anything else.*

I know, Oscar, it's written all over you. I'm touched by that. But better we skip the sentiment. You're a wonderful, transparent man. I'm very drawn to you, too. I'm not a loose woman; I don't sleep with men casually. You are a beautiful, sensitive man. And very sexy. I've thought about getting you into my bed since that first moment in Rubenstein's class.

[Jesus, is this really happening? Man, how did she get so totally in charge here? You've hardly thought about anything else since you first saw her, too, Oscar. You ready for this?] Well, I hope you don't mind terribly, Maudie, I mean is it going to be a total freak out for you that I really do love you? I mean I'm afraid I really do, out of control.

Quiet, Oscar, that's quite enough. Talking's over.

Maudie leaned toward Oscar holding his face between her hands. With her long, strong fingers she massaged the corners of his jaw, smiling. She pulled his face toward hers, opening his lips with her lips. Her tongue darted into his mouth, probing. She leaned against him, her breasts pressing into him. He moaned, his erection bulging. She reached down and took hold of him through his pants. Oscar jumped to his feet.

It's OK, Oscar, I promise I won't hurt you. She smiled again.

Hurt me? Not the problem. You almost just brought this whole sweet moment to a hasty close. I nearly shot off when you grabbed me like that.

Sorry, dear boy, didn't mean to startle you. Shall we start again? Please.

Maudie stood and began slowly, deliberately, undoing his belt,. He took hold of the top button of her blouse. And it all tumbled into a blur of kissing and searching each other with their hands, their mouths, rubbing, moaning, their clothes falling in a heap on the floor, until Oscar was standing in his boxer shorts, the cotton fabric pushed up, comically, by his raised penis. The sight of Maudie's tiny half bra and black thong made Oscar feel like he might hyperventilate, surrender the little breath he still had. Maudie took hold of his shorts and yanked, they dropped to his ankles. As he stepped out of them, she took a step back and, with frank interest, looked him over.

My God, you're a rare specimen, dear man; you're even more beautiful naked than you are all dressed up

She reached for his penis, gently stroking it. Oscar's knees went rubbery.

Oh my God, Maudie, I can't do this very long; I want to come when I'm inside you, not like this.

I'm going into the bathroom for a moment, Oscar, and then I want that impressive erection inside my body where it belongs. Don't move.

She was back in seconds, naked, her breasts and her buttocks the same bronze color as the rest of her. Her large dark, purple nipples hard, her thick pubic hair jet black. Oscar couldn't stop himself from staring.

So, what do you think? Maudie asked, smiling.

Think? Oh Christ, Maudie, my brain just gave up thinking. You are so fucking beautiful!

Maudie embraced him, most of her tawny skin in contact with his pale skin. [*I'm like anemic, up against this gorgeous brown woman.*] She leaned into him, pushing him toward the bed. With a little shove she tumbled him backward onto the bed, climbed on top of him, taking hold of his penis, guiding it into her moist pouch. Shifting her position, she straddled him, her knees flexed on either side of him. She grasped his hips, pulling them into her. Her eyes closed, her face tilted up toward the ceiling. Oscar was writhing beneath her.

Oh Oscar, go; yes, now; go Oscar!

Oscar thought he might have lost consciousness for a moment. Bright colors flashed in his head. Just when his heart seemed about to burst through his chest he felt everything let go, releasing his pent up energy and breath. Strobe lights flashed behind his eyes as if he'd received a blow to his head. Maudie screamed, her hips pounding into Oscar, driving him down into the bed.

Oscar thought he must have shouted, too. He lost all track of time. Were they in that coupled position for a long while, or only seconds? [*Sweet Jesus, make it be forever!*]

As they began to return to awareness, Maudie laughed.

What's funny?

You, Oscar, and me, pretending to be sophisticated Wharton graduate students, but really just two feral animals. She laughed again. *Sweet man, this was a happy surprise. For a stuck-up Anglo, you're one hell of a lover. I thought you pale boys were s'posed to be tame.*

It's only because—thanks to you—we never got to the old missionary position; that's when I revert to my wimpy roots. With you jumping around on top of me like that, I just about forgot what species I was, let alone what tribe I come from.

Well, we may have to rewrite the book on Whitey; your frisky member would make a Ndebele chief envious.

Maudie lifted her hips and held his sticky, wet prick as he slid out of her. She reached for a tissue on the bedside table, folded and gently wrapped it around his member, rolling off him onto her side next to him in an easy, athletic move. She cupped the back of his head with her hand and pulled his face to hers. They kissed, open mouthed, full tongued.

I could get to like this, she said as she pulled back just far enough to focus on his face.

Oh God, Maudie, I could die now.

Well don't, love, there's more work to do, and a lot more play.

Their love-making never failed to end in wild abandon, rich fare for two over-achievers who lived life so much in their heads. It was an unlikely chapter, love junkies skipping lectures, forgetting appointments, stealing time to bed down together. But Oscar felt they never again quite reached another moment like their first, when he felt every cell in Maudie was in synch with every cell in him. They both knew—alas—neither was hedonist enough to let this delicious sex shape their entire life. [*Though,*] Oscar considered more than once, [*given the choice, maybe . . .*]

[*There's more work to be done*]. It haunted him. Ever since he was a small boy at his father's table, dominated by politics and the world's problems, Oscar had been determined to spend his life making a difference, working to alleviate suffering and poverty. But he'd never run into anyone—certainly no woman—who matched Maudie's determination, her single-mindedness. It intimidated and frustrated him.

[*Maybe I am a hedonist, after all.*] He'd had girlfriends, one serious, whom he had thought he might marry one day. But being with Maudie was of a different order. With the others he had always pictured the two of them working together in noble causes.

With Maudie he could give a damn whether they ever did anything for anyone else. [*I'd become a drug dealer if that meant I could spend my life with her. I thought I was in love with Leigh; Jesus Christ, that was a schoolboy crush, nothing like this.*]

But, except for those moments of explosive orgasm, Oscar never again felt it was for Maudie quite what it was for him. After they'd made love—though it required him to exercise uncommon self-control—he learned not to try to leverage that moment to maneuver her into a conversation about their future. As if explosive sex might have weakened her resolve.

Nobody knows the future, she'd reply, her voice gone flat, businesslike. *This time is about right now, Oscar. Don't be pushing me. My life and my vocation belong to Zimbabwe. I've known that ever since I was a little girl. Anything that distracts me from that, I will purge from my life.*

Once Oscar's longings and frustration got the better of him: he hadn't meant for his voice to rise: *So, what about babies? What about the rest of your life, other than saving Zimbabwe? Don't you trust your heart as much as your head to tell you the truth when we're together like this?*

The warmth drained from Maudie's eyes. She pulled away, seeming to withdraw deep within herself, frightening Oscar. Her voice sounded remote:

Don't you ever fuck with me about this, Oscar. If you try to use our sex to manipulate me, I'll walk away from you without so much as a glance back at you.

Oscar never did again, though it was never far from his mind. Their love-making was unfailingly great, but for the first time since the initial, unbalancing rush of puberty, Oscar understood that even the greatest sex can't fill every space in your life. Like a good drug, it wasn't long before he wanted more. And not only more sex. Oscar wanted more of Maudie—the more, he knew, that she could never give him.

* * *

IS THIS WHAT AMERICANS MEAN BY "FALLING IN LOVE?"

Maudie: [*What is this nonsense about being in love? American boys can't tell the difference between fantasy and real life. They think their lives are a movie. No wonder they keep electing child/men, actors to be their presidents. Puer aeternus. It can be beguiling in a boyfriend. For a while. Can these guys who are in training to run the world really think this being in love, leading with their glands, provides a dependable guide for life? Or is it another of those poses my friends warned me they take on to try to get some free sex?*]

* * *

Oscar's Issues

As it was for Maudie, Oscar's most unresolved conflict was with his father, whom he admired and who perplexed him. Though not outwardly pious like other priests, his father devoted his life to the work of the Episcopal Church. After a brief tenure as a parish priest, he had become director of the Presiding Bishop's Fund For World Relief, a multi-million dollar fund that did good works around the world.

Oscar had been told that when his father was first ordained he was the only white man who could safely walk the streets of Hough in the years it was controlled by violent, angry blacks. And Oscar marveled that he seemed to have equal access to the board rooms of Wall Street.

Oscar saw what it cost his father to straddle that huge divide. Kissing the asses of the business leaders, confirming the outrage of unemployed blacks and their labor bosses, all in the name of a God Oscar sensed his father had long since ceased to believe in.

Once, after his father had taken his regular turn celebrating the Eucharist at Trinity Church on Wall Street, Oscar, then a junior in college, turned to his father at lunch, and asked, *Dad, there's a hell of a lot of hocus pocus in that service. Do you actually believe all that shit?*

Oscar! his mother, always protective of his father, pretended to be horrified, *that's no way to speak about the most sacred commitment of your father's life.*

Now Mother, his father said—Oscar hated it when his parents called each other mother and father; it felt like they were in a Thornton Wilder play—*despite the scatology, that's a perfectly legitimate question.*

It sure as shit is, Oscar pressed in, *if what you mean by believe, which I suspect most church-goers do, is you think some great being hears prayers*

46

and changes things in response, or that there is some supernatural magic in the consecrated bread and wine. So, if it's not too rude to ask, what do you believe? And if it's not what you say most people in church believe, do you pretend so you can hang onto your job?

Oscar, that was uncalled for, his mother protested.

It's OK, Mother. He smiled. [*Indulging me.*] *I'm happy you trust me enough to ask, though I doubt I can answer your question so it will satisfy you, Oscar, since I still haven't been able to answer it very satisfactorily for myself. But I can tell you that something about my being ordained makes it possible for me to be a part of people's lives and play a role in complex conflicts in ways that most people can't.*

So, Dad, you put on that dog collar the way Clark Kent puts on his Superman suit, giving him supposed mystical powers?

His father laughed, his mother was silent.

I've never thought of it quite like that, Oscar, but maybe it's not that far off. I have always wondered whether Superman's strength was about his secret powers, or about what people believed. The power they gave him.

That sounds more like Christian Science than the Apostles' Creed, now his mother was the one who sounded edgy. *Are you saying your vocation* (Oscar had heard his father use that term before, but never his mother. His mother pretty much stayed out of talk like this.) *is like a costume you put on to do your job? And take off when you're not working?*

This is beginning to sound like one of those endless, unresolvable fights we have in diocesan convention every year, liberals and conservatives beating each other up. (Oscar guessed they'd pushed him about as far as he was willing to go.) *What say we enjoy our roast beef and give this God-talk a rest?*

* * *

OSCAR, MEET AFRICA

MARCH 2021

Maudie invited Oscar to go with her to Zimbabwe for spring break their first year at Wharton. At dinner one night in the Presidential Palace, President Mugabe suggested that Oscar and Maudie take the long drive south, through Masvingo to the Lowveld, through the rural countryside and some of the huge sugar cane, citrus, and tobacco owned by European whites until the recent land redistribution. *Your press has made much of this*, her father said, *making it sound as if it were merely our petulant payback. But you cannot possibly comprehend its true significance until you see the vast area and wealth involved. We won our political independence, but all the big money remained until recently in the hands of those who colonized us.*

Oscar tried to ignore his father's voice in his head: *Check the statistics, Oscar, for before and after Mugabe's land grabs.*

Driving the rural road south, they stopped at a bottle store for a soda, needing relief from the oppressive heat. The woman at the counter had a whining infant tied to her back by a colorful piece of fabric. As the young mother handed them their drinks, Maudie engaged her in conversation in Shona.

Back in the car, Oscar asked her what they had talked about.

I asked her about her baby. She said her baby had a high fever and hadn't been able to keep down any nourishment since the night before.

Did she say she had taken the baby to the doctor?

She said the healing man was coming to her house this afternoon.

Healing man?

Witch doctor, for lack of a better name.

Did you tell her she needed a real doctor, not a witch doctor? The baby is dehydrated, could even have cholera and die if it doesn't get IV fluids.

You know, Oscar, for a sensitive, supposedly worldly man, you have some pretty chauvinistic western ideas. Witch doctors have been the main medical—and religious—people in this region for longer than there has been a United States. Just because they don't have a degree from Harvard Medical School doesn't mean they don't know anything.

So, Maudie, I would be most grateful if you might begin to give me a little guidance on this Shona witch doctor/shaman business. In the two weeks since I arrived it's become obvious that if I'm ever going to make any sense of what's going on around me, I'm going to need some good coaching on how to curb the western rationalism steeped in my bones.

Oscar knew Maudie would pick up the sarcastic edge in his voice, but [*maybe,*] he decided, [*it's time I pushed back a little on some of this voodoo stuff*].

You know, Oscar, it would be a pleasure for me to be your coach for some of that if I thought there was anything in you that might be able, or willing, to make you actually seriously consider it. Sorry if it seems like I'm belittling you—there's lots about American culture I still don't get, like what makes you think deregulating markets makes them more fair or automatically more efficient. Or how it is a movie actor can be your president?—It's just that some things, if they haven't been a part of you since you were born, will always seem too weird to believe. No matter how well they can be explained I don't think I'm ever going to understand doctors and lawyers advertising they way they do in the States, as if they were soft drinks. And I doubt you're going to make sense of traditional African medicine.

In Philadelphia, Oscar had begun to feel he and Maudie had a powerful emotional kinship. He loved Zimbabwe, found it fascinating and stunningly beautiful, from the moment he stepped off the airplane. Like Maudie herself, whose beauty could still startle him. He wanted in the worst way to absorb the way she saw the world. He knew it required his quieting his skeptical mind.

[*Some of it is how exotic she seems. Naked, or decked out like the president's daughter, she still can seem like a woman out of a dream. Not someone I would be taking a trip with in real, waking time.*]

Oscar and Maudie drank their sodas in the sidewalk café—that's what Maudie called the two packing crates held together by a corrugated tin roof on a dirt side road in Masvingo. Maudie warned Oscar that the gradual descent from Harare's 5,000 feet, down to sea level and the Lowveld, was going to feel like they were driving into a furnace.

You'd best drink a lot of fluids as we go, Oscar, or you're going to get a splitting headache.

Maudie had loaded several bottles of bubble-gum-colored Fanta drinks into a cooler before they left. They were a putrid color and Oscar had politely declined to drink them until, after an hour or so, he began to feel slightly disoriented. Too late, his nasty headache told him he had been stupidly stubborn.

Oscar could see the building heat was getting to Maudie too—small beads of sweat dotted her forehead—but she seemed relaxed and comfortable sitting across from him in the folding metal chairs on the red dirt.

Half-naked children tried to sell them chewing gum and cigarettes. Oscar felt awkward, but Maudie smiled sweetly, turning them away in lilting Shona. Her easy smile and her effortless way with the children soothed him, made his headache bearable. He was grateful just to be with her.

He knew this infatuation couldn't last; he'd eventually have to see her as a person, not some goddess. [*You worship goddesses, not marry them.*] It made Oscar melancholy. And it made Maudie seem even more inaccessible.

I'm not being disingenuous, Maudie; I really am fascinated. I want to understand.

I believe you do, Oscar, but there's just no way. Romantic poet you may be; you're still the consummate western man. You know, even though it's a barrier between us we'll never be able to cross, it's actually one of the things that attracted me to you. So different from the men I grew up with. Alas, it's also one of so many things that would make it end in disaster if we ever seriously tried to merge our lives.

[*Shit.*] Oscar wished he'd never brought it up. He tortured himself to avoid mentioning anything that focused on these differences. Some days everything seemed to etch it deeper. From their first date Maudie had, very matter-of-factly, even in their most intimate moments, insisted that their relationship couldn't evolve into anything permanent.

When Maudie first brought up the idea of his coming to Zimbabwe for a visit—assuring him her father had welcomed it—Oscar's heart leapt. Maybe she was softening. Maybe . . .

Why not take one of the government Mercedes? her father had offered when they were planning the drive down into the Lowveld. *I have so many at my disposal,* he laughed. *And they're air conditioned. That little Toyota you rented surely doesn't have air conditioning.*

Oscar sensed he was being tested. Rich white American can't cope with African heat.

Thank you, Mr. President. That's more than generous. But the Toyota will do nicely, and we won't be burning your government's petrol.

Suit yourself, Oscar. It's going to get beastly hot down there. I would never make that trip without air conditioning. But then I'm an old man.

Afterwards Maudie poked fun at Oscar: *Tough guy. Who needs air conditioning? Noble, Oscar, but . . .* He held his ground. [*I give in to her about everything; I can hang with this.*] He soon came to regret his posturing.

Maudie didn't tell Oscar about the tense conversation she and her father had about whether they would be permitted to make the trip without CIO agents.

It is against my better judgment, Maudie, but I know you are going to be only in rural, remote places. And I trust your good sense, and Oscar's diligence in watching out for you. You deserve a chance for some true away time. But you must promise me you will go to the safari camp and remain there until you return home.

So many disorienting moments for Oscar. [*Beastly. Does anyone say beastly unless they're pure Limey? Every night at formal dinner—table set with English china and heavy sterling silverware—there is a moment reserved for pissing on England. But set aside his skin color, where we are, and his politics, and he is Oxford educated, English MP. Or maybe PM.*]

Maybe, Maudie—Oscar was silently scolding himself for having clumsily stumbled into yet another cultural divide, wishing he had taken her father up on the government Mercedes, his head pounding—*but you forget that my father is an Episcopal priest, not a hedge fund manager. I was raised in a counter-culture that not only worked for racial and economic justice, but was supposed to believe the center of life is communal eating of a dead demigod, and drinking his blood. It's not as if I don't have some primeval history pretty deeply imbedded in my own culture.* [*That may have been a little overdone, Oscar.*]

Maudie laughed that full-bodied, head thrown back, shoulders shaking laugh that made Oscar love just being with her. **Give me a break, Oscar,** (her father spoke like a Limey and Maudie often used slang like a young American,) **You're asking me to believe that what goes on in Shona folk religion in the African bush, and in an Episcopal Church on Fifth Avenue in New York City are somehow equivalent?**

Hang on a minute, Maudie. Your mother was a devout Anglican, a stalwart supporter of the old Rhodie dean of St. Mary's Cathedral, and of the American dean who came after him. I suspect she would have been right at home at St. Bart's on Fifth Avenue.

Maudie's eyes narrowed. Oscar knew he'd just tread on hallowed ground. Again. [*Shit, I've fucking done it again.*]

Don't you ever try to pretend you understand about my mother. To suggest that a devout Anglican in Zimbabwe is even close kin to an American Episcopalian is ridiculous. Let alone an Exeter/Harvard snot taking communion at St. Bartholomew's. My mother was a sophisticated, worldly woman who could function in any setting anywhere in the world. And did. She may have had a Swedish father, but she was African to her bones, everything African women aspire to. Including me.

O.K. Babe, I'm so sorry. I apologize. Just consider it another of my endless stupid missteps into yet another pile of shit. So sorry.

Maudie laughed again, giving Oscar a moment's relief. **Some of our people burn buffalo chips for fuel and heat. We use it for healing wounds; for all sorts of things. Sometimes stepping into shit can be a good move. But that's the Ndebele who revere buffalo shit. They're hunters and warriors. We Shona are farmers and we don't appreciate buffalo and elephants trampling our crops. So we're not so keen on their shit. Maybe you'd best wait until you go to Bulawayo and Vic Falls, where the Ndebele run the show. Then you can step happily in their shit.**

Maudie's fun could torture Oscar. He scrambled for some subject that would seem neutral, innocuous.

Wasn't Masvingo called Ft. Victoria under colonial rule? I've always wondered what it's like to live in a country that has a revolution that changes the names of all the cities

Africans have always called it Masvingo, never referred to it as Ft. Victoria unless we were with old Rhodies. That's one way—there are

a whole lot more—you can tell who doesn't accept that they aren't still running things in this country. They still call Harare, Salisbury, and Masvingo, Ft. Vic.

(Oscar remembered that his father, when he told his father of his upcoming visit to Zimbabwe, his father said he had once gone to a World Council of Churches meeting in Salisbury, just before Ian Smith declared Unilateral Declaration of Independence and was expelled from the Commonwealth.

It's Harare, Dad, not Salisbury. That was its old colonial name.

Oh, sorry, right you are, son. So hard to track the changes in Africa. Seems like there's a new nation, with new city names, every week.)

We better get going, Oscar. Maudie broke into Oscar's reverie. *We for sure want to make it before dark. Once we get below Ungundu Halt, the roads get pretty dicey, just one tarred lane, animals, people walking on the side. When you pass a vehicle coming the other way you have to keep your left wheel just off the shoulder, and the buses don't give you any room. Can be pretty scary. Triangle and Chiredzi are still over an hour from here.*

Though it was a slight slap at his masculinity, Oscar was glad Maudie had insisted on driving. He'd never driven in conditions like this, or on the left side.

I've got my international license.

Your international license doesn't remotely prepare you for driving on these treacherous roads. Nor on the left hand side. Not to mention the eccentric habits of Zimbabwean drivers.

The awkwardness about who would drive didn't detract from Oscar's loving this long drive with Maudie. He had her undivided attention, a rare pleasure. Even on their dates in Philadelphia she always seemed preoccupied with some issue at home. Oscar once asked if she might leave her cell phone behind so they could enjoy some quiet time together. That was one of the early moments he was blind-sided by her anger.

Oscar, ever since I was 15—when my mother died—I have been the one person my father trusts and confides in. He lives under stress almost no one can imagine. When he needs to talk with me, he needs to talk with me right then. You want to be my boyfriend, you become my cell phone's and my father's boyfriend.

But out here in the bush beyond the reach of cell service, Maudie seemed relaxed, content to be alone with Oscar with no distractions.

Incredibly kind of your father to invite me, Maudie. And to let me take you away for a while. I hope he knows how grateful I am.

He knows, Oscar. He trusts you. I never dreamed he'd agree to our taking this trip without CIO guys. He trusts you more than he does most of the people he works with every day. And he understands and appreciates that you, too, are a generous and thoughtful person, not just a taker. He knows that you understand the reciprocity of these things.

Oscar felt his heart thump, skipping a beat. [*That comment wasn't casual, not just the legendary African courtliness. Reciprocity?*] He kept himself from asking what she meant. [*Enough shit between my toes for one afternoon.*]

Just ahead we take a left turn at Ungundu Halt, Maudie said, *and we begin a more rapid descent into the Lowveld. And it's going to start getting really hot. Good thing we're getting there toward the end of the day. Sometimes in the middle of the day you have to keep putting cool water on your hands to be able to hold onto the steering wheel.*

Jesus, Maudie, hotter than it already is?

You people from northern Europe really probably should stay away from Southern Africa, Oscar.

[*There are just too many piles of shit all over the place, I can't miss them all.*] They drove the next 15 minutes in silence, 15 minutes, 1,000 foot drop, and a 10 degree rise in temperature. As they neared the desert floor, Maudie suggested they close the windows even though they didn't have air conditioning. The heat coming in the windows was unbearable. She tolerated it much better than he did but Oscar could see even Maudie began to look wilted.

[*Holy shit! This heat's unbearable. That comment about northern Europeans in southern African was more than just a tease,*] Oscar conceded to himself. He was finding it hard just to take in enough air.

Oscar nodded without responding, [*Walking on eggshells here*]. He was surprised, on edge from the heat, and Maudie's seeming testy.

Not far down the road they passed a small community of mud rondovals. Several of the huts had smaller huts a few yards from their front door.

What are those little rondhovals, Maudie? They look way too small for anyone to live in. Almost like dog houses or something.

Those are for their ancestors. There are small altars inside, and places to burn candles when families go inside to welcome and worship their ancestors.

Worship ancestors?

Maudie laughed. *Oh, Oscar, I keep forgetting where you come from. I begin to think you grew up here, like me. Yes, worship ancestors. Your politicians refer to it as 'family values.' It is our form of respect, asking for protection from venerable people who are no longer squandering their energy getting and spending.*

But you said your parents are Anglicans. I've never known an Anglican who worshipped ancestors.

Oh, you most certainly have, Oscar. How about your mother, who is a member of the Colonial Dames? A few years ago both the Anglican and Roman Catholic Churches decided they had to make some decisions about their followers who were still practicing ancestor worship. The Anglicans decided they needed to wipe it out, that it was a form of idolatry that violated the first commandment.

And the Roman Catholics?

Oh, they said, "Ancestor worship? We know all about that. We call it the Communion of the Saints." It was such a sensible and humane decision that, had it not been for celibacy and the Pope, it might almost have persuaded my mother to convert.

Wildly contrasting origins, young, black, African, Shona woman, young, white, preppy, American man, doing a complex dance around ancient boundaries, edging uncertainly toward a future that transcends cultural constraints. Or perhaps testing whether an infatuation older than human culture itself—the mating call—is strong enough to drown out the constraints of our endless parochial divides.

*   *   *

WHERE THE WILD THINGS ARE

They drove to a safari camp deep in the bush, in Gonarezhou National Park, a game preserve where they would spend two nights. The drive into the park was adventure enough for Oscar. As they left the main road—barely a road by Oscar's reckoning—they continued on narrow trails, through dry river beds (and one that still had enough water to make Oscar wonder if they would founder).

Maudie, how the hell do you know where we're going?

She laughed that loud laugh that Oscar never knew was because she thought he was naïve, or because she got buzzed watching him getting buzzed by these exotic African moments. *What makes you think I do? Do you really care whether we ever find our way out of here?*

When they arrived at the camp, miraculously, Oscar thought, he was totally taken in by the look of the place, right out of a travel movie. Concrete buildings open to the air, wood shutters for covering windows at night, an ablution block in the middle of the camp, all a first for Oscar, unlike any place he had ever been. [*A little wilder than Boy Scout camp.*]

They arrived at dusk. *You'd better go over to the ablution block and take care of your business before it gets dark, Oscar, because the lions and hyena love to come around at night to see if careless campers have left anything tasty behind.*

Lions? Here? In the campground? Got another big laugh from Maudie.

At 3am they were wakened by growling.

Holy shit, Maudie! Those lions sound really close!

Not to worry, Oscar, they don't much care for either the indoors, or white boys.

Jesus, Maudie, all that growling; they must be mating.

Of course that's what you'd think, you horny man; they're claiming their territory. Mating comes later, once they have won their pride.

Wow! So they fight each other, and the winner gets the females?

Sort of, Oscar, but not exactly. They threaten each other and try out their scariest voices while the females observe. And then the females decide which male is their best bet for making strong babies.

That didn't sound much like any animal mating behavior Oscar knew anything about, but out there in the middle of the bush he figured was no place to challenge whatever Maudie told him. He understood this was all part of his initiation.

Oscar love Maudie. Maudie loved the bush. Q.E.D. Oscar loved being in the bush. In fact, Maudie quite aside, he really did.

* * *

Oscar's Last Stand
March 2022

They all but lived the second half of the last semester together (Maudie, knowing her father's CIO agents were always nearby, went home every night to her own apartment, even if it was nearly dawn). Maudie, though unfailingly uninhibited in her lovemaking, remained resolute in refusing to return Oscar's declarations of love. *American romantic love is for the movies, Oscar.*

You're a lovely man, Oscar, she reassured him, when he begged her, after a particularly passionate night. *As I've told you often, you're way more exciting than the reputation American men have among African women. I hope it will be some comfort that I may be able to help repair your national reputation.* Maudie loved teasing Oscar about this, and he laughed rather than take offense, even though it stung. *But I've tried to be honest with you, no permanent connections for me. Not with anyone.*

Oh for Jesus' sweet sake, Oscar complained, *take a good look at us*! It made him feel at such a disadvantage, his being gaga and her so calculating. Looking down at her firm brown breasts, her waist narrowing to the perfect black V of coarse, pubic hair, still made him light-headed, as if he had taken a potent drug. [*Best drug I'll ever do.*] *We're like a married couple already*.

Oh Oscar, can you not face reality about how far we are from such a thing? You may be every woman's dream of the lover they wish for—you're mine—but lover and husband are two entirely different things. Maudie reached down and held Oscar's penis lightly in her hand, smiling. He began to stiffen again despite being spent from their athletic, near sleepless night.

Oscar pulled away, petulant, embarrassed at how easily her lightest touch could divert him. *Seems like it's not asking all that much for you just to tell me you love me. Or am I some piece of meat, servicing you like a stud animal?*

Enough of that, Oscar. Whining doesn't become you. Maudie pulled her hand away.

Yeah, right, sorry. But when all this began between us I had no clue it was going to be this powerful. How can you stay so focused on this mission you keep talking about, as if everything that's gone on between us means nothing. It's completely changed me. Come on, Maudie. Admit it. You must have some desire in you to live a normal life. Listening to the sound of his own voice embarrassed Oscar. [*You sound desperate, Oscar. You got any self-respect?*]

And this normal life you keep talking about, Oscar, Maudie's tone betrayed her growing impatience. *A stay-at-home wife in a house on the Main Line? You want an American housewife, get yourself an American girlfriend. I'm African, Shona. My father is president of Zimbabwe. He fought a war for that. For me that is normal life. I don't mean to make it sound like I think bourgeois comforts are shameful—we're still fighting for our people to have them. But they're just not for me. Not in this lifetime. We're lovers. That's great. Yes, it's had a big impact on me. But if being lovers, knowing it must end, is not enough for you, then you'd better leave now.*

And what if it doesn't work out for you to succeed your father? It may not work, you know. From what I know of Africa politics, it sounds like a long shot. Oscar never ventured here, but his fatigue and the looming deadline of graduation were upping the ante. *I mean, who the hell can predict the future anywhere, especially in a volatile, new country like Zimbabwe?*

Maudie sat up, pulling the sheet around her shoulders. Her brown eyes narrowed, icy cold. *This is the last time I'm going to say this, Oscar. Don't you ever try using our relationship to undermine my future in Zimbabwe. I promise you it'll end up costing you your lover.*

*   *   *

A New Wrinkle

Wharton. April, 2022

Thanks a lot, Dad, for your interest, but I really don't think McKinsey is the right fit for me. Oscar's father, The Rev. Andrew Anderson, Director of Social Justice Ministries and World Relief on the staff of the National Episcopal Church in New York, had sat next to Gretchen Mallory at the annual Martin Luther King Dinner at the Waldorf Astoria two nights before. Gretchen had been Chief of Staff in Andrew Young's office when he was mayor of Atlanta, and was now a major player in the politics of racial justice. She had been Managing Partner of McKinsey Global Institute's overseas division for some time. Andrew had mentioned to her Oscar's interest in hoping to find ways of using his MBA to empower economic change in the third world.

Maybe not, Oscar—Andrew knew his modulated preacher's tone would infuriate his son—*but what could it hurt to give Mallory a call? You'll be looking for some sort of job after Wharton. Gretchen is incredibly well connected in the third world you're so interested in, and she could probably at least open some doors.*

Oscar hated the rush he got when his father mentioned McKinsey. Most of the people at Wharton would kill to get hired by McKinsey. The competition for an interview was tougher than it had been to get admitted to Wharton. That night he waited for Maudie at her apartment so he could talk with her about it.

Look, Oscar, I have never been able to figure out quite what it is you're looking for. I hear the excitement in your voice when you talk about

---

McKinsey. And why not? Everyone in the class would give their life just to get an interview. But I also hear your uneasiness, your guilt about I don't quite know what. Is this more of that purity thing? That you don't want your father's help, or that you think McKinsey's an exploiter? I mean what's the issue you're struggling with here?

Stick with me, Maudie, Oscar struggled not to slip into his begging voice. *Don't lean on me too hard about this. I'm not sure what the issue is either. I'm just thinking out loud, hoping to get a handle on it. I could use your help in getting a little clearer what the issues are for me.*

Oscar, you're a grown man; isn't it about time you gave up these little innocence games you love so much, and claimed your place in the grown-up world? How about you just step up and make a decision about how you want to use all this hard-ass B School stuff? In six weeks we graduate from this place.

Oscar's skepticism about cutthroat capitalism hadn't kept him from being in the top 10 percent of the class, along with Maudie, both years. [*If it hadn't been for Maudie, I probably would have dropped out after the first semester.*]

When he called Gretchen Mallory the next day she had already spoken with the Dean.

Oscar, I'm so glad you called. Your father wasn't sure you would. She sounded like an old friend, not like the formidable managing partner Oscar had heard his classmates gossip about. *Why don't you come to New York one day next week—say Wednesday—and you and I can have lunch and talk about your future. Your father tells me you're not much interested in the corporate world. After 20 years in that rat race, I can't say as I blame you. But it'd be a pleasure to meet you, and just sit and talk, no pressure, no obligations.* She didn't have to tell him he shouldn't mention this to any of his classmates.

* * *

ANOTHER FORMIDABLE WOMAN
NYC. APRIL 2022

Their conversation was in Gretchen Mallory's private dining room in the corner of the building at 55 East 52nd Street with the big window looking over the East River. It triggered the ambition fantasies Oscar struggled so hard to persuade himself he didn't have.

So you're interested in the third world and economic justice. Any thoughts about how you might put those together?

The give and take was easy, so relaxed that it took Oscar by surprise when Gretchen sprang on him a special project McKinsey had been talking about that she thought might interest Oscar.

Did you know McKinsey has been working with the Economics Ministry in Robert Mugabe's government in Zimbabwe?

[*Dad told her a lot more than he admitted to me.*]

No, I didn't know that, Oscar tried to sound casual, hoping to keep his excitement from showing.

Your Dad tells me you have a particular interest in Zimbabwe.

My girlfriend is President Mugabe's daughter. Oscar figured she knew all this. He thought it pointless to continue the verbal fencing. *I suppose that means I have a particular interest in the country.* He hated the defensive tone he heard in his own voice.

That would be Maudie Mugabe. We're told she may well succeed her father as president. What do you think?

[*Yellow flag! Caution, slippery slope.*] Maudie wouldn't talk with him about the ins and outs of Zimbabwe politics even when the two of them

----

were in bed together. Oscar knew better than to risk revealing anything [*as if I have anything to reveal*] to this charming, unknown woman.

I really know very little about that. Oscar wasn't being totally forthright, but in truth he hadn't quite figured out what to make of Maudie's future in her father's government. He often wished he knew more. He'd been present when her father spoke with her about being the future President. Oscar had wondered how much it was wishful thinking, or whether he could actually make it happen. *I suspect you people at McKinsey may know a lot more about that than I do.*

We only know what we read in the papers. Oscar, despite being a novice in this international world of covert information, understood Gretchen Mallory had just told him a lie. It was common knowledge at Wharton that McKinsey provided major cover for CIA operatives all over the world. That was one reason all those young sharks would love to have a job there. Gretchen clearly possessed a lot more information than what she read in the papers.

Well, Oscar, we've been approached by Mdziwe Baunda, Zimbabwe's economics minister, to ask if we might find a recently trained economist who would act as his aide. When I talked with your father the other night I wondered if—with your unusual resume—you just might fill that bill?

Gretchen, Oscar tried to sound more comfortable than he felt, calling her by her first name as she had insisted, *I'm about to be a brand new MBA with only the pitifully meager experience of a couple of internships. I've visited the country once, for two weeks. Can you imagine asking the Zimbabwe Minister of Economics to take me on as his aide?*

As a matter of fact I can, she answered. *He's looking for someone young, unusually bright, and low profile enough not to attract media attention. And he specifically asked for someone who hasn't already formed so many firm opinions, someone already so committed to American style capitalism, that they'd be an ideological nuisance. That's an awful lot of different things, rarely all found in one person.*

Let me put this to you straight, Oscar. Gretchen's manner turned intense. *There are huge numbers of problems in that government right now and they're only going to get a lot worse. The IMF is unhappy about Mugabe's vast personal wealth, and about the troops he's sending to the Congo. The World Bank is angry about how they feel the government has botched what they euphemistically refer to as land reform. Their treasury has been printing money promiscuously, thinking they can solve their political unrest by paying off people with worthless, inflated paper. Our clients, and they're a motley bunch on all sides of the political divide in that beleaguered country, are looking for someone to go there who not only knows something about economics, but who also might be able to provide a channel for solid information for these agencies that are getting impatient with the country and threatening to cut it off from any further aid. The IMF can't justify continuing endlessly to pour money into a failing country as they have been. But they also think cutting the cord at this critical point would be an even bigger mistake.*

We may have been given a unique opportunity. Minister Baunda, a member of the rival Ndebele tribe, is nonetheless a cabinet member in Mugabe's Shona dominated government. Because of their fear of losing the critical next IMF payment, Mugabe has agreed to Baunda's request for a McKinsey intern. If we can find the right person, perhaps it will provide the opening for the information the IMF has been frustrated in getting up until now.

And you think I'd fit that bill? Oscar was weary. The lunch had been rich and the warm afternoon sun had just passed over the top of the window. His head felt heavy. He shouldn't have eaten that peppermint ice cream with the chocolate sauce.

I don't honestly know, Oscar. The warmth was back in her voice, making Oscar feel even more cautious. *But you do have some curious credentials, not easy to match, and Maudie Mugabe isn't the only one.*

It could turn out that my relationship with Maudie might be a negative for what you're asking, Oscar warned. He wasn't about to tell this tough woman about the complexities of his relationship with Maudie. And the truth was that he had no clue himself how their relationship [*if she'd even agree to having it continue*] would mesh with what Gretchen was suggesting. [*What does she know about Maudie and me?*]

It wouldn't be long before Oscar would understand that in the world in which he was about to be immersed, he'd do well to assume that people know everything about you before they ever meet you. Everything.

*   *   *

WHO'S ON WHICH SIDE?

Wouldn't that be interesting? He was surprised that Maudie actually seemed to take to the idea when Oscar told her about it that night when she picked him up at the airport. *But* [*here comes the caveat*] *I hope you don't think you'd have some sort of inside track with either Minister Baunda or the president because of me.*

Look, Maudie, I still think this is the weirdest, most fucked-up idea I've ever heard of. It scares the shit out of me. But a couple things have me considering it. The first is that it is by far the most interesting possibility I've heard u̇ till now in the interview process. I mean, ∧ *would I rather live in Brooklyn Heights and stay up all night checking the grammar in a new bond issue, or get to be in on a government's attempt to bring prosperity to a struggling infant nation? The second, and—I have to be honest with you—most important to me, is that it would mean I would be somewhere near you instead of thousands of miles away.*

You know I'm flattered, Oscar. The thought of being near you appeals to me, too. But I think you better put those two things in reverse order. Nothing's changed about what I have told you so many times about my future. Not only am I not going to have a lot of time for a personal life when I go back, but think for a moment about how tricky it would be for the two of us. You are on McKinsey's payroll, advising our government about their loans from the IMF. Not only will I be constantly in the public eye, but I will be among those working to secure those loans for our impoverished country. I'm not saying we could never see each other. Maybe we could find occasional moments to sneak off for some down time together. But think about it. You are a white westerner from a parastatal company potentially playing a key role in our country's fortunes. And I am President Mugabe's daughter. And heir.

*   *   *

Oscar Signs On: What's My Line? NYC. May 2022

In their last conversation before Oscar signed on with McKinsey for this weird job, Gretchen Mallory had tried to prepare him for the inevitable emotional and political turmoil, the disconnect he was going to experience between what he thought he understood, and how things would actually play out in Zimbabwe.

We're asking you to pay particular attention to what Mugabe's real intentions may be in his government's confiscation of the big, commercial white farms. We've known for a long time this was coming, maybe before Mugabe realized himself that he had no choice if he wanted to stay in power. That last election—he actually lost, though he rigged the recount—woke him to the reality that he better come through on those promises he made before independence about putting productive farmland into indigenous hands.

You'll hear them refer to it as "land reform," or "redistribution." And I suppose you could have made a case for calling it that, at least in part, if they had set up some reliable system for compensating the white farmers. And if they'd had the sense to leave at least some of the most efficient farms in place. The big white farms and tourism were the only real source of foreign currency the country had. Both completely destroyed.

Gretchen read the discomfort in Oscar's face.

Whatever you make of the justice of the thing, Oscar, or of the colonial history that gave the white farmers all the best land, this precipitous, violent invading of working farms has totally wrecked, not only the agriculture sector, but also tourism and safari hunting. They've managed to wipe out virtually their entire access to foreign currency with one ill-considered policy.

You're going over there not only to help them keep orderly books for the IMF to inspect, but to try to help interpret to them how this is playing in the rest of the world. What the consequences may be beyond their own short-term political interests. We're not sure just where Baunda is on the issue, but as Finance Minister he plays a key role. We need to know more about that, and we need to find out how reliable the figures are that come out of his ministry.

Oscar was haunted by mental replays of that conversations with Gretchen. It was the closest she came to saying outright that he was being hired to spy on his client. [*Christ, wouldn't you think McKinsey might want to make their CIA shadow just a little less obvious?*] Now, whenever anyone referred to "land reform," he heard an echo of Gretchen's caustic voice. It made Oscar's stomach turn over.

As he knew from the start he would, Oscar quickly give in to his excitement about the job and the chance to be on the same continent as Maudie. He told himself he needed to keep in check any hopes that this might end up changing Maudie's mind about the two of them, but he gave up trying to maintain the fiction that he cared about the job, or anything else, mattered to him much as being near Maudie.

*   *   *

Maudie Vexes Oscar (Again)
July 2022. On To Zimbabwe

Though she never weakened, never offered Oscar encouragement about a future for the two of them, two weeks after Oscar arrived in Zimbabwe Maudie took pity on Oscar and arranged with a friend for the two of them to spend an evening alone in the friend's apartment. Maudie gave Oscar elaborate instructions about where to park and how to make his way so he'd have a chance to enter the apartment building without being seen. It was his first sense of what was going to be required for them to see each other, and how seldom that likely would be possible. He was nervous about following his instructions, and even more about how different it might be, being with Maudie in Harare rather than Philadelphia.

The public announcement of Maudie's appointment as deputy president had been made leaked to the press, adding to Oscar's apprehension. And, he was embarrassed to admit, to his excitement.

[*I've never slept with a vice-president, not even of a sorority.*]

Maudie's greeting and her skillful swift seduction erased Oscar's anxiety, at least long enough to reassure him that the pleasure of their being together was undiminished. And that pleasure did in the resolve Oscar had made to himself on his way over. He asked Maudie if perhaps she arranged this meeting because she had been rethinking their relationship.

[*At least I asked without whining.*]

Try to think of it this way, Oscar.

That Maudie could carry on what sounded to him like a contract negotiation, lying next to him, naked—both of them damp from love-making—was yet another dimension to Maudie that made her seem beyond reach and exotic.

[*Could I seem even remotely exotic to her?*] He felt the farthest imaginable from exotic as their conversation began.

Maudie rolled over toward him, heightening his self-consciousness. Despite their easy, familiar intimacy, when she focused her attention on him like this, she seemed to him like another species, her body and her intentions a seamless whole, her entire being single-focused, seeming to bypass her consciousness.

Oscar, on the other hand, was chronically plagued by self-consciousness. He'd once joked with his therapist that he'd know he was cured if he ever had a single, spontaneous, unexamined moment.

What have you come here to do? If you had accepted that Fulbright, Maudie said, *you'd be in some unheated room in Oxford right now, trading clever ironies with a bunch of other brilliant writers, one of whom would no doubt already be so celebrated in the literary world—and unknown by everyone else—you could impress your grandchildren one day, telling them you used to sit around bullshitting with him. Maybe you would even be the one the others bragged about having known way back when. Kind of a long distance from Zimbabwe's finance ministry.*

Look, Maudie—Oscar pulled up the sheet, covering himself, a gesture he regretted even as he watched himself doing it—*when I said I feel all at sea here, it wasn't because I wish I hadn't turned down the Fulbright.*

Maudie smiled. She gently stroked his member through the sheet.

No need to be defensive, Oscar. I meant it as a compliment, trying to tell you what a brave, principled decision I think you made when you decided to come here. I know you wish it included a piece about a future for the two of us, but I also have learned a little something about your integrity. And I know you wouldn't have accepted the heavy responsibility if you weren't prepared to give yourself to it.

Oscar felt himself begin to stir under Maudie's stroking. He would have thought he was all finished for the afternoon. [*I wonder how much that blood rush is from Maudie's hand, and how much because she said she thinks I was brave to come here instead of Oxford?*]

I'm not making fun of you, Oscar. I'm Zimbabwean. There are paradoxes that go with that. Even though we fought a nasty war against the Brits, we have still been powerfully influenced by them. We'll never say this in public, but we're all closet Anglophiles. You notice we all stop work at 10am and 3pm every day for tea. Zimbabweans, at least those you'll be dealing with, think being conversant with Keats, or having an Oxford degree are signs of having made it. I can't think of any of my Zimbabwe friends who would turn down a chance to spend time at Oxford. Even if it's only for that foolish summer session you see advertised in magazines.

My father would never admit it, but his Oxford degree means almost as much to him as being president of this country. And it's an honorary degree.

God, Maudie, maybe it's because I'm trying to get my sea legs here. I'm so off-balance I can't tell when you're complimenting me and when you're dissing me.

You'll know if I mean to diss you, Oscar. Don't be so hard on yourself, dear man. We are who we are, all of us. And I suspect that's pretty much decided by the time we learn to walk. You may not realize what you're like to a woman brought up among men, both African and Western, who swagger to show off their strength. I have seen how your ambivalence embarrasses you. I actually find it rather charming. Endearing. Integrity can be pretty sexy when you've spent half your life among political bottom feeders.

Of course it can also put you at a real disadvantage when you're negotiating with the likes of one of us.

Oscar knew all this, had heard it for years, though in a somewhat different tone, from his parents. *You can't get by on charm forever, Oscar.* He'd repeated that to his therapist who had roared with laughter. *Likely, not, Oscar, but if you could bottle it, you'd be the richest man in the world.*

He resisted his urge to keep the conversation rolling, fishing for more compliments. He lay as still as he was able with Maudie's hand resting lightly on top of the sheet, casually caressing his lap. [*Is she even aware she's doing that?*]

Oscar turned to face Maudie, his head propped on the pillow. He raised himself on an elbow and leaned toward her, kissing her on each eyelid. He lowered his head and brushed her nipple with his tongue, the tiny bumps like the skin on a tropical fruit. Maudie shuddered. Her eyes closed.

They were hot and spent after an hour of love-making. The temperature was in the 90s but Maudie had turned off the air conditioning. *I want your man smell, Oscar.* They both wanted to make this time last. This was the first time they had been alone in the two weeks since Oscar had arrived in Zimbabwe. The two years in Philadelphia already seemed like long ago.

Though neither mentioned it they both knew Maudie's appointment as Deputy President meant the end of just about any chance for private time.

The already edgy matter of a close relationship with a white American consultant from McKinsey—a functionary within the Zimbabwe Finance Ministry—now became much more edgy.

Before you agree to this, Oscar, Maudie had warned, when he was considering the job, *you need to understand there will be precious little, maybe no, opportunity for us to be together.*

He knew she'd leave in a few minutes. The afternoon now seemed to Oscar like it could be an ending. [*Good night moon. Goodnight dreams. Goodnight Maudie.*] Her warm, ocher skin, her taste on his tongue, sensations he couldn't bear to imagine letting go, already haunted him, like a junkie about to go cold turkey.

Maudie moved her hand from his lap, stretching, her arms extending full in front of her, then over her head, her legs flexed, toes pointed.

[*She's like a great cat!*]

I'm afraid I really must be going, Oscar. The president has called a meeting of Agriculture and the Judiciary to discuss all the issues that will be coming up around our implementing the government's land reform and redistribution.

[*Land reform? I fucking hate this.*]

It makes you uncomfortable, doesn't it Oscar? My calling it land reform.

Maudie swung her legs over the side of the bed, spearing her tiny panties with her big toe. She leaned down, neatly sliding them onto her left foot. As she stood, pulling up her pants, Oscar's apprehension about land reform and land confiscation faded, giving way to regret, as Maudie buckled her bra, cupping the breasts Oscar had just been tasting.

Well, my dear man, I have spent enough time in the States to know that it is simply impossible for you to see it as we do. Nor will I waste my breath trying to persuade you that African land—once redistributed, finally returned to Africans—serves the cause of justice, and ultimately of economic reform. Even though I assure you it does.

Oscar and Maudie both burst into laughter.

Think about it, Maudie, how many negotiations about international loans and power politics do you suppose have been conducted between people who were naked?

Likely a lot more than you might imagine, Oscar.

Come to think of it, Oscar, when I hear myself put it to you like that, maybe I will try to convince you. Even if part of why you were sent here was to try to turn us away from following through with this, maybe you can begin to see why this issue cuts way more deeply than if it were merely economic or political. It's the very heart of our revolution. And it takes precedence over everything else even, for the moment, over the poverty we hope your IMF will help us address.

I do understand your situation, Oscar. McKinsey and the IMF hope you can persuade us to delay land reform until our economy is stronger, so their loans won't seem so risky. Well, I hope you may help to persuade them that they're investing in something much more important than merely next quarter's GDP.

Oh Maudie, you know by now I haven't got a noble, principled bone in my body. And that I don't begin to understand or trust my own motives. About anything. I'm totally double-minded about this land business. And, despite your kind words, did I take this job just for the chance to spend an afternoon like this in bed with you? Probably. But maybe you're right that that's not the whole story. Maybe I had some small hope of being some help. Land reform? Illegal confiscation? Who can say?

Maudie, fully dressed in black pin-stripe power suit, her hair coiffed into a perfect Afro, looked as if she had spent the afternoon in conference, devising strategy for presenting numbers that would convince the IMF they were on track to justify payment of the upcoming installment on their loan. Though still new in Zimbabwe Oscar, too, had been quickly caught up in the crisis atmosphere caused by the IMF threat to hold up the loan if the farm takeovers continued. Maudie and Oscar had signed out of their respective offices, so they each wrote in the log, for a strategy meeting to organize the numbers for presentation to the IMF.

[In a way, I guess you could say we did] Oscar thought.

In contrast to Maudie, Oscar still looked like the unmade bed he was lying in. He sat on the edge. Maudie leaned down and gave him a moist, soft-lipped kiss.

Till then, Love, she said, and was out the door before Oscar could get to his feet.

[*I wonder if we'll ever actually have to sit across the table from each other to do that negotiation? I wonder if that really may have been what this afternoon was about for Maudie? I sure hope not.*]

*   *   *

Dinners with Dad

Zimbabwe's land issues came up between Maudie and Oscar often during their time at Wharton, and even occasionally in the early days of Oscar's tenure at the Zimbabwe Finance Ministry. The subject fascinated Oscar, who understood their government saw it as key in every way—politically, economically, emotionally—to Zimbabwe's coming of age. It triggered issues of self-respect and claims as a legitimiate independent nation.

For Maudie the passion the matter aroused was etched deep into her by many of the conversations at her father's dinner table.

Dinner in the presidential palace formal dining room, Maudie and her father alone at the long table, the state china, crystal, silver. Once Maudie's favorite times with her father. But more recently she felt less of the old easy intimacy, the bantering and teasing, gossiping about world figures and ministers of his own government. Much less laughing at themselves about how outlandish it was for black Africans, so recently lackeys of the imperialist Brits, to be the ones now dining like royalty. Much as she loved those dinners, they reminded Maudie how much she still missed her mother. [*What must it be like for him? No one to share his bed. Not as if he lacks women eager to fill that gap. Old maybe, but his African male appetites seem intact. Still, even the occasional tryst isn't the same. He has to miss Mother. No one can get him to relax and laugh at himself the way she did.*]

Tension she sensed growing between them which she never felt in earlier years, wrecking their easy banter, made Maudie miserable. Her father blamed it on the years she spent in Europe and the U.S. Maudie worried her father was becoming increasingly intransigent, suspicious, even of her. Their first open clash came the night George Mudziwe, the Minister for Internal Security, joined them for dinner.

Mr. President, he addressed her father in a squeaky, obsequious voice. [*Disgusting! Nobody's dealing straight with him anymore.*] It spooked Maudie. But even worse was the smile it brought to her father's face. [*It can't be that he doesn't see through that fawning.*] The two men had embraced in the traditional Shona manner. To Maudie the embrace seemed different from the usual comradely greeting. It seemed furtive, almost prurient.

The dinner conversation turned to two opposition MPs who had recently started an independent newspaper. It was the first challenge since independence to the Harare Herald which, semi-independent in theory, was understood by everyone to speak with the government's voice.

What do you have on those two fags? her father asked Mudziwe. [*I've never heard him use that nasty term before!*] She knew of her father's contempt for homosexuals, a prejudice deep-seated in African culture. Maudie was embarrassed at his open contempt when she had used the western term "gay," though she was not altogether comfortable herself with how her attitudes about this had wavered during her time in Europe and the U.S

Well, Mr. President, they have been seen going into The Spot, that bar down near the Holiday Inn which is known to be a gathering place for western perverts.

I've been to The Spot, several times, Maudie protested, ***it's no . . .***

Maudie! her father shouted, ***this matter is none of your concern. Comrade Mudziwe and I are discussing potentially important matters of state security. You must not interrupt.***

Maudie was badly shaken. And angry. Since her mother's death she had been her father's hostess and his confidante. She was by his side to receive heads of state and ministers of government. It had been only weeks she had officially been made Deputy President. He never before had spoken to her in this voice. Never embarrassed her in front of another minister.

[*What's this? What's going on?*]

Please continue. President Mugabe made a show of turning his chair to face Mudziwe so his back was to his daughter. Maudie felt her anger rising. This was a new experience and it felt ominous. [*I've got to hold my tongue until Father and I are alone.*]

These two homosexuals are trying to use their so-called newspaper as cover to make their disgusting sexual deviancy fade into the background. You have only to see what nonsense they print to know they are not serious journalists. Of course the western press is always trying to portray us as animals, sub-human, claiming their AIDS epidemic started with our people mating with monkeys. It is dangerous perverts like these two, trying to ingratiate themselves with our former masters, who give African manhood a bad name. Unless we stop them they will try to introduce western sexual decadence and disease into countries like Zimbabwe.

Maudie felt like she was in a nightmare. Her resolve to keep still was faltering. *Mr. President*—she took care to address her father by his formal title. She was desperate to change the direction of the conversation. *With all due respect, I have spent two years at a Business School affiliated with one of the world's leading medical schools, and we learned quite a lot about AIDS there. I must tell you . . .*

Silence! The crystal goblets teetered as her father shouted, pounding his fist on the 17th century mahogany English dining room table. *If you insist on interrupting state business I will have no choice but to banish you from the room.*

Don't be too hard on her, Mr. President, these men have taken in many, even of our own people, who do not understand how dangerous they are to the morals of our country. She has spent the past years being exposed to western ideas. But you needn't fear. The Deputy President has inherited her parents' wisdom; she will soon regain her healthy African perspective.

Comrade Minister! Mugabe again rattled the crystal. *I am perfectly capable of disciplining my own daughter. I do not need you to advise me.*

Yes, Mr. President, voice yet squeakier.

Maudie's heart sank. Her father's intolerance of anything other than the toadying had grown far worse than she had realized. What a disaster if she no longer enjoyed his confidence, could no longer speak frankly to him. What use would she be? What catastrophe might he walk into, unnecessarily, simply to reassure himself of his own authority?

Would you think, Comrade, he turned again to Mudziwe, as if their conversation hadn't been interrupted, *that the time has come for us to make a decisive move against them? We cannot permit this cancer to grow unchecked in our body politic indefinitely.*

We must be thoughtful and cautious in how we go about this, Mr. President. Western journalists will be only too eager to portray this as an issue of freedom of the press, even though you and I understand it is nothing of the kind. It is a well known tragedy that the west has lost all sense of personal morality and dignity, and will shamelessly overlook sexual license as if it is no longer a matter of consequence. My suggestion is that whatever move we make against the paper be done through anonymous third parties, those with no official connection to the government. It might be best that it come from an angry reader, an ordinary citizen, with CIO encouragement in the background, seeking personal revenge for an outrageous breach of the common good.

I follow your excellent reasoning, Comrade Minister.

Her father's smirk made Maudie feel sick to her stomach. [*This is a cheesy Cold War novel in the making. Father, you can't have unraveled this much. As for you, Mudziwe, you slimy bastard, may you get AIDS in your lascivious pub crawling through gay Harare nightlife.*] It was well known among the president's inner circle that Mudziwe frequented the most sordid gay nightclubs in the city. [*Is it possible Dad doesn't know? Surely he couldn't be that clueless. God save us.*]

Maudie was silent for the rest of dinner, excusing herself immediately after the final course, before coffee and brandy. She drove herself home, turned on CNN, watched distractedly for a few minutes, turned it off, put in her iPod earphones. James Taylor in concert at Tanglewood, a recording that always helped calm her. Her father hated Taylor's music, called it the whining of an American hippie drug abuser. They used to laugh at their different taste in music. Now she suspected her father might destroy the iPod if he discovered her listening.

Rock-a-bye Sweet baby James . . . Maudie felt the tears rolling down her cheeks. She never cried in front of anyone since her mother died, but lately she found herself crying by herself. Oscar sensed her sadness, pleading with her to talk about it with him. She couldn't do that. She trusted him more than anyone, didn't worry that he would try to take advantage of her weakness (and she did regard tears, other than in formal mourning, as weakness). But she disciplined herself to keep whatever differences she had with her father and his government between the two of them. What's more, Oscar was working for Baunda, and even though Baunda was a minister in her father's government, he was Ndebele. Maudie wanted to protect her relationship with her father, and she had a powerful, innate sense of discretion. As had her mother. Even when she had disagreed profoundly with her father, no one outside their family would ever know. Though it sometimes frustrated Oscar—for whom candor trumped secrecy—and made the distance between them seem greater, her steely discipline was another exotic fascination about her, and made Oscar's infatuation with Maudie even deeper.

But as Maudie sensed the growing distance from her father, her loneliness and growing need to gain perspective on how best to carry out her role, made her drop her resolve and begin to confide in Oscar. [*This is likely to go bad.*]

Maudie, her father said to her on another night when it was just the two of them at dinner, *I hope you know that I do understand that I've been asking you to become something I probably have no right to ask of you.*

I've asked you to become, at least in the way you manage your emotions, more a man than a woman. The dangerous direction Zimbabwe's politics are taking makes it unwise for me to confide in anyone else in official position. I know you are aware that I believe you are brighter and tougher than any of my ministers, and I have come to rely on you more than on any of them. And I do know that requires you to exercise male, not female, emotional discipline.

Maudie had absorbed another, deeper dimension of feminism in America. Her mother's feminism, though unrelenting, was subtle, softened by her deference to her husband. Maudie was at pains not to concede how much her father's fears about American influence had been realized, but she found it hard sometimes to conceal how much his entrenched African sexism made her bristle. But she still considered herself a child of old Africa. She understood her father's meaning. Even while it unnerved her, her father's charge thrilled Maudie. *I pledge to you I will do my best, Father, to honor what you ask of me. I hope it is of some comfort to you to know that I have absorbed much of the emotional discipline I admire in you.* And she had. But in earlier days—while she scrupulously maintained traditional respect for her elder parent—their exchanges had been reciprocal. He was candid with her and listened to her opinions. Now something seemed to be changing. The change was ominous and made Maudie feel terribly alone.

And now, increasingly, she began to confide in Oscar in ways she had previously been careful to avoid.

So it was particularly unsettling on another night at dinner. Again, just the two of them—roasted tenderloin of pork and the traditional Shona staple, sadza, mealie-meal, accented with a mellow Italian Merlot. Maudie felt relaxed with her father for the first time in many weeks, safe, almost in the old, familiar way. Until her father shifted their lively conversation about the Zimbabwe cricket team's recent stirring victory over Bangladesh, to the subject of Oscar.

How's Oscar doing over at Finance, Maudie? I haven't seen or heard much of him for a while?

You know, Father, now that you mention it, neither have I. I guess he's very busy, what with the IMF due here soon to discuss the next payment on our loan. Why don't you invite him to dinner here with you at the palace and ask him how things are going? He'd be flattered, and you know Oscar; he'll tell you what he thinks. He can't help being open and candid even if it means violating a state secret.

[*That may not have been the smartest thing to say to the president about Oscar.*]

Maudie, do you have any doubts about Oscar's being dependably loyal to us, to our interests in these matters, not a stooge for the IMF or any of those other agencies that get their hooks into every IMF matter—the CIA and their cronies?

[*This conversation doesn't feel so cozy anymore.*] *Father, you were the one who pushed to put Oscar in that position. I've never had any reason to doubt his integrity. Have you?*

Well, no, not really, but he is an American, and he was recruited by McKinsey. And we both are aware that McKinsey is well known for making their people available for clandestine work. And Minister Baunda is, after all, Ndebele, from Bulawayo, and ZAPU.

Father, it wasn't very long ago that you told me Oscar was the son you always wished you had, despite his being the wrong color and from the wrong country and hemisphere. I confess that made me a little uncomfortable, wondering if you were suggesting him for a prospective son-in-law. Because as you know, I'm committed to serving Zimbabwe and you, and that means not making any life pledges beyond my responsibilities to the nation, certainly not marriage. But no, I've never had any cause to question Oscar's loyalty. I interpreted your expressions of affection for him to mean your trust in him was nearly as great as your trust in me. What makes you raise this now?

No reason, really. Our Director of the Central Intelligence Organization brought it up with me last week. Of course it's his job to remain constantly vigilant, even to risk overreacting so as not to be caught unaware. The President watched Maudie for her reaction.

And? Maudie was now on high alert.

Well, he said Oscar makes several phone calls a week back to Gretchen Mallory at McKinsey. The CIO Director refers to her as Oscar's "handler."

That's absurd! Typical spy paranoia. Of course he speaks with Gretchen Mallory. She's his boss. Maudie's eyes flashed with anger. [*Don't overreact,* Maudie.] **Why are they monitoring his phone traffic? Has he done something suspicious to warrant being spied on like that, violating his privacy?**

No need to get so exercised in defending your American lover, Maudie. It's the job of our intelligence people, routine to keep tabs on people. He may be your boyfriend, but don't forget that he is from the country whose president has referred to me as a pernicious dictator.

[*Don't bite, Maudie, on the lover, boyfriend bit.*]

So, Father, tell me, do you have my phone tapped? Maudie spit out her words.

President Mugabe laughed. *We haven't had sparks fly like that at this table since your sainted mother died. But you mustn't take offense, my dear daughter. He's in a sensitive job, privy to information most of my top ministers don't see. So we keep our eye on him as we would anyone in his position. He's an adult, he knows the ways of the world. I'm sure he expects us to do tha*t.

Maudie wasn't placated. *You didn't answer my question.*

Maudie, don't push me. I would imagine both your and my phones are tapped, with the exception, perhaps, of the ones that have scramblers they haven't yet defeated. And since we rely on our security people for the scramblers, well . . . If not by ZAPU, probably by my rivals in ZANU, our own party. It is naïve to think otherwise. When you became my closest confidant you surrendered not only your anonymity, but your privacy. Just as I did when I became president. It is an unhappy reality of life at the pinnacle of power.

That may be, Father, but if so, when—if ever—might we assume we can be candid, open, without fear we're being overheard?

The president looked behind him in a gesture she took to mean that he was looking around for who might be listening at this very moment.

Well, we never can be certain, my dear daughter, can we? Do you recall reading that piece in the London Times last year about Gorbachev being confronted with a transcript of a conversation he had with Raisa when they were in bed at his Dacha? He never knew whether the listener had been the CIA or his own KGB. So how are we to know whether someone may be listening to us? I think we must always assume someone may be, and that their interests will undoubtedly not always be in prefect concert with ours.

Maudie was now in full pursuit. *So, assuming everything we say is overheard, just how are we to go about conducting our business? Not to mention our personal lives?*

Above reproach. Her father threw back his head and roared laughter.

You really do find that amusing, that you never have a private moment?

Amusing? No, darling daughter, I find it sobering. As you should. The steep price for my ambition to become the leader of our nation, a difficult and much sought after job. And if you feel it is too great a burden, you'd best tell me now, because, as I hope you never forget, I have been preparing you for that job since before your mother died.

Maudie shifted nervously in her chair. *How, for instance, do the servants know not to enter the room while we're having this conversation?* She was deliberately avoiding the challenge he had thrown at her, an issue she had turned aside when Oscar had tried to get her to talk about it. Of the many unsettled pieces of her life, the loss of all privacy caused her perhaps the most anxiety. [*Is there anyone I can really trust?*]

They know not to enter until I press the buzzer at my feet. But you have said nothing about the matter I mentioned. Is this surrender of personal life more than you are prepared to take on?

Mr. President—they were on formal ground now, no longer father and daughter enjoying dinner—*you know better than anyone that everything in my life has been to prepare me for this. I have become, frankly, useless for any other purpose. It is quite irrelevant whether I like thinking I may never again enjoy a private moment. If that is a condition of what I am to do, then it is. It is what life has thrust upon me. I can't believe you or anyone else would willingly, knowingly choose it for himself. Had I known at 15 what I know now, would I have? Who can say? But the question became meaningless some time ago.*

Quite right, Maudie, and in fact, for my sanity I choose to believe I do still have private moments. But I can never be certain, and I know, alas, from the intelligence reports I receive about even those closest to me, how sophisticated and difficult to detect these tiny surveillance devices can be.

Maudie looked uneasy. *Did you mean me, when you spoke of those closest to you?*

My dear daughter, I have chosen to trust you absolutely. I have given strict orders that your privacy is never to be violated. Yet, even though I am president, I cannot control everyone in the government. Nor can I always know what agents of other governments may be doing. And if you are to sit in my seat one day, you must learn that you, too, cannot trust anyone, absolutely. No one. Even your own father, you must assume, will betray you if, God forbid, he should find it necessary.

[*Even your own father! Where does this end?*]

Maudie knew this terrible reality would haunt her, probably for the rest of her life. Who could ever have imagined a life in which you couldn't trust anyone? [*Thank God I was never tempted to succumb to Oscar's begging me to marry him. Preposterous as it seems now, when we were together in Philadelphia, I think I really did let myself fantasize about it a couple of times. I don't think Oscar ever had any idea. He once asked if I didn't long for a "normal" life. He'd decompensate if he overheard this conversation with Father.*]

*   *   *

An Invitation for

Oscar, Too

Oscar was to have his own innings with President Mugabe. Though never able to put out of his mind what his father and Gretchen said about the president, Oscar had come to quite like and respect the old man. And fear him. And there was always that other lurking; he was the father of the woman Oscar loved.

Oscar's list of the bizarre since arriving in Zimbabwe was long, but this led the list so far:

Maudie's father, His Excellency—the message on his answering machine announced—*The Honorable Robert Gabriel Mugabe, President of Zimbabwe, wishes to extend an invitation to Oscar Anderson to join him for dinner at the Presidential Palace.*

Oscar's first instinct was that it was a gesture, not a serious invitation. When he mentioned it to Maudie he tried to sound off-hand, wanting her to know he understood there was no way the president really wanted to spend an evening with him. She laughed. Oscar didn't ask Maudie what her laugh meant. [*Doe she think I'm an asshole, so impressed by being invited?*]

Apparently not. She began coaching him about what to expect.

Maudie warned him not to let his being flattered by the invitation to the palace cause him to lower his guard. *My father is every bit as charming as you are, Oscar—when he chooses to be. But unlike you, he is not transparent. He is crafty, never lowering his guard, aware every moment in every encounter how the power is flowing. I hope you know that he genuinely likes and respects you. But you are an American with ties to the IMF, and he is president of a country that needs money desperately.*

The easy intimacy with Maudie from their time at Wharton seemed to Oscar to have become rare and fleeting once they were in her country. In Zimbabwe there were several times in every day that he felt at sea, unsure how to navigate. He had expected to feel off balance in a strange culture; he was discovering he had been naïve in thinking the weirdness wouldn't extend to his relationship with Maudie. Looking to her to provide a safe and familiar place where he could let down is air, ignored reality.

Was he expected to make a formal response to the invitation? [*This is driving me nuts, never knowing if I'm about to step in yet another pile of shit. Or whether I am the pile of shit. I'm supposedly here to help put the country's finances in order, but whatever that's supposed to mean sure has nothing to do with any accounting I ever learned. The stupid numbers have nothing to do with anything except what someone wants them to at the moment. Maudie's on her way to becoming president, but not word one about the Constitution calling for popular election. What ever made McKinsey think it was a good idea for me to come do this? What made me think so? You know the answer to that, lover boy.*]

When Oscar gently probed her about how the succession thing could get around the constitutional problem, Maudie patiently tried to explain it to him. *I am the daughter—the only child—of the nation's first and so far only president. Yes, we have a constitution that provides for elections, but our constitution isn't 200 years old like yours. It has already been changed several times to reflect the fast changing circumstances.*

Despite the constitution, the issue of succession is far from clear. We may not be a mature enough democracy to have a full blown election when it comes time for a new president. I know you take such a thing for granted in the States—or you did before 2000—but you have been through it many, many times in the U.S. We have yet to do it. It's not yet clear we are even securely a nation. Were it not for our borders having been drawn by colonial commercial interests, it is likely that Zimbabwe would today be at least two countries rather than one, with the two main tribal groups dividing east and west. But we are what we are. Reality takes precedence.

For the sake of order and the well-being of Zimbabwe, it may turn out that my succeeding my father in office without the uncertainty and chaos of trying to hold a national election, is the best option.

Oscar's mouth fell open in astonishment. *Even if you wanted to, even if you thought it was the best choice, could you actually pull that off, Maudie? I mean, assuming you want Zimbabwe to become a working democracy, don't you think that would set the country back? Wouldn't you risk turning the country into a family monarchy?*

You mean like the Kennedys, or the Bushes, or the Clintons?

They both broke into laughter, breaking the tension. Another reminder for Oscar that his assumptions were often no more than unexamined prejudices that would evaporate when confronted with the realities.

We're not at Wharton any more, Oscar, and we're not working out a marketing case study. Nor are we a carefree couple enjoying the freedom and irrelevance of graduate school.

When the call came from the president's personal secretary, despite the earlier invitation on his answering machine, Oscar was still taken aback. The voice on the other end identified himself as the president's personal assistant, whom Oscar had met. Oscar felt they had made friends, but now his tone was formal:

The president would like you to come to the Presidential Palace for dinner on Thursday night. You may come in smart casual dress. He will expect you at seven o'clock, and you will use the diplomatic entrance on the side opposite the Sports Club. Security will be expecting you. But you must not be alarmed if they put you through rigorous screening. Depending on who is on duty at the diplomatic gate, you could be frisked. A few of the men are extremely cautious, which is why they hold those strategic posts. It is not personal; everyone receives the same scrutiny.

He hung up before Oscar could respond. [*That wasn't an invitation, it was a summons.*] Never mind that he'd had a date on the calendar for that night for weeks, with the president's daughter, whom he hadn't laid eyes on in a month. He tried to dismiss the thought that the president—or his daughter—might have known that. [*Paranoia will only make things worse. You're playing by their rules and you've never seen the rule book.*]

Oscar dialed Maudie's number.

The recording: *The deputy president is in conference. Because of her heavy schedule over the next several days, it may be at least that long before she is able to return your call.*

Maudie—Oscar didn't mind leaving a message, though he wished the recording was Maudie's voice rather than the generic voice-over—*your father's secretary called to summon me to dinner Thursday night. He hung up too fast for me to try to explain that I already have a date . . . I assume it's ok to thank him for his kindness, and demur?*

Hi, Oscar. Her voice was light, cheerful. *So, you're going to dinner with the president.*

Is this for real? Are you going to be there, Maudie? It wouldn't be a substitute for an evening with just the two of us, but at least . . .

No, Oscar, I won't be there. It'll be stag on Thursday at the Presidential Palace. And, yes, it's for real. The president is not in the habit of issuing casual invitations.

The amusement in her voice did nothing to reassure him. [*Shit. I'm not going to ask her if she already knew about this. Or maybe set it up? Or if this is a state occasion, or maybe when I'm going to be moved in on, asked for some inside shit from the U.S., become some kind of double agent.*]

But what about our date? Looking forward to an evening together has been my lifeline these past long weeks. [*Cool it, Oscar, you're whining.*]

Oscar, do I really need to remind you? You're in Zimbabwe on loan from McKinsey to the American State Department as special assistant to our finance minister. Not to carry on our courtship.

Give me a break, Maudie. I understand about all that, but there's more to life than . . .

I'm not sure you do understand, Oscar. And unless you can, unless you're ready to discipline yourself—as I am—putting personal issues aside while we address the critical matters this country faces, you're going to fail at the job you were brought here to do.

The president wishes to spend an evening with you. That in itself should be more than enough reason to set aside whatever else you may have planned. Here, as in the United States, when the president calls, you answer. Aside from the honor—he rarely dines with anyone other than a state visitor, or me—there is the critical reason you are here. The economic morass we find ourselves in could destroy everything the president has worked for. Perhaps you haven't realized how much the president and I are both counting on you to help us break through this impasse with the IMF.

Maudie, Maudie, it's me, Oscar. Give me a break. Do you think I would ever have been asked, or would have considered taking this job, if it weren't for you? I mean, let's get real; if it weren't for you there's no way I would have ever been considered in the first place, right? You make it sound like I'm the fucking secretary of state or something. I'm a flunkie, a rookie consultant. Of course I hope I can help, but, Jesus, I'm not exactly a major player in all this. Maybe you forget, I'm a first time consultant.

Oscar, we're not in some Hollywood movie; This is governing under difficult circumstances—reality—it isn't therapy.

Please, Oscar, I know this is all more weighty than you signed on for. But whatever weird circumstances may have brought you—and me—to this point, there is critical work to be done. And those circumstances have appointed you and me to do this. So forget all that modesty business. Whether other, more suitable people might have done better, here we are.

If this is more than you are prepared to do, maybe you'd better become clear about that before you get in any deeper because, not trying to get too dramatic, this may be the last moment you'll be able to walk away clean. [*Feel familiar, Maudie? An echo of the conversation the other night with your father?*] *From here on I can promise you it's all going to become less clear and more demanding. So maybe you want to find yourself a girlfriend who is willing to make warming your bed and your porridge the focus of her life.*

Oh please, Maudie, that was a cheap shot, so unfair, and you know it.

Maudie sighed. *I apologize, Oscar. That was uncalled for. Things are heating up so fast, Oscar, my nerves are pretty frayed. I never meant to let this happen, but, besides my father, you've become the only person I talk to about all this. I know you think I'm tough, but I do still need someone I can trust and talk to. A white American might not have been first choice for either Father or me, but sometimes these matters overturn how we design things, or even our judgment. He trusts you, Oscar. And so do I. I hope to hell you don't prove us reckless.*

I never meant to lure you here under false pretenses. What Zimbabwe is facing—what I'm facing, and, unless you bail out now, you're facing—is going to have to push all our personal issues aside.

Maybe it's too much to ask someone like you, from white, middle class America. I'm only a generation removed from guerilla bush warfare. That's where my toughness comes from. You probably can't build it any other way. You didn't have to fight for what you have. This isn't even your country. I wish you would stop telling me about your having come here because of me. That's not going to be enough to sustain you for what's coming.

Don't misunderstand about my father living like a successful westerner. It doesn't mean he thinks the way you do. The way he lives is a political symbol. It shows we've replaced British prerogatives with our own. I don't let myself indulge in them. Sorry if I sound to you like some hard core revolutionary, Oscar, but if you're going to be able to help us, you need to understand this stuff. It's just not like anything you've ever known.

Maudie's passionate speech made Oscar's heart sink. [*It's like she's explaining her nation's mission to the UN.*] Every phrase increased the distance between them. It didn't help that he heard in her voice an echo of his own telling his skeptical father that his passion for working for justice in the developing world was more important to him than anything. [*Is it still, Oscar?*]

You never misled me, Maudie. You're right about my whining, wanting us to make a life together. I'm afraid a big part of my coming here was hoping it would give us another shot at putting our lives together. When we were in Philadelphia, listening to you tell me about what you—and then I—would be coming here to do, was like watching a play. It was a big high and I wanted in on it. So much more exciting than anything I ever imagined myself doing.

But you know, my dearest, right now, embarrassing as it is to admit, I think I bullshitted myself. There's a lot more middle class American in me than I might wish. And I'm afraid that has so far translated into caring more about how to seduce you than about how I can become a soldier in Zimbabwe's revolution.

I know, Oscar. Nobody can ever really talk themselves into this hard shit. I don't think any less of you for it. But maybe it really would be better for you to fess up and resign. And go home now. Before the choice is taken away. I have no wish to torture you. And if our relationship is what's keeping you here, it's going to end up a disaster.

You know, Maudie, I may be scared shitless, but this is by far the most compelling thing I've ever gotten myself into. And even if it can't end up the way I've always hoped, I want in. I'm already in so far over my head I feel like I'm drowning. But like a drowning man I'm seeing my whole life pass before me, and if doing this means going under, so be it. Who knows, maybe I'll even actually learn to swim in this deep water. Maybe I won't drown. [*That's a ton of metaphor, Oscar; who're you performing for?*]

And I'll never apologize for wanting to be where you are.

The following two days were a whirlwind. Minister Baunda was preparing for the visit from the sharks from IMF.

The production numbers were some of that deep water Oscar was thrashing around in. Who knew the figures were at best rough guess, and at worst trumped up? Everybody? Oscar couldn't imagine how anyone who had their eyes half-open the past months could believe the optimistic estimates. The next installment on the IMF loan—virtually the only source of revenue the country could hope for—was, as everyone in Zimbabwe and the IMF knew, dependent on improved agricultural yields, along with the president and his ministers curbing their lavish spending. And the finance ministry needed tp convince the IMF that their numbers reflected reality.

Oscar knew—certainly Comrade Baunda knew—that not a single one of those things had happened. Did the IMF know? President Mugabe surely knew. And how could Maudie not know? If the loan were held up—as the IMF threatened—it would bring the country to its knees.

Oscar's job was to collate the numbers as they came in from the various sectors and get them into coherent form to present to the IMF auditors. *Not to judge their honesty or accuracy, Oscar,* Minister Baunda reminded him. *Only the agricultural overseers of the different sectors can vouch for their accuracy.*

Oscar's encrypted conversations with Gretchen Mallory at McKinsey [*are they really secure?*] erased any lingering doubts he may once have had about her being under cover CIA [*not very damn far undercover*]. And a stooge for the IMF. *The IMF is pressing very hard on this, Oscar,* she told him. Oscar knew they would insist on getting him alone to pump him for what he knew about the reliability of the numbers. That's what he had been sent to do; how could he play dumb? Why would he even consider it? [*Who am I pimping for here?*]

[*How can you ever know who knows what? Maybe this just one big global charade in which the players all understand the figures will be presented in a seemingly orderly way, and everyone except me? And just winks at what they all know are bogus numbers. And we go ahead playing the game, conducting our business as if it's all on the up and up? Incredible! It sounds more and more like what I've read about that huge economic collapse back in 2008. Everybody sees it coming, knows the numbers are bullshit, but nobody has the balls to blow the whistle. Because everyone's in on it.*]

It was hardly a secret—the NY Times and the London Times wrote about it regularly [*even if the Harare Herald reports the government numbers as gospel*]—that ever since the government began kicking white farmers off their land and giving it to so-called war veterans [*everybody knows they're cronies of the president who've never farmed*], crop production had all but come to a standstill.

Oscar had argued with his own father when he said he'd seen the terrible crop numbers since the government takeover of the farms. The whole western world considered Mugabe just another African tragedy, a once brave, patriotic leader who freed his people from colonial tyranny, but who now, like every other post-colonial black African leader, had driven his country into desperate poverty, caring only about his personal power and wealth.

[*What's really fucked up is, they're right. Or they're right when you look at it while you're sitting in Washington or New York.*

[*But it just doesn't look all that clear to me any more. Yeah, I know, people will say I'm being co-opted, blinded by my leftist leanings, not to mention because I'm so crazy about Maudie. And that's not really wrong either. You can't possibly understand all this without being here. But being here doesn't change the numbers. And those guys at the IMF don't give a shit about anything else. Or do they? Maybe I shouldn't.*

[*I've gained some real respect for Minister Baunda. I wonder what it means that he's Ndebele? You have to wonder what that may have to do with the way he handles these numbers? Is he laying some kind of a trap? Or is he happy just to have a job in a country with 90 percent unemployment? And some pretty nice perks.*

[*I mean, how the hell does this work, the Shona controlling the government, throwing an occasional bone to an Ndebele, a strategic ministry like finance? I haven't seen anything to make me think he isn't loyal to Mugabe's government.*

[*I don't suppose it's all that different from when President Obama appointed Bush's defense secretary, Robert Gates as his defense secretary.*] At least that's what Oscar told himself hoping to preserve at least a little of his comfort level that was shrinking every day.

Tuesday, seven o'clock sharp, Oscar pitched up at the diplomatic entrance of the Presidential Palace, his uneasiness about the evening mingled equally with his excitement.

*   *   *

ARE YOU SURE YOU WERE
EXPECTING ME?

The other two times Oscar had visited the Presidential Palace, he arrived as a passenger in Maudie's Mercedes roadster and they had been passed through the checkpoints by smiling guards waving their Uzis in friendly greeting. Maudie offered to drive him again this time, but Oscar felt he needed to go on his own. [*No need to look like I need Maudie to hold my hand, though I wouldn't mind if she did.*]

And this time was quite different. In his aging Mazda Oscar got a taste of what it was like for most who came for a meeting with the president. President Mugabe's personal secretary had called him several times—as recently as that afternoon—to tell him how eagerly the president was looking forward to their dinner.

All the palace guards have been given your information, Oscar—your photo, your eye scan, plate number—with instructions to pass you through straight away. But I hope you understand one or two of them may seem somewhat hostile, insist on putting you through a vigorous check.

Please be assured this is not personal. We are still a very young country with fragile institutions. Even a presidential order cannot always make everyone relax their vigilance. Please be patient and, whatever you do, do not challenge them. They take their responsibility to guard the president very seriously. I'm sure you are aware of how many assassinations there have been in our neighboring countries.

At the third checkpoint, all within several yards of each other, a huge beefy man [*he must be Ndebele, I've never seen a Shona that big*] took a long, slow look at the three forms of ID Oscar offered, looking down at his papers, then back at Oscar, silently, as if he were uncertain whether he might have forged them.

Please step out of your vehicle, keeping your hands in plain view.

[*I should have taken Maudie up on her offer to drive me through the gates.*]

As he unfolded his 6'5" frame from the low slung Mazda, Oscar came eye to eye with the massive man. [*He must outweigh me by 100 pounds.*]

Spread your feet wide apart and place your hands on the roof of the vehicle.

[*I have never felt so fucking white.*] Oscar had seen white cops make black men assume this posture in West Philadelphia. He felt alone, vulnerable, at a loss as what to expect next, totally at the mercy of this giant man with his deadly weapon dangling casually over his forearm. [*Why should he be so goddamn cautious with me? He has to have been told I am here at the personal invitation of the president.*]

Of course Oscar knew the answer—[*I'm white*]—which only heightened his anxiety.

The guard frisked him, running his large hands roughly down his sides, back up the insides of his legs, knocking his testicles, making Oscar flinch. While Oscar remained in that spread-eagled, humiliating position, the guard shined his flashlight on Oscar's ID, examining it for what Oscar knew was an unnecessarily long time, obviously meant to intimidate. [*Good job.*] Oscar forced himself to focus on what the president's secretary had said, about the solemnity of their job and the numbers of African leaders who had been assassinated.

He was determined not to betray his anxiety [*anxiety? I'm scared shitless!*], as he stared into the muzzle of the Uzi pointing at him while the guard continued to study his ID at a leisurely pace.

As Oscar was about to hyperventilate the guard handed his cards back to him. **Pass on**, he said, motioning with his Uzi to a parking place only 10 yards ahead. On a sawhorse in front of the parking place, **Oscar Anderson** was stenciled in large black letters.

Oscar pulled into the spot, took a long, deep breath, and got out of the car. Andrew, President Mugabe's longtime aide and bodyguard, whom Oscar had met often enough to call by name, stood just in front of the car, seeming to Oscar to have materialized out of thin air. Andrew stepped forward as Oscar emerged from the car, embraced and kissed

Oscar on each cheek, in the manner of Zimbabweans who had spent time among Europeans.

Wonderful to see you, Oscar. I trust you were warmly welcomed as you entered the palace grounds.

You are most gracious, Andrew, Oscar responded, trying to keep a neutral tone, wondering how much Andrew knew of his encounter with the guard. Or [*Jesus, I really am becoming paranoid*] whether the guard had been following an order, maybe putting Oscar to some sort of test?

The president is grateful for your doing him the honor of giving up an evening to him.

The honor, I assure you, Andrew, is entirely mine.

The ritual requirements apparently satisfied, Andrew motioned Oscar through a heavy wooden door into a paneled, high-ceiling room with two couches covered in yellow muslin facing each other. A large flower-print, soft-cushion chair was at one end of the two couches, set precisely at the midpoint between them. Behind the chair, 10 feet away, was a large mahogany partner's desk, bare except for a Zimbabwe bird carved in ironwood, a blotter, and a gold pen-and-pencil set in an ivory holder carved from the tusk of an elephant. On either side of the desk and slightly behind it, were the Zimbabwe and Shona flags. Two obviously old oil paintings [*English, no doubt*]—one of the African bush, one of Victoria Falls—in heavy gilt frames. [*Probably—if only I knew anything about art—famous paintings.*] On his two previous visits to the palace he'd seen several art objects he felt certain he ought to recognize.

On the far wall were photographs of President Mugabe, one with Nelson Mandela, one with Queen Elizabeth.

Although he had been to the palace before, this was his first visit to the president's formal office. Something about it struck Oscar as eerily familiar.

[*Of course. It's a nearly exact replica of the Oval Office in the White House.*]

The president will be here shortly, Sir. Please make yourself comfortable.

[*Nadang! Where had he come from?*]

May I bring you a drink while you wait, Sir?

Nadang and Andrew were permanent fixtures in the presidential retinue. Oscar supposed they were combination protocol officers, cronies, and personal bodyguards. Despite his affection for them, Andrew's uneasiness ramped up.

What does the president normally like to drink, Nadang?

Oscar hoped for some guidance about what was expected.

He is partial to single malt Scotch Whiskey, Sir.

That sounds quite nice, Nadang. Oscar silently chided himself for, once again, falling into imitating the stilted, British English of so many educated Zimbabweans. [*I know these guys see right through me, are laughing up their sleeve at me. They know I've never had a single malt Scotch, don't know it from a double malt. If he'd said the president drinks Castle beer maybe I'd have connected a little better.*]

Very good, Sir.

With a slight bow Nadang disappeared through a door that was so skillfully hidden in the wall Oscar hadn't realized it was there. Oscar stood in the middle of the room feeling self-conscious. He assumed he was being watched, though he couldn't find the cameras. He made one sweeping look around—not wanting to appear on camera as a voyeur. He was particularly interested in what books were on the shelves of the two bookcases on either side of the room.

Dickens. Of course. One whole shelf of leather-bound Dickens, just beneath the shelf of leather-bound volumes authored by President Mugabe. Oscar had read two of the president's books before he came to Zimbabwe. The man could write. And he had a lot to say.

[*How do you put the pieces together? A tribal African, guerilla fighter, Oxford, London School of Economics, and an office designed for the head of state of a major western nation?*]

Oscar! What a pleasure. Thank you so much for coming.

Oscar was afraid he must have jerked around suddenly, awkwardly, startled by the president's silent entrance.

Mr. President! Was as much as Oscar could manage.

President Mugabe strode across the room in three athletic strides and gripped Oscar's shoulders, pulling him into an embrace—Oscar's second two-cheek kiss of the young evening. Although Oscar had met the man perhaps a half dozen times, he marveled again at his energy and self-assurance. Intimidating Oscar. In Oscar's last conversation with Gretchen Mallory—the one that confirmed in Oscar's mind that she was at least partially undercover CIA—Gretchen had emphasized her interest in Mugabe's health, how he was aging.

We know he's at least in his mid 80s, Oscar, but everyone says he appears to have the stamina and vitality of a man 20 years his junior. We'd love to have your take.

Despite Oscar's physical advantage—6'5" to Mugabe's 5'7", 200 pounds to Mugabe's 145, 27 years old to Mugabe's 80 something—as they embraced, Oscar felt overmatched. Psychically, and, oddly, even physically.

I've been looking forward to this evening, Oscar. It is long overdue. My daughter is an astute judge of character, and I presume you know how highly she regards you.

Thank you, Mr. President. Very kind of you to say so.

Your assistance to Minister Baunda as we struggle to emerge from our economic malaise is proving extremely valuable. The challenges are legion. We have much to discuss, Oscar.

[*So, it's a work night.*]

Nadang appeared through the invisible door with two old-fashion glasses on a silver tray.

[*Oh, Jesus, the single malt scotches. I better nurse mine all evening. And no ice to dilute it.*] Oscar reached for his glass. [*This is likely to prove more complicated than trying to figure out who wrote all Shakespeare's stuff.*]

You would be every father's dream of the man his daughter might marry, Oscar . . .

This was Oscar's first one-on-one with President Mugabe. He had gotten to know him just enough to have learned how much he enjoyed the long pause he often left between clauses. The next clause was designed to put the person he was speaking with off balance. Oscar waited, figuring if he responded to that first surprising phrase he would end up looking like the donkey he already felt like. He had practiced in front of the mirror, struggling to keep a neutral expression rather than the friendly, boyish grin that had won him so much approval over the years.

Early on Maudie asked him about it. *Why do you smile so often, have a big grin even when nothing funny or even particularly happy has happened?* He had no answer. He had no idea. He was unaware how much he smiled until Maudie pointed it out. And now he was self-conscious about it. Especially with Africans who seemed always to present a neutral facial expression until something provoked them to betray emotion.

Looking down the long mahogany table—Oscar and President Mugabe were seated at opposite ends—his discipline crumbled. He could feel that miserable, shit-eating grin creeping across his face as if an alien had taken charge of his facial muscles.

President Mugabe's face now broke into its own wide grin.

You'd be this father's dream if you had been born black African and were a card carrying member of Zanu PF.

And now here came the laugh, boisterous, full bodied, and totally—so it seemed to Oscar—at Oscar's expense.

[*At least I think my stupid grin has been replaced with a look of confusion.*]

I've offended you, Oscar. My apologies. I intended a joke we could share, softening this unusual situation you and I find ourselves in. I would never risk such a thing with someone I felt was unsure of my affection and respect. I assure you I meant no offense.

Of course, Mr. President. No offense taken.

[*Offense,*] Oscar thought, [*is hardly the issue. This guy didn't get to be the first black warrior to overturn a white colonial regime and become president, by being considerate of other people's feelings. Maudie nailed it; this is about letting us both know who has the power.*]

The waiter—in tuxedo—came through the swinging door, tray held high, balancing two tall crystal dishes. Somehow he managed a slight bow, without spilling, as he ceremoniously placed the shrimp cocktail in front of the president. Mugabe gave no acknowledgement as the waiter walked the five steps to Oscar's end and placed his dish in front of him, packed with plump shrimp covered in red sauce. Oscar hoped his astonishment at being served shrimp cocktail wasn't obvious.

Perhaps you are surprised to be served shrimp in an impoverished, landlocked nation the world press enjoys telling the world is facing starvation. We have endured hardships before, always at the hands of those who enjoyed their own luxuries at our expense. But we manage to embarrass them by our refusal to become beggars, not licking their feet. How pleased Ian Smith would be to think I had been reduced to eating mealies from maize we received from international relief agencies. Instead, Oscar, we dine on the finest shrimp from Mozambique.

Mr. President, having come to know your daughter—the most worldly, sophisticated woman I have ever known—I would have expected no less. [*Liar.*]

President Mugabe threw back his head and laughed again, this time longer, louder. **Oscar, my daughter, as I have already said, is an** *unparalleled judge of character. As president of a young, struggling, African nation—disparaged by the western world—I knew you would be puzzled, perhaps even disappointed, were I to fail to make a political statement against the injustices that have caused us such misery. It is my solemn duty, always, to remind my guests that our revolution is not yet complete.*

Now that we have that behind us, may I welcome you to my table, and say how privileged I feel to have you accept my invitation. Not only to dinner tonight, but to come and offer your considerable skill to Minister Baunda and our nation. My I propose a toast, to your good health, to the future of Zimbabwe, and to a growing friendship between our nations.

[*I will never be the equal of this fox,*] thought Oscar, as he raised his glass, remembering not to actually drink. [*He has fenced with the world's best for more than 30 years.*] Oscar was grateful for the interlude provided by their turning attention to their shrimp.

As they ate, Oscar took advantage of lifting the fork to his mouth to consider his host, taking a long look at him trying not to seem to stare. [*Gretchen wondered what kind of shape the old man is in. If it wasn't so well known, you would never believe he had celebrated his 84th birthday last July. In an extravaganza the London Observer claimed was financed by China, and alleged to have cost almost as much as Zimbabwe's GDP.*]

Deep, black, unwrinkled skin stretched over his high cheekbones. Tight black curly hair [*he must color it*]. Foreign leaders who met him inevitably spoke of his vigor, his ramrod straight posture, firm handshake. His Savile Row suits and Church wingtips—made, so it was widely reported, by his personal tailor and cobbler in London—would have seemed pretentious, even offensive, on most African dictators.

[*Somehow, you can hardly hold such finery against Robert Mugabe. It suits his dignity. Such hypocrisy, our insisting that leaders of poor countries should have modest tastes. You may be caving here, Oscar.*]

How are you finding Zimbabwe, Oscar? I believe most westerners find us a bit of a puzzle.

Maudie had told me how beautiful it is, Mr. President, but it would have been impossible to prepare one for the reality.

*　　*　　*

Zimbabwe's Beauty;
A Passport

Maudie had indeed told him, mostly to coach him in the importance of meeting a Zimbabwean, any Zimbabwean, with extravagant praise for the country's beauty. His first test came days after his arrival when he was stopped by one of the roadblocks it seemed one encountered every few kilometers. The soldier, dressed in fatigues, looked teen-aged, which added to Oscar's nervousness as the young man leaned into the open window, gesturing with his Uzi toward the seat next to Oscar.

Seatbelt must be fastened! the man barked.

Oh, of course. How careless of me.

License! The young man demanded.

Oscar fumbled for his wallet, leaning to his left, trying to pull his wallet from beneath his right back pocket.

No! License! The young soldier put the stock of his rifle on his hip, as if to take aim.

Yes, in my wallet, Oscar tried to explain, pulling his hand away from his hip.

You get out. The soldier trained his Uzi on Oscar with one hand while he pulled open the door with the other. Oscar emerged, cautiously, careful not to do anything that might seem menacing. Standing made it easier to reach his wallet, which he did, handing it to the soldier. It fell open to his license, his photo, under plastic. The soldier examined the photo, then looked up at Oscar, not seeming intimidated by his being nearly a foot taller.

Mazza chu zetts, the soldier read, slowly, **What is this Mazza chu zetts?**

Oscar was puzzled for a moment until he understood the man was reading the name of the state that had issued the license.

Mass a chu setts, Oscar repeated with the same cadence, **is a state in the United States. I come from Mass a chu setts.**

You American? His voice seemed to take on a friendlier tone. [*Some places in the world, it's still OK to be American.*] **How you like Zimbabwe?**

I think it is the most beautiful place I have ever seen, Oscar said, half because he really did think so, and half because he remembered what Maudie had told him.

Yes, of course, the soldier said, his face breaking into a wide grin as he handed the wallet back to Oscar. He held the door, gesturing again with his weapon—this time without menace—**Pass on**, he said as Oscar settled back into the driver's seat, making a point of buckling his seat belt before putting the car in gear. Watching the soldier in his rear view mirror, he remembered the conversations he had with old Africa hands at the State Department, warning him the only way to work your way through any confrontation in Africa was money, bribing.

[*Never even occurred to me. Didn't seem like he was looking for money. Maybe effusive praise for the country is as good as a bribe.*]

*   *   *

Dinner Continued; Many Courses And Much Fencing

Everyone is impressed by the country's natural beauty, Oscar. And there is so much you have yet to see. Maudie tells me you have not yet been to Victoria Falls—the president had broken into Oscar's flashback to the roadblock. *You must reserve your judgment of the country's majesty until you have seen that World Wonder. You know, no one had ever seen the Falls until Cecile Rhodes discovered them.*

Oscar froze.

Another burst of laughter from Mugabe. *Oh, my apologies, Oscar. It will take time for you to become accustomed to our unusual humor. Much of it is rooted in the indignities we endured during our colonial past. Like the humor your American blacks have inherited from their slave ancestors. It may seem bitter to you, but it served as one of the chief means of our survival during those long, difficult years.*

[*Over your depth, Oscar. En garde.*]

The shrimp had been cleared and two new waiters—in black tie—set in front of each of them a small Spode plate on which sliced figs were artfully arranged around the edge of the plate, with wafer-thin slices of prosciutto ham on top of honeydew melon in the center.

In the course of the evening Oscar lost count of the number of courses, each accompanied by a different wine, from France, Italy, Australia, even California. Oscar—a one-beer-a-night drinker—knew nothing about wine. But he knew if he drained his glass each time a new one was poured, he would likely end up asleep before dessert, his head on the table. Maudie had prepared him for this, too.

You need only bring the glass to your lips, Oscar. But you must do that.

All through dinner as his host shifted, without warning from matters of state to international intrigue, to personal intimacies, to trick questions, Oscar felt off balance. One moment the conversation seemed more intimate than Oscar felt entitled to, the next packed with ominous reminders of the uneasiness between their two countries. He found the president's referring to himself in the third person curious.

I wonder what advice you would give to an old Madala, Oscar, who led a successful revolution more than 30 years ago and now finds himself still occupying the seat of authority? The demands and needs of people throwing off tyranny are different from those people in a developing nation. Most of our people were born after the revolution. And technology has changed the world faster than this old leader can change?

Oscar was grateful that President Mugabe went on without waiting for a response. *And Maudie, Oscar, how do you think Maudie is readjusting to life in Zimbabwe? She has been away for many years. And now she returns, without time to become accustomed to life here again. But regardless of how hard that may be, she has to bear significant new responsibility.*

I think Maudie is a true wonder, Mr. President, your daughter in every respect. She is the most resourceful person I have ever known. Whatever challenges may be waiting for her, there is no doubt she will be more than equal to them.

The president let that hang in the air for a little longer than was comfortable for Oscar, who wondered if he may have gone overboard in his praise.

You are very fond of her, aren't you, Oscar? Of course it is a challenge for you to understand her situation and the needs of our young country. I can imagine how difficult it must be for someone from a country like yours to understand putting the nation's needs ahead of personal desires. As much as we admired your President Clinton, we cannot afford such diversions as he enjoyed while we are still in so precarious a moment in our development.

[Don't bite on that one, Oscar.]

She has never failed to be transparent and above board with me about her priorities, Mr. President.

Another long silence. *Life presents us with challenges, Oscar. They can often take from our hands the future we may have envisioned for ourselves. None of us is clever enough to be able to design for ourselves the way events will unfold. That is in God's hands, not ours.*

[*Didn't Maudie say he's a Marxist atheist? Two ears, one mouth, remember, Oscar.*]

I wonder if Maudie ever speaks to you about me? Or about the affairs of our state? About whether you think she would govern as I have? Of course she is of a different generation, and has a very different experience, both of life in Zimbabwe and of the world.

He had slipped it in so easily, as if this was what they had been comfortably chatting about through the whole dinner. Oscar was grateful he had taken Maudie's suggestion, bringing each wine to his lips without taking even a sip. ·

Mr. President, aside from her obvious love and admiration for you, Maudie has never spoken with me about how you carry on your heavy responsibilities. Nor do we discuss what she may be thinking about her future role in Zimbabwe.

Of course, Oscar. She is as circumspect as her late mother. God rest her soul.

Here it was again. Maudie told him her father had once been a devoutly religious man, when her mother was alive. But now would have nothing to do with the church, except when it became embroiled in politics.

[*I get it. He's just like our politicians, trotting out the deity when the moment suits it. Meaning nothing.*]

Mr. President, getting to know Maudie these past couple of years has been among the happiest and richest experiences of my life . . . [*listen to yourself, Oscar, you're beginning to speak as if you were a character from Dickens.*] *I would be fascinated to learn more about what your family life was like as she was growing up. Knowing what you went through, it's hard for me to imagine how you managed to raise such a strong, worldly, yet modest daughter. My affection and admiration for her make me want to know all I can of what has shaped her life.*

The president's face froze. [*Oh shit, I've stepped in it again. What this time?*]

Oscar, we are a tribal people. You northern Europeans regard our tribal origins as primitive. I have spent time in the bush as a guerilla fighter, in a prison run by the Selous Scouts, and studied economics at The London School. I have been tortured, and I have received honorary doctoral degrees from universities in both hemispheres. Your people are now so far removed from your tribal origins, or from the hardships of birthing your country, I fear any attempt I might make to explain my daughter's upbringing would be incomprehensible to you.

Oscar realized he was staring down the long table at his lover's father, clueless as to how they had arrived at this awkward moment. Or how to navigate his way through it. His host had turned to the plate in front of him, concentrating, furiously drawing his knife across the pork tenderloin on the plate as if it were tough as buffalo.

I'm afraid I may have phrased my question awkwardly, Mr. President.

[*There's that fucking squeaky, obsequious voce, Oscar.*] He hated himself when that voice took over.

I admire your daughter more than just about anyone I've ever known.

Of course you do, Oscar, Because you think it quite miraculous that the daughter of an African guerilla fighter could be so clever and so sophisticated.

Oscar felt a mixture of anger and frustration. And fear. Maudie's advice had been, no matter how provocative her father might become, never to take the bait.

[*In for a penny, in for a pound, may as well go right at it, Oscar.*]

Do you think it possible, Sir, that all white westerners might not be exactly alike? That someone born in a majority black American city like Cleveland, and raised in a diverse world capital like New York, could have a different view of the world than a Rhodesian tobacco farmer?

Mugabe finally looked up from his plate, making eye contact with Oscar. Even though his host's fierce expression continued to unnerve him, Oscar was glad for even this much acknowledgement.

Forgive me, Oscar. You must excuse an old man's bitterness. You are a fine young man, a tribute to the healthy changes your country has made over the past decades. Had I not respected you, and believed you come from a generation that has largely overcome your nation's racist and imperialist past, I would not have trusted you to come here and assist Minister Baunda in this essential effort to strengthen our struggling economy.

This is not personal. It is not your fault that you have generations of racial dominance in your bones. And are heir to the global divide—south, north, black, white, east, west—that is unlikely to be fully breached in either of our lifetimes.

If you are truly interested, I am happy to talk with you about our young nation, how we came to be, what we hope, and the ways we would like you to help us. As well as the ways we would not wish your help, even though you believe it is being offered in good faith.

But do not ask me to explain where we have come from or why we regard the world as we do. Or why we believe white racism is as fundamental a part of your country as baseball. We have each been formed by our historical circumstances. We can perhaps learn to respect our differences, but it is too much to expect us to ever fully understand each other's views.

[*Jesus! Maudie times 10.*] The president looked down the table at Oscar for another long moment. Oscar understood the matter was closed. [*And what was the matter, again?*].

The remainder of the evening went more smoothly, if skirting the issue most important to Oscar could be considered smooth. Despite having called Oscar off the Mugabe family history, the president seemed genuinely interested in Oscar's family history, how growing up in an Anglican priest's family influenced his view of the world, and the way it may have shaped his choices about what he intended to do with his life.

Oscar wished there might be a way to restore some balance to the conversation [*He insists my being a white westerner means I'm racist. Does he ever consider that where he comes from likely makes him at least equally prejudiced in different ways?*]

The president seemed to sense Oscar's discomfort. Before President Mugabe dismissed Oscar for the evening, he reopened the conversation one more time.

Oscar, you must not take all this to heart. You read the classics at Harvard, enjoying the generosity of a liberal community in which you were being prepared not only to put to good use the knowledge and skills your education gave you, but also to become comfortable with the access to the privilege and power assumed for you from your birth. At a similar point in my life I was in the African bush, hoping to survive.

None of us gets to choose our origin, Oscar; it is an impenetrable mystery. And though we can rise above it, not let it trap us like a caged beast, we cannot erase it from our bones.

Mr. President, you are a most complex and brilliant man. I will not pretend to understand all you are trying to explain to me. Much of what I think I am coming to understand here seems contrary to some of the deepest convictions I have formed over my lifetime. Because of my awe for all you have lived through, because of my respect for your intellect, I am having to reconsider things I have previously regarded as settled, beyond debate. This must be the steepest my learning curve has been since I learned to speak.

Mugabe's satisfied smile widened into a huge grin, and he finally broke into that startling belly laugh Oscar couldn't read, whether genuinely amused, appreciative, or maybe scornful.

You are an earnest young man, Oscar. So was I, once, briefly, before events required me to hold onto life more loosely. I, too, was in love with a young woman whose parents told her she could never share my life. She defied her parents. It cost her more than she could have imagined, finally even her life. Being part of the birth of our nation, and even more the gift of Maudie—so she assured me before she died—she considered to be worth the high cost.

I am genuinely sorry that you and Maudie cannot replicate the happy choice her mother and I made. The press of events and Maudie's sense of national duty makes it impossible.

She has left no doubt about that, Mr. President. Nor about her absolute loyalty to you and to the vision you both share for Zimbabwe.

Ah yes. She, too, is young, idealistic. I have no doubt of her loyalty to me. But none of us can know what may yet be required of her. You have seen enough by now to know our country is still profoundly unsettled. It is by no means clear what course will be required for us to proceed.

I was the person appointed by history to bring us to independence. That was more than 30 years ago. Someone else should have emerged by now to succeed me for our next chapter. But largely because of our historical tribal divisions, and the treachery of our former masters who have not yet accepted the verdict of our victory in the war for independence, the person for that duty has not yet emerged. But the time must soon come. Although God has given me unusual health and vigor into my old age, I am not immortal. And Maudie alone among our younger leaders combines the array of gifts required to lead us into that next chapter. But the needs of that chapter may prove so unpredictable and complex that they could yet conflict even with her loyalty to her aging father.

[*Is he using me to send a message to Maudie? What message?*]

I can't imagine such a thing, Sir.

Neither can Maudie, Oscar. Life sometimes presents us with cruel choices we never could have imagined. Could not bear to imagine.

[*What am I supposed to do with that?*]

Before you go, I wish to express again my thanks to you, for being such a valued friend and supporter of my daughter, and for setting aside your career to come and help Minister Baunda make sense of our economic records. It is my hope that you will have absorbed enough of what we are about here to be able to interpret to the IMF why it is that we believe the production numbers by themselves tell only a part of the story, and are hardly sufficient to determine their decisions about the loans.

Mr. President, you are right that working alongside Minister Baunda and spending time in Zimbabwe make the issues all look quite different from how they seem from an office in New York or Washington. But I'm sure you understand that I play only a small role, if any, in the Fund's decisions about their loans.

Oscar, you perhaps have yet to see how central a person you have become in this matter. I understand you are young, and your job is described as a mere intern, but circumstance has trumped all that. How much of life often becomes inscrutable.

That—inscrutable—pronouncement turned out to be President Mugabe's dismissal of his dinner guest. It marked what seemed to Oscar a seemingly abrupt—although not unwelcome—end to the evening.

Thank you very much for doing me the honor of dining with me, Oscar. I am no longer a young man and I require rest for the heavy duties facing me every day. I bid you a good night.

He rose, and with a slight bow, turned and exited through the door beside the kitchen. As if in response to some signal, a palace guard appeared at the door behind Oscar and announced that he would escort Oscar to his car.

Oscar was relieved that Maudie's father had not wanted to linger over brandy and cigars as Maudie had told him was likely. Oscar had never been able to choke down brandy, and cigar smoke made him feel nauseated. But he wondered if perhaps the reason for the abrupt ending was Oscar's having said he doubted he would have much influence in the IMF loan decision.

[*Does he really think I can influence the decision about the loan? I don't think he understands where I really fit in all that. Or is it maybe that I don't understand?*]

Just suck it up, Oscar, Maudie had counseled him, laughing. ***You want to be a player with the big boys in the international scene, you'd best learn to tolerate old world affectations that go along with it. I'm not sure those men really like cigars and brandy, but they're part of the ritual.***

[*Not tonight, thank God. I'm exhausted just by a two hour dinner. Imagine doing this as regular fare. And I'm 60 years younger than that old fox. Don't think I'd ever make it in this world.*]

On the ride home Oscar's head spun with all that had gone on during dinner. He was spent. He had to fight to stay awake on the short drive. He parked his car, let himself into his apartment, sat in his chair, intending to read the crop reports he had brought home from the office. Seconds after he picked up the first paper, his head dropped onto his chest and he slipped into deep sleep.

*   *   *

DEBRIEFING

Oscar was startled awake by the Zimbabwe National Anthem—Ishe Komborera—the ring tone he had downloaded onto his phone after he was offered the job. Maudie thought it was hilarious that he considered it a kind of protection in case he ever got into trouble with the police. *Like that "Support Your Local Police" sticker you Americans put on your bumpers, Oscar? I suppose you're going tell the policeman to wait a moment while you boot up your phone and play it for him.*

He was disoriented, having fallen asleep sitting in his wing chair reading harvest reports from the maize farmers. Even exhausted as he was, he had thought he was too stirred up by his dinner with President Mugabe to be able to sleep.

[*Guess not.*]

He checked the screen. Maudie's private number. Thrilled as he always was to see her number on his phone, he was beat. He didn't have the energy to talk with her.

Hi Maudie, sorry to let it ring so many times. I guess I fell asleep.

Maudie knew he went to bed earlier than she did, but she felt free to call him when she had something on her mind. She never apologized for waking him.

How was dinner with the old man? Fuzzy as he was from sleep, *old man* put Oscar on alert. She'd never used such a homey title; it was always *The president*, or *Father*.

It was a very challenging evening, Maudie. I'm not sure I've ever spent an evening like that, when I felt I needed to be at the top of my game every second.

Maudie laughed. *Sounds like he got your number. Not to feel badly, he gets everyone's number. That's why he is where he is.*

Maudie, I'm all done in. It was about the most complex evening I've ever spent, anywhere, and I don't think I can do the evening justice right now. I wonder when we might be able to talk?

How about tomorrow morning at 6:30, Oscar? If you'll park in the Hilton underground garage and walk through Miekle's to the alley behind my building, no one will see you come in through the back entrance. Certainly not at that hour.

Oscar looked across at the glowing green numbers on the digital clock: 11:47. He mentally counted the number of hours.

I'll be there.

It had been three weeks since he'd seen her. They talked a couple of times each week on the phone, but her schedule and her concern that the press was going to start rumors made face-to-face meetings all too rare.

After they hung up Oscar barely managed to strip to his shorts before falling into bed, too tired even to shower. He fell asleep as his head hit the pillow. A few minutes past 4 he woke, still exhausted but his mind at full speed. His meditation training deserted him as he tracked back over the dinner conversation.

[*Does Maudie believe that shit about western racism? She couldn't. Not and have become my lover. I don't think. For Christ's sake, Oscar, for once in your life, just take things at face value. The old man is a first generation African revolutionary. What do you expect? But Maudie? She's spent half her life in Switzerland, London and Philadelphia. Yeah, right, and just what is it I'm supposed to make of that?*]

Oscar briefly considered turning on the light and reading. But he was so weary. [*I'll just lie here, not fight with my mind. Maybe I can get a few more minutes sleep.*] When the alarm went off at six he wasn't sure, but he thought he might have drifted off. If he had, it didn't feel like it had put a dent in his exhaustion.

He drove to the Hilton in a trance. As he made his way toward the parking garage the sun had just begun to color the horizon. The doors on the bottom floor of Miekles were always open—a passageway between downtown streets—and his energy began to return as he reached the alley and went through the door to the back stairs of her building. He punched her lighted buzzer. Her voice on the intercom made his exhaustion evaporate.

—

Come on up, Oscar. Door's open.

Oscar got into the elevator and pushed 7. The door opened onto the hallway outside her apartment. Oscar could see the door was slightly ajar.

In here! Maudie's voice came from the kitchen.

Oscar went through the living room into the kitchen. Maudie was in the kitchen all right, standing at the sink with her back to the door through which Oscar came.

She was naked.

Oh, Oscar, it's you! What a surprise!

The rush of his blood to his nether region made Oscar light-headed. He barely managed to stay on his feet.

You in a big hurry Oscar, or can we wait breakfast for a few minutes?

Before he could gather himself for a clever response she was on him like a hungry leopard. Her arms around his neck, legs gripping his torso, she had a death grip on his hair as she pulled his face into hers and plunged her tongue into his eagerly waiting mouth.

As Maudie locked her heels behind Oscar's knees his legs buckled, crashing him backwards to the floor. She roughly yanked his pants down; his undershorts came with them. She landed on top of him, hooking his pants with her toe, freeing his right leg.

He grabbed for her buttocks as she mounted him, moaning. She bunched his jersey up under his chin, her breasts pressed against his chest.

Oscar had her buttocks in his grasp, Maudie astride him. She reached down and guided him into her, thrusting herself forward until they both exploded in a furious climax. Her scream nearly burst his eardrum—or was it *his* shout, so loud it shocked him—as if it came from someone else. Two people possessed.

Though their coupling was over in less than a minute, their sweating bodies slipped and suctioned to each other as if they had spent all morning making love in a steam bath.

They lay motionless, silent, for several minutes, still joined. Maudie sighed and rolled off onto her side. The two of them were on the kitchen floor face to face.

Maudie laughed, lightly at first, gradually building, infecting Oscar, until the two of them were roaring with laughter—two bare bellies bouncing, one pale, one chocolate.

Finally Maudie caught her breath. *Well, dear boy, in case you're wondering what happened, you've just been royally fucked by an untamed African.*

Holy shit, Maudie, you and your father sure have different ways of greeting your guests!

Over the coming months as Oscar became more immersed in the riddle of Zimbabwe politics and his ambiguous place in them, the dinner with the president and the morning after with Maudie became bookends of Oscar's life in Zimbabwe. Not exactly a matched set. They quashed his every effort to make the disparate pieces fit into a coherent puzzle.

*   *   *

In Country,
Months Later . . .

The initial strangeness Oscar experienced being in a new country on a different continent gradually eased. He was absorbed by the work at the Finance Ministry. And he was drawn into the growing urgency about how to rationalize the undeniably disastrous yield numbers from agriculture [*Not that the numbers from any other sector are better. Better find some way so they can be presented to the IMF*]. It was obvious there was no hope of the IMF coming through with the money otherwise. And without that money . . .

He found the work fascinating, challenging. He admired Minister Baunda's steadfastness in the face of seemingly certain ruin. As he became increasingly committed to making the numbers convincing, Oscar tried to keep in mind the warnings from Gretchen and the state department people who had trained him. They counseled him to be alert to the subtle ways the different culture and ethic in which he would be living and working would influence him.

[*They presented it as if I would of course resist it. What if being here just makes me think I was wrong about some things?*] The biggest being land redistribution. [*Yeah, it's been done stupidly, corruptly, but for God's sake; white Europeans took the land without compensation over 100 years ago and have gotten filthy rich on the backs of African labor. Why isn't this turnabout fair play?*]

Oscar wished he could talk with Maudie about all this. But Maudie was not only too busy for even a brief phone check-in most days, she had a major hand in running the programs those IMF guys asked him to keep a skeptical eye on.

And he hadn't dared ask her how serious she thought her father's political opposition was becoming. Now that inflation had ramped up to a level they were unable to even measure at the finance ministry, signs of political unrest were popping up everywhere. The work was absorbing enough to keep Oscar's mind off his frustration about so seldom ever seeing Maudie. Most nights he at least put in a call to her. The nights she picked up after hearing his voice on her answering machine provided the payoff, however small, he required to keep going.

But I haven't laid eyes on you in 10 days. As he talked to Maudie on the phone, Oscar watched out the window of his third story flat overlooking Samora Michele Avenue. The street was lighted by torches burning across the street. Demonstrators, maybe 400 of them, were milling around the park. Must be the small black growers he'd heard were beginning to organize, angry about the new ceiling the government had put on the price of maize.

Oscar, we've talked this to death. I'm first vice-president, deputy president of this country. I can't just take a break whenever I feel like it. And what about you? From what I hear you've got more than enough to keep you occupied over there in the Finance Ministry. Last time I checked, inflation was running up to something over 200 percent.

Shall we talk about that, Maudie? About what's going on that the economy should be so volatile? Oscar knew he was out of bounds, but after six months in the country he was exhausted and feeling increasingly fragile. Yes, he'd come to work for the economics minister, and though he could have cared less that he wasn't piling up a personal fortune doing the Wall Street or Silicone Valley gig like so many classmates, he hadn't bargained on the loneliness and confusion of being in a foreign country surrounded by people whose motives and habits totally eluded him.

Go easy on that, Oscar, Maudie warned. *We may come at it a little differently from each other, but we're both here with some serious heavy lifting to do. We're not at Wharton doing case studies any more. Our little romance can take a rest while you and I do our best to see the nation through these hard labor pains.*

That "little" stung Oscar.

[*I've got to stop looking to Maudie to fix it for me. But she's the only person in this whole goddamn country I can talk to and think we're remotely on the same page. Yeah, I know, she spelled all this out before I took the job. I hope to hell I wasn't kidding myself when I figured the job would be exotic enough to keep me interested, keep up my morale, no matter how things go with Maudie.*]

But just the thought of Maudie being a five-minute drive away, seemingly within such easy reach, ate away at Oscar's resolve.

I'm not asking you to run away with me or anything, Maudie. How about just meeting me for a cup of coffee before work tomorrow?

This was the hardest part for Oscar, harder than all the agony of sorting his way through the labyrinth of African custom and politics. No matter how much she demurred, Maudie held title to his heart. In Philadelphia at Wharton they got so they could complete each others' sentences, anticipate what the other was thinking. He'd never felt closer to anyone. Now there were times when Maudie seemed to him just like the people in the finance ministry who made him crazy. Oscar felt foolish to have thought that she was more like him than like them, American, not Zimbabwean. [*God,*] he thought, [*I'm already thinking about 'them' and 'me'. This gig is coming apart.*] The one person he'd found he could even to talk to, Tony Lane, was the political attaché at the American Embassy. [*Or maybe CIA chief of station?*] It didn't require spy training to figure out that Tony's friendship with Oscar was motivated by more than mere mutual affection.

[*It's the wrenching loneliness. Tony's the kind of guy I'd have become buddies with in a nano-second at Harvard. But here, like this, I never know whether I'm talking with a friend or a spy.*]

Of course, Oscar, I'd love to. Maudie's voice lightened an octave and some of the tension left Oscar. **I'm sorry; I'm just so strung out. Do you know the president** [*she used to refer to him as "Father"*] **never gets more than three hours sleep a night? The rest of the time he works, and just about everyone close to him does the same thing. I'm actually sleeping at the palace many nights, never make it back to my own apartment. And I feel incredibly guilty, even though he never says anything if I slack off.**

You know you could have a more relaxed living arrangement, Maudie, with some pretty nice perks. Someone who would cook and clean. A working house-husband. [*Oscar, will you never learn?*]

Give it a rest, Oscar. You know better. The president's deputy and daughter living with a white American who also just happens to be here working for McKinsey, the American consulting firm that has been linked

to the IMF, not to mention the CIA. Now there's a formula for a bright political future.

[*Back off, buddy, deep water.*] Oscar hoped Maudie was right that her phone calls were scrambled and could be read by no one, even the CIO, Zimbabwe's intelligence agency.

Come on, Maudie, Oscar complained, *my salary may be paid by McKinsey, but at the moment I'm working for the same government and the same ends you are. No need to trot out all that media bullshit. I understand the boundaries. But they don't mean we can never even see each other.*

Sorry, Oscar. But it's no good to kid ourselves that your and my interests in all this are identical. Trying to sort that out can only lead us into places neither of us wants to go. It'll work itself out over time. Yes, thanks, I'd love to have coffee with you in the morning. 6:30? Holiday Inn?

See you there.

Oscar heard the click before he could say good bye. He turned on his laptop and waited for the reassuring tone of the modem connecting. These days e-mail was his lifeline, his only companion, his link to a world that now sometimes seemed more like a movie he'd once seen than the real life he was living. Some nights he even went alone to see movies he would never have gone to back in the States, just so he could have a slice of America, portrayed in all its Hollywood stupidity. He was embarrassed by the mindless affluence and gratuitous violence the movies made seem standard American fare, and even more embarrassed by his hunger to lap it up on the big screen. He was fiercely homesick—more than he even admitted to himself—so, hang the embarrassment, he went to every two-bit American movie he could.

The first email was from his friend Russ, who rode the Africa desk in the state department back in D.C. Russ had asked him before he left the States if he'd like to be cut in on the non-classified message traffic about Zimbabwe. Neither Russ nor Oscar was sure whether it was a good idea, since email was certainly the least secure means of communication. But the information was accessible to anyone who really wanted it, and Oscar was desperate for someone to talk to, even electronically, and for information. Even information that was of questionable reliability.

[*Reliable information? What makes you think the U.S. State Department puts out reliable information; not just spin?*] Now he was doing what he'd been warned about by his mentors, and especially by Maudie.

116

Oscar, she'd said, *You're going to find yourself doubting what everyone in Zimbabwe tells you, simply because you're in Africa. I know you don't think of yourself as a racist or an American super patriot, and you're certainly not by any usual measure. But you are an American; it's in your bones. It's subtle and you're going to have to first own up to it, and then curb it best you can, or there's really no point in your going at all.*

What's going to be even harder is that what you are fed by your own people, McKinsey, your State Department is going to be colored by their interest in what you are doing here. So you will have to filter everything through that reality. You can expect to lose all the bearings by which you are used to figuring out where you are politically, economically, culturally. You're going to find yourself a man without a country, suspicious of what Zimbabweans tell you, and equally suspicious of what your own handlers in the States tell you.

[*Handlers? That seemed like such exaggeration then; now it turns out to have been way too gentle. Makes the loneliness unbearable.*]

Forrest Luther, the State Department bulletin began, *financial analyst for southeastern Africa, announced today the third quarter estimates for Zimbabwe's economy. While recent rains have given encouraging signs for this year's maize crop, it is feared that the government's recent ceiling imposed on the market price of the crop will discourage farmers from planting a second crop. The cost of fertilizer—if it can be found at all—is prohibitive and, even with the ceiling, the price of a 40kg bag of mealies is beyond reach of a growing number of even formerly middle class Zimbabwe families.*

Inflation continues at an unacceptable pace, now running at more than 200 percent per annum. Shortages in basic commodities such as diesel fuel, and rumors of the government's failure to release funds to pay for electricity from the regional grid have scared off the few investors who were still active. Reports of large demonstrations in Harare by farmers and students have raised questions about the long-term viability of Mugabe's government.

Mugabe has recently hinted that he will now push ahead with greater determination the land reform he promised when he was first elected. Since this likely means continued seizing of the large white-owned farms that make up the vast majority of the productive farmland in the country which provide more than half the country's access to foreign currency, the world economic community sees this possibility as self-defeating for the country's regaining its financial footing.

Sources close to the IMF indicate there will likely be a re-examination of their engagement with the country, and specifically of the IMF commitment to paying the next installment on the loans they have negotiated.

Oscar pressed the power button on his laptop and leaned back in his chair as the screen went dark. He had felt shaky enough before reading the email. He wondered if Minister Baunda had seen it yet. Worse, what about Mugabe? And Maudie? What if she's read this message? She'll be angry, berate him as if he'd written it. [*Oh please, God, let us have a lovely coffee tomorrow. Holy shit, what's happening to me? I don't even believe in God, and here I am, praying like a goddamn monk. I'm fucking losing it.*]

Between a rock and a hard place—his father's favorite expression which he'd always hated—was how his head felt right now. As if it were in a vise. He wondered if Maudie really thought he could have any effect on America's policy toward Zimbabwe. [*What if—please no, God—that was what was behind her willingness to stay connected to me?*] Their connection now seemed frustrating and fragile.

He lay on his couch, hoping the pounding in his temples might calm down. He watched the torches rising and falling, creating a light show on the walls of his apartment as the demonstrators left the park and headed up the boulevard toward Parliament. The jacarandas were in bloom, a soft lavender in the torchlight. He wondered how long they had been flowering. This was the first time he had noticed.

Oscar woke at 2 am. He'd fallen asleep with his clothes on. He considered staying on the couch for the rest of the night. He was meeting Maudie in just over four hours. But cold and stiff, he rose, went to the bathroom, emptied his bladder, brushed his teeth, stripped to his tee shirt and undershorts and got under the covers in his bed. Nights in Harare were surprisingly chilly—he had expected tropical, like the Caribbean—and he went to bed with cold feet and a dripping nose every night. He'd have given anything at that moment—including a trumped up optimistic report on the state of the Zimbabwe economy—to have Maudie in the bed next to him, warming his body and reassuring his troubled mind.

*   *   *

Breakfast At Harare
Holiday Inn

Oscar, your eyes look like two piss holes in the snow! [*There's an expression you not only didn't learn growing up in Zimbabwe, and would so scandalize your father.*] He hadn't seen her come across the café floor. He had meant to compose himself, try to look at least a little together before greeting her.

You, on the other hand, he said, struggling to regain himself, *look ravishing*.

Get off it, Oscar. No one looks ravishing at 6:30 in the morning.

Maudie, in fact, did. She was dressed for work, in a maroon tweed jacket and knee-length skirt that set off her tan complexion and accented the red highlights in her coiffed afro. The expensive silk blouse—[*from Nordstrom, I bet*]—and matching leather heels and handbag, lent Maudie an air of elegant importance. Every head in the café turned to watch as she walked confidently across the room.

[*Does everyone know her? Her picture's never in the papers, but people must know who she is. I wonder what they think of our meeting like this? Maybe they think it's business? Maybe it is. You've got to stop obsessing like this; it's Maudie and me this morning, or is it? Can it ever be again? Has it ever really been?*]

Oscar stood and came around to pull out a chair for her across from where he was sitting. In his peripheral vision he saw two men two tables away, subtly but unmistakably keeping close watch on the two of them.

Your goons? Oscar asked, shifting his eyes towards the men.

Part of the life, Oscar. Don't take it personally.

So how are you, sweet Maudie? Oscar was determined to ignore his weariness and distress, focus on how glad he was to see her.

Really quite wonderful, Oscar, thanks for asking. I've had days recently when I really can see what a good thing it was that I put in those two years at Wharton. Gives me a perspective on our place in the world I don't think I could ever have gotten in London. And how about you; how're you doing with your culture shock? I'm hearing good things about the contribution you're making over at Finance. They tell me you are one quick study, you already make better sense of the numbers than most of the people who have been there for years. No surprise.

Oscar was torn. Being praised by Maudie was the sunshine breaking through the clouds. But it was more confusing now than it used to be. He wasn't sure now whether her praise was from his lover or from a high government official. And since he had felt so far like a useless cipher, wandering the halls of the Finance Ministry like a blind man, he wondered who could have told her he was effective. And he'd come here this morning hoping to drop the chaos of work and just enjoy a few minutes with Maudie. He had missed her terribly. Sitting looking at her he admitted [*The truth, Oscar, you took this job 95 percent because of Maudie. I almost didn't give a shit about the finances of Zimbabwe. But you know, I think, maybe I'm actually starting to.*]

Oh, I'm chugging along, he answered, hoping he sounded casual, *but, even though the work is pretty damn interesting, I sure miss seeing you.*

And I miss you, too, Oscar. But this is exactly how we both understood it was going to be. There's a crisis an hour in the president's office as we struggle to build this country's credibility, and claim our place as a functioning nation in the world. There's no time in my life for just about anything except tending to the crises. Maudie reached across the table and took Oscar's hand, massaging his palm with her fingers. Her touch sent an electric current through him. She fixed Oscar with a deep, longing look, as if she were asking him to understand, not to push her about this.

Maudie, as he struggled to respond, Oscar was aware of how exhausted he was; he had no reserves. Maudie let her hand linger on his. Her touch soothed like a warm compress on a torn muscle. He felt his guard lower. For a moment he was afraid he might cry. *Your father is incredibly lucky to have you by his side right now.*

You really think so, Oscar? I sometimes wonder if someone not so close to him might serve him better.

Maudie, I don't know whether you're looking to be reassured, but for all sorts of reasons—only one being your kinship with your father—there's no one in this country, close kin or not, who could be making a bigger contribution or have a better understanding of what's needed right now than you.

As he lay awake last night, Oscar had cooked up a plan to try to lure Maudie away from Harare for a few days.

Hey, Maudie, I've been in this country for more than six months and I haven't seen Vic Falls. Last time I checked, the Falls was still one of the Seven Wonders of the World. I don't want to be like my friends who have lived in New York all their lives and never seen the Statue of Liberty or been up the Empire State Building.

How about we both take a couple of days off, fly out there, and you can show me your country's biggest boast?

Then maybe you can take me to Great Zimbabwe. I've heard so much about those amazing stone structures.

What do you say?

Oscar, you definitely should go to The Falls, but I don't see a day off in my near future. And I'm not the one to take you there. Not only because I can't take the time, but in case you didn't do your homework about our country, the western part of the country is Ndebele, not Shona.

I'd a whole lot rather go with you, Maudie. You've got to take some time off or you're going to burn out like a comet at the pace you're going. And what's this bit about Ndebele and Shona? I thought Zimbabwe became one nation in 1980.

Don't get self-righteous with me, Oscar, pretending you don't understand. I've heard your father's stories about what it was like for him to go to Mississippi and Alabama in the 60s. We are one nation, but we have many of the same bitter regional rivalries as you do.

The president travels to Bulawayo when he has business there. He is the president of the whole country. But there are still lots of feelings from tribal rivalries that go back long before western colonialists came to organize us to suit their own commercial interests. They were mostly kept under wraps while we were struggling against, first the British, and then Ian Smith. But now we must deal with them on our own terms.

We've begun. But they have roots that go back further than the founding of your own country. We fought together and we have formed coalitions. Your Minister Baunda is perhaps the most prominent but by no means the only Ndebele in our government. We've still got a long way to go, and it can still be needlessly provocative for high profile Shona to travel there except for official business.

But that should in no way deter you from going to see Victoria Falls. You can read about them, see pictures, but nothing can prepare you for the incredible size. Standing in the spray and that deafening roar of the falling water, you'll understand why the Ndebele name for them means "the smoke that thunders."

And you should go now, right after the rains, when there is so much water falling.

*　*　*

An Early Alert

Oscar knew more than he suspected Maudie would like him to know about the Shona-Ndebele rivalry. About how Cecil Rhodes had allied himself with the Shona. Oscar's old anthropology professor at Harvard with whom he had spoken when he knew he was going to Zimbabwe, said that Rhodes had feared the warrior Ndebele and decided to exploit the ancient rivalry by befriending the less aggressive Shona, arming and educating them.

No one knows, his professor told him, *how many Ndebele died in those early days of British colonial rule. But best guesses put the casualties as much as one-third of those who lived in the westernmost part of the country.*

After independence, when Joshua Nkomo, the leader of the Ndebele party known as ZAPU, turned down an offer to become part of the new government, Mugabe sent his notorious Fifth Brigade, trained by North Koreans, into western Zimbabwe where some say they slaughtered maybe as many as 20,000 people. That led Nkomo to give up his fight with Mugabe and ZANU/PF, the Shona political party, and take the token cabinet position that caused his followers to believe he had sold them out. He said he did it to stop wholesale slaughter of the Ndebele, believing Mugabe was willing to murder them all if that was required for ZANU to take uncontested control.

What you ought to understand, Oscar, is that Mugabe began as a fierce patriot and liberator. But without serious threat from the old colonialists, Mugabe fears he has lost the focus for the support that won him the election back in 1980. He is afraid of any opposition and the Ndebele are the Shona's most ancient and implacable enemy.

The defeat of his attempt to change the constitution by referendum in 2000 took Mugabe totally by surprise. It made him even more certain that he was in danger of losing his support and the job he has come to regard as his personal fiefdom.

That's when—and why—he began the invasion and confiscation of the white farms. He believed, probably with some basis, that the people were angry that 20 years after independence, most of the best farmland was still in the hands of prosperous white farmers.

The white farmers had only just begun to sense their holding onto 90 percent of the most productive land was unsustainable. They started turning pieces of their tobacco and sugar cane farms over to their most trusted workers, teaching them how to farm the land efficiently. They gave them some of their older tractors and other equipment. They regarded their meager gestures as heroic, and resented criticism from England and the U.S. about too little, too late.

But for Mugabe the die was cast. The rest is known to the whole world. The white farms—unjust or not—had provided a huge cash crop that was the country's main source of foreign currency, as well as export maize for all of southern Africa. The farm takeovers brought that to a halt and the country's economy plummeted.

In an incredibly short period Zimbabwe changed from the breadbasket of southern Africa to a nation of starving people, dependent on foreign aid for survival.

The world outside of southern Africa blames Mugabe's megalomania. But many of his ruling colleagues in neighboring countries blame the west's colonial legacy. Both can make persuasive, maybe even legitimate cases.

Oscar wondered if he would ever have a conversation about all this with Maudie. [*It all fit sort of neatly into categories when Dr. Stewart explained it back then. Doesn't seem so neat now that I'm in the middle of it.*]

He wanted to see the Falls whether Maudie went with him or not. He wasn't going back to the States and tell people he never got there. And maybe he could pick up a little more about the western, Ndebele part of the country.

Maudie, you're right, I've decided to go to the Falls. I've got some time coming to me. And Minister Baunda seemed delighted that I would want to go and has approved a week's leave. I think I'd like to drive. I've never seen the western part of the country.

—

It'll be a nice drive, Oscar. But be sure and take along a replacement fan belt. Somehow those things always seem to break when you're in the middle of nowhere.

Thanks for the advice, Maudie. I'll do that. But I'm embarrassed to admit I wouldn't have the faintest idea of how to put on a new fan belt.

Maudie laughed. *Of course you don't, dear Oscar. But you've never had a problem in the middle of nowhere in our country. People will stop and help.*

Even the Ndebele? How do they feel about white Americans?

She laughed again. *Oscar, if there's one thing neither politics nor tribal rivalry, nor anything else, can keep an African from, it's offering hospitality to a stranger. For us it is right up there with breathing oxygen. We do it without thinking about it, as much for our own survival as out of kindness.*

[*The more I see of this place the more I feel like we're different species. They're still pissed about white western colonialism, but they'll stop to help a white man if I break down? Not like Mississippi in the sixties.*]

Right, Maudie. I've heard you on this hospitality thing before, but I don't think I really quite get it. I remember Dad's stories about traveling back roads at night in rural Mississippi when he was doing voter registration in the sixties. He said he and the guys he was with just assumed if anything happened they'd end up like those two white guys and the black guy whose bodies were found later in that earthen dam.

I promise you Oscar that you will be totally safe driving to the Falls. By the way, if you want just a hint of what things were like in this country before independence—for good and for ill—you might want to stay in the Victoria Falls Hotel. Even though it's fallen on hard times, you can see the somewhat shabby remnants of the old colonial days.

Do I really want to see that?

Well, yes, I think you do. Because, odd as it may sound, there is a secret, unacknowledged piece of many Zimbabweans that is nostalgic for those days. Well, not exactly nostalgic, because we'd never want to go back to toadying up to the Brits. But it looked pretty cool, that life. And though you'll never get any of us to say it out loud, we couldn't help wondering, when they still had their foot on our neck, if we got lucky, someday we might be able to throw off that foot and taste that good life ourselves.

Yeah, but Maudie, you know first-hand, having lived in Switzerland, the UK and the US, the emptiness of all that opulence.

Oh, Oscar, you children of western privilege never will get the subtleties about life in places like post-colonial Zimbabwe. Do I want British colonialism restored to Zimbabwe? No. But do I enjoy the perks of life that money and power provide, just like everybody? Yes, I do.

You go to the Falls, and do stay in the Vic Falls Hotel. Unfortunately it is no longer sufficiently ornate or sumptuous to cause you that wrenching conflict of a full taste of the great life you western imperialists enjoyed while so many of our people were mired in misery. But it'll give you a little taste.

And then what, Maudie? What am I supposed to do with that little taste? Find it bitter and upsetting? Wallow in guilt? This was one of those moments when Oscar had no idea whether Maudie was toying with him, enjoying watching him squirm, or giving him a glimpse of the anger imbedded in her bones about what her country had been put through. .

Just go, Oscar. Maudie's voice was cold, dismissive. Oscar had skirted this subtle boundary before. He couldn't understand or anticipate it much better than when he first knew Maudie, but now he at least knew when he was coming too close. And he knew better than to venture any closer.

I'll do that, Maudie.

When Oscar spoke with Minister Baunda [*is he really my boss, or is he standing in for others? And which others? Mugabe? CIA? McKinsey?*] about taking off for a few days and going to the Falls, Baunda seemed pleased that Oscar wanted to go see one of the country's most celebrated spots.

Yes, Oscar, by all means you must go. All the world celebrates the Falls. Quite properly. And then you must go to Great Zimbabwe, the real glory of Zimbabwe's history, whose origins the world pretends is shrouded in mystery, because it's impossible that such rich civilization could have flourished in Africa long before the beginnings of European culture.

But Oscar, while you are at the Falls, you must remember that you are in Matabeleland, a part of the country that is still adjusting to Shona majority rule.

This was the first time since his arrival in the country that Oscar had heard anyone besides Maudie speak so explicitly about the tribal rivalry that Oscar's professor had described to him before he came. And even the couple of times he had broached it with Maudie, she made it clear the subject was taboo.

I appreciate the reminder, Mr. Minister. Is there anything in particular I should be on the lookout for?

Oscar was fishing. Did Baunda know that Oscar was aware he was Ndebele? Though Oscar had pretty much given up hope of sorting out who was on what side of any issue in this country, he always hoped to pick up useful new information. And while he tried to be careful not to seem too curious, he wanted to take advantage of any chance to unpack a piece of the mystery that only seemed to deepen every day he was there.

Oscar, you are in the employ of the government of Zimbabwe. You are an American. You are white. You are a full head taller than almost everyone in this country. Though the Ndebele are taller than the Shona, few of them are 6'5". You must assume wherever you go people will immediately be aware of you. And many more than you imagine will know who you are and what you are doing here.

Oscar found it curious that Minister Baunda hadn't said anything about being Ndebele himself. Surely he couldn't think Oscar was unaware of that. He was grateful Baunda hadn't mentioned Maudie, but he suspected he was meant to understand she was high on that list of the things people would be aware of about him.

*　　*　　*

ON THE ROAD

Oscar loved the trip. Almost as much because of what happened when, as Maudie had predicted, the fan belt on his old Mazda *did* break, as for the Victoria Falls Hotel, and the Falls themselves.

Standing by the side of a remote road, the car's bonnet raised [*to signal my distress, not because I have the faintest idea what to do*], Oscar waited 10 minutes before another vehicle came by. A noisy, dilapidated Toyota pickup with two men pulled off in front of him. They got out and walked toward Oscar.

Some trouble, Boss?

Fan belt broke.

Oh. Maybe we have panty hose. It hold you to next town if you drive slow.

Oh no, I've got an extra fan belt. I just don't know how to put it on.

Oscar saw their expressions brighten. *We fix it, Boss.*

The one who had been driving the Toyota went back to his truck and rummaged around the bed. He turned and, big smile on his face, triumphantly held up a crowbar. Both men set to it without another word, leaning over the engine of Oscar's Mazda, tugging and murmuring in Shona while Oscar stood watching, feeling useless. He reached under the seat of his vehicle and found the spare fan belt, handing it over when asked. In short order they rose up, beaming.

Start up the engine, the driver man said.

Oscar got into his car and turned the key. The engine turned over. The men stood studying their work while Oscar kept his eye on the temperature gauge, sure it would again run up into the red. It climbed slowly until it reached the midpoint where it stayed. Oscar was elated. He jumped out of the car.

Thank you so much! Here, please let me pay you. Oscar pulled out an American $20 bill, which he knew was much coveted in Zimbabwe.

No, Boss. No charge. Smiles even broader.

Oscar made two more attempts, finally sensing he was insulting their hospitality.

Where you going? Driver man asked.

Bulawayo, what about you? They were due to leave the road they were on and take a smaller road 10 km further on, to their jobs. After thanking them effusively, until he felt it was becoming offensive, Oscar got into his Mazda and pulled onto the road. He watched the Toyota pull out behind him. Twenty km down the road he saw they were still behind him. To his confusion and discomfort they obviously hadn't turned off as planned, but followed Oscar all the way into Bulawayo, until he pulled into a petrol station.

Then they honked and waved as they passed by.

The next morning he drove the rest of the way to the Victoria Falls Hotel. He found a weird kind of relief in enjoying luxury (even shabby luxury), having been given permission by Maudie not to feel guilty about it. He was especially taken with the oversize statue of Cecil Rhodes in heroic posture, hand on his hip as he looked across the Falls. [*Wonder why the government left it here? Maybe they get a kick out of the inscription on it saying that Rhodes discovered the Falls.*]

After he returned, he persuaded Maudie to have an early breakfast so he could tell her about the trip. She seemed preoccupied, but then she usually was. Oscar searched for ways to divert the conversation away from business, back to the two of them. The effort was futile and the breakfast aborted when one of the omnipresent men from the adjoining table came over and spoke to Maudie. *Excuse me, Miss Maudie, but the president asks that you return immediately. He says it's extremely urgent.*

Sorry, Oscar, she said, a sad smile begging his understanding, *got to run. I'll be in touch very soon. I promise.*

*   *   *

The Wheels
Are Coming Off

And she was, but not as Oscar expected, or hoped. When Oscar returned to his apartment he read the remainder of his email. One was a disturbing message from Russ, encrypted—which was a warning itself, since he had never been cleared for such messages—about a report in Reuter's of two Zimbabwe journalists who had written in the opposition newspaper that the real reason for Mugabe's sending troops into the Congo was because of his personal financial interest in a diamond mine in that country.

Oscar, the message concluded, *we don't know how much credibility to give to this, but suggest you be on high alert. There's no tradition of press independence in Zimbabwe and we think this could present a challenge serious enough to push the president over the edge. If he digs in his heels and things break wrong with this, we believe it could be enough to embolden his adversaries, maybe even be the beginning of the end for his presidency.*

One report says the journalists have been arrested. This is an ominous development.

And be advised the IMF is watching these events with great concern.

* * *

The Deputy President Takes Issue With The President

I will not stand for this sort of insolence among these arrogant journalists! Maudie and her father were alone in the small private office just off his official office. She sometimes wondered if anyone besides her could detect her father's complexion change when he was angry. He was so beautifully black—nearly purple in his official photographs—most people could never see the change. But she could, and she knew it meant he was close to being disastrously out of control.

Baba—Maudie called him this now only when the two of them were alone—*it's hard to keep still about this because it's so grossly unfair. But if we want Zimbabwe to stop being treated as a pariah by the international community and be given the respect we deserve, we're going to have to at least appear to tolerate some degree of independence in our press. It's just the way the whole world is tending now. And there's no reason to think anyone is going to take these two hack reporters' ridiculous story seriously. You know that.* [*I hope to hell it's a ridiculous story.*]

[*Jesus, Dad, diamonds? You're not getting involved with the diamond trade in the Congo, surely. Tell me you're not!*]

Maudie was concerned to see that her father hadn't shaved. His eyes were a jaundiced yellow, as if he hadn't slept or had drunk too much of his beloved French brandy last night.

I don't give a damn about which way the world is going, he shouted. *I am the leader of this country and I decide what the limits are. And this goes well beyond them. Who do they think they are, accusing me,*

—
131

the president, of sending our young men to die in war only to protect my personal financial interests? Why, making such an accusation against a head of state in time of war is treason under the laws of any country. And treason is punishable by death. These traitors deserve to die.

Maudie shuddered. Maybe the only good thing about how much her father had isolated himself was she felt pretty sure he hadn't yet talked with anyone else about this. And she knew for sure that no one else any longer dared to challenge him if they disagreed. She felt the weight of this, even while she appreciated the pressure he was under; pressure she understood had caused him to act like this. When her mother was alive she used to be able to calm him down, restore some perspective. But Maudie lacked her mother's trump card, access to his bed. And her mother hadn't been concerned with her own political future. Maudie was.

Baba, reporters are always going off half-cocked. Everyone understands they exaggerate to make stories seem sensational, sell a lot of papers and win prizes. When you make a fuss and oppose them you only give them credibility. If you let them print their lies and simply dismiss them as absurd, not worthy of a response, they'll hang themselves. And you will receive praise and support for being confident in your position, and for tolerating a free press, even when they make unjust accusations.

Oh Maudie, her father shook his head wearily, *I knew you never should have gone to that American university. They have corrupted your mind with those ridiculous ideas Americans think should govern every country in the world. Can you imagine the chaos in this country if we allowed the press to go off snooping and printing slander and gossip, whatever they please, the way they pretend to tolerate in America? Freedom of the press is a slogan the Americans brag about, but it is no more a reality in the United States than it is in China. They're just more subtle and underhanded in the way they control it. The Washington Post, The New York Times, they know who pays their salaries. We, too, must make it clear that journalists have a responsibility to advance, not detract from the nation's fortunes.*

Look, Baba, I'm not going to carry the torch for American so-called freedom of the press. I'm just telling you the loans we're looking to the IMF to pay could dry up in a hurry if international opinion gets stirred up over our putting these reporters in jail. I'm making the case for being practical, putting our need for that money ahead of our anger at these reporters and their cockeyed story. [I hope to hell it's only a cockeyed story.]

—

Maudie, The IMF has made a solemn agreement to pay that installment. There were no conditions, nothing about not interfering with the press, placed on it. We are a sovereign nation, not a tool of the IMF. If they try to coerce us, attempt to use their wealth to manipulate us and force us to weaken our country, we'll go our own way.

Maudie knew when he talked like this he was feeling desperate. She remembered how her mother used to go over next to him and stand very close, just stand there, silent, looking at him. She would tousle his hair, cluck to him, kiss him. It always worked. When he almost married Angel, his long time secretary, Maudie had hoped there might be someone again who could probe that soft side. But she worried that Angel was motivated more by her own hunger for power than by her affection for her father, and she'd been secretly relieved when it hadn't worked out. Since then it had become increasingly clear there'd be no one else, only Maudie, in whom he would confide. At moments like this, she missed her mother terribly, and felt the oppressive weight of being his only confidante.

Baba, can we take a moment to review the facts? What's actually happened so far? What steps have you taken about the reporters?

Merely instructed the army to arrest them and hold them while we investigate who they've been talking with. They're not being formally charged with anything yet.

Arrested? The army? Maudie was unable to disguise her horror. Her father glared at her. *You can't have the army arrest civilians. That's unconstitutional. They haven't even been charged. Oh Dad, surely you see how this is playing right into the hands of your enemies? Don't you see where this could lead?*

You sound like one of those weak-minded ACLU American lawyers, Maudie. I wrote the constitution of Zimbabwe. These journalists are tools of the old colonialists, white Europeans, using this subterfuge as opportunity to try to return us to the old ways when we served their interests rather than our own. I can't stand by while the forces of reaction use these so-called journalists to try to turn back the clock on our infant nation. I spent 11 years in their prisons. Our comrades shed their blood to free us from their yoke. It's my duty to protect our people from these imperialists who want to take from us what we won in war.

Maudie knew better than to argue with her father when he had worked himself up like this. And much of what he said struck a responsive cord in her. But she knew the cost in the international community was going to be dear and would eventually encourage their political enemies who were lying in wait for just such an opportunity. She thought about Oscar going to work this morning and wondered what Minister Baunda might have to say about this. He was, after all, Ndebele. And while he had been even more helpful than they had hoped—managing the country's finances honestly and relatively transparently—he couldn't have forgotten what happened to his tribesmen in the 1980s.

[*How in the world,*] she wondered, [*will Oscar cope with this one?*]

She had seen the reporters' story in yesterday's paper, and she, too, had been outraged at the accusations against her father of sending Zimbabwe's young men to fight in the Congolese war just to protect his interests in the diamond mines. Maudie knew her father had built great wealth and she heard the rumors about how much of it may had been siphoned from the nation's treasury. But she knew him better than anyone, and much as she knew he enjoyed his perks, she was confident he would never risk Zimbabwe lives just to defend his own riches.

Oh Baba, I understand about your protecting our nation from neo-colonialists. But you need to listen to the kind of advice that can help you do it in a way that doesn't make you vulnerable to your enemies, abroad or at home. And I fear that what you're doing with these reporters could do both.

That's why I have you here, Maudie. Maudie was relieved to see his shoulders drop, the muscles around his jaw relax. *I know I can trust you, and you've been around long enough to understand the way these things work. I listen to you. You're no sycophant, you tell me the truth. That's why you're being groomed to follow me in this office; no one else in the country is so well suited, or prepared.*

She watched him light a cigarette, take a deep drag and expel it through his wide flared nostrils. At 84 he still cut an awesome figure. Bad as things had gotten, and paranoid as he could become, Maudie's admiration for his warrior spirit was undiminished. He stood ramrod straight, his brown eyes darting, jaw thrust forward, as if daring anyone to challenge him. When she was a little girl, Maudie used to beg him to tell her stories of how he and his comrades had fought their guerilla war against Ian Smith's Rhodesian Selou Scouts. She'd heard stories about how he had been cornered more than once, about the big reward for his capture, dead or alive. But somehow—even the years he spent in their prison—he had always outsmarted them, those arrogant Brits, snots,

trained at Sandhurst. He rarely would talk about all that, but he took great delight in explaining that the Shona and the Ndebele knew the bush, and once it became clear that's where the country's fate would be decided, the outcome was never in doubt. She never tired of his broad smile as he told of the old Rhodesians' worst fears being realized when he, the most hated and feared of all the guerilla fighters, was elected the country's first president by a large majority.

I always try to tell you the truth, Dad, for your sake and for the sake of this country. But Dad, I'm your daughter. I love you and can't bear to hurt you. You need some other people you trust, who have a little more distance.

She saw him stiffen and knew she'd touched another hot button. *This is not a matter of our close personal relationship. You are my daughter by an accident of biology,* he barked at her. *You are, by historical and political necessity, my trusted advisor and my appointed successor. I expect you to set aside the bourgeois sentiments you learned in those western schools, as I have, and as a disciplined African revolutionary choose what is best for our country. There is no place for sentiment in determining what is at stake in Zimbabwe.*

Maudie felt outgunned, could muster no response to his fierce determination for her to remain his closest confidante, and to pursue his rage at the reporters. She believed he was right, even while she suspected both of them would soon find themselves facing circumstances in which they would wish that the reality of international pressure, and of making themselves vulnerable to their political enemies might have carried as much weight in their thinking as their righteous revolutionary fervor.

* * *

JOURNALISTS REPORTEDLY TORTURED; EDITOR DEMANDS RELEASE

Oscar winced as he read the headline in the Independent. He'd had to get a pirated copy from the U.S. Embassy; every newsstand had sold out. As Tony Lane had asked, laughing, *Who do you think might have wanted to buy all those papers before people could read them?*

The lead paragraph was all Oscar needed to read. **The Editor of the Independent has asked the Supreme Court to sit in special emergency session to rule on the constitutionality of the army's having seized the two men. The Chief Justice has said the court would hear arguments on Monday.**

They always pull these stunts on Friday, Tony explained to Oscar. *So it takes at least three days before anything can be done about it. By then everyone has gotten used to the idea; the opposition has been sobered by three days of being beaten in their nasty jail, and the've lost whatever stomach they may have had for holding out for their principles.*

Look, Tony, I know it looks bad, but let's wait until we know a little more about what's going on before we form hard opinions.

I understand what an uncomfortable spot you're in, Oscar—Tony liked Oscar and believed in his integrity—*But you don't have to be in on the cable traffic from Washington to know how this is playing back there and in the whole western press. It stinks.*

*   *   *

McKinsey

Performance Review?

Maudie, I've really got to talk to you. Oscar wondered who might be listening to this conversation. *Something important has come up and I really need to run it by you. It's extremely urgent.*

Have you been reading the papers, Oscar? Maudie's tone, withering sarcasm, sent a shiver up Oscar's spine. *Do you think I've got two seconds to talk with anyone, with all that's going on right now?*

Look, Maudie, I've received a summons from McKinsey to fly back to Washington for consultation. I leave first thing in the morning. I'd really like to see you before I go. And I think it'd be a good idea for you, as well as for me, if we could at least make a stab at being on the same page before I get into a conversation with them about what's going on here.

What sort of summons? What do they want? Maudie's tone had changed. Oscar had figured this would get her attention.

On the phone, Gretchen Mallory talked about a six—month performance review. But this is the first I've heard of any six-month review. I have no doubt they have something else they want to talk about. And you and I both can guess what it is. I'd sure like to have some straight talk with you before I go. Not that I hold out any hope of figuring out who I'm working for. Oscar immediately wished he could take that back.

If you'll stand on the corner in front of your apartment, I'll be by and pick you up in an hour. She hung up without waiting for a response.

Oh, Jesus, she knows me, Oscar smiled to himself. *She knows I'd cancel an appointment with God Almighty to spend some time with her.*

He picked up the phone and dialed the secure number of his boss, the Deputy Minister of Finance. [*I think he's my boss.*] When his secretary came on the line, Oscar explained that he had been called back to Washington for his semi-annual review and needed to get ready to leave the following morning. ***My plans are uncertain right now***, he explained when she asked when he would return, ***but I should see you within the week***. When he hung up he wondered how much anxiety would be stirred in the Ministry by his call. He knew they wouldn't buy the semi-annual review story, but he couldn't come up with a better one. Lately it had seemed to him as if his colleagues at work were skeptical of almost everything about him. But they were still willing to go along, never openly challenging him. He worried about what they thought they might be gaining by cutting him so much slack.

[*Man,*] he thought, his anxiety rising, [*they think I have the inside track with the IMF. Worse, I'm afraid they may be right. And I don't have any idea what I'm supposed to do with it.*]

*   *   *

LOVE AND DANGER

Hop in. Maudie leaned across the front seat of the steel gray Mercedes roadster convertible and flipped open the door. The top two buttons of her sea green silk blouse were undone. She leaned just long enough to give Oscar a glimpse of her cleavage. His breath caught in his throat. As he slid in beside her he tried not to stare at her legs, bare to the thighs, her tweed brown skirt hiked up so she could shift her lovely feet from accelerator to brake.

How did you manage to shake your goons? Oscar asked, thrilled to be alone with her.

I can get a little leeway when I demand it. she smiled. **But I'm not counting on our being completely on our own. So hang on!** Maudie swung the wheel hard to the left and gunned it. Oscar was flung back into his seat. She did a U-turn in the middle of Samora Michele, causing several cars from both directions to swerve and stop. A taxi driver swore at her in Shona. Maudie smiled and waved.

For the next five minutes she drove like a madwoman through the streets of Harare, turning down alleys and tiny unpaved ways Oscar had never seen. Finally she seemed to relax as she pulled out onto a small road in Barrowdale, a suburb, houses with high walls topped with barbed wire.

Where're we headed, Maudie?

Not to worry, my sweet man, she answered. **You'll know soon enough. Does it really matter to you?** She reached across and stroked Oscar's crotch. He felt himself spring to life.

No, really, it doesn't. Not an iota.

Maudie pulled the roadster into the driveway of a modest bungalow on a side street. She reached above her and punched a small box clipped to the sun visor. The garage door opened and Maudie pulled the car in and punched the button again. The door closed behind them.

So whose is this?

Oscar, consider yourself on a need-to-know basis. And all you need to know right now is that we have this place for the next two hours and no one is going to find us here. She turned toward him, putting her hand on the back of his neck, pulling him into her. As she explored his mouth with her tongue, Oscar felt his knees go rubbery. His whole body shivered, as if he were suddenly freezing cold. Maudie leaned away from him.

What was that?

That, my love, was my treasonous body, declaring unconditional surrender to my captor.

Maudie took him by the hand, leading him from the garage through the kitchen and into the bedroom at the end of a narrow hallway. The king-size bed filled most of the space in the small room. Being alone like this, once routine, as if they were a married couple, now felt exotic to Oscar, erotic, forbidden. He was light-headed, as if he might hyperventilate. Maudie breathed heavily into his ear. She stepped back and pulled her blouse over her head. She wasn't wearing a bra. Her nipples were hard. She stepped toward him again.

Wait, Maudie, he gasped, *I didn't realize . . . I didn't bring anything . . .*

Don't you worry, Oscar, I've taken care of everything.

Their lovemaking was fresh and urgent. The months of abstinence and political intrigue had given them each a sense of danger and impermanence. Their bodies, flesh to flesh, neatly fitted as ever, groin to moist groin, toe to head, was intoxicating.

After an hour's lovemaking, they were spent, their fingertips touching lightly as they lay naked on their backs on the bed, near sleep.

Maudie, Oscar felt reluctant bringing this up, wishing the intimacy could be all this day was about, *what am I going to say back in Washington when I'm asked about the two journalists being jailed?*

You're going to tell them the truth, that you don't know anything more than what you've read in the papers.

And the hemorrhaging of Zim dollars into the Congo war? Am I going to say that even though I've spent the past six months immersed in Zimbabwe's finances, I know nothing about that either?

Well, Oscar, maybe you can begin by telling me what that looks like from your perspective in the Finance Ministry. Maudie's tone was all business, no longer seductive. Oscar's reverie was gone. They may have been lying naked, side by side, but now both understood it had become a business meeting.

Maudie, I'm so done with this cat and mouse game we've been playing about this stuff. I mean, we can't pretend we're strangers, or playing parts in a James Bond movie. Can't we just be straight with each other about this?

Oscar, sometimes you're such a dreamer. I mean, do you have any idea what's at stake here? What you mean by straight, and what I may mean, likely could turn out to be very different. It doesn't take a political scientist to understand that our interests in all this aren't identical.

Maudie, we both know I'm going to get grilled hard about all this stuff, and it would be a big help to get some idea from you what you and your Father are hoping I'll say.

Oh Oscar, Maudie rolled over against him, running her finger along his eyebrows, *I guess you're just going to have to call it as you see it. I see no reason you need to get all worked up about this. You came here to help Minister Baunda, not to feed information to McKinsey or the CIA.*

Now who's being the dreamer, Maudie? You know as well as I do that McKinsey, and whoever they may be in bed with, the CIA, the IMF, UNICEF—whoever—are not going to be satisfied with some perfunctory report from me. They're looking for substance, reassurance that this country is being governed by people who know what they're doing, and aren't just feathering their own nests. We're talking billions of dollars here. You think they'll buy my pleading ignorance, or being vague?

And this reporter business is sure to be spooking them. It's the only thing that can explain the sudden, out of the blue timing, summoning me back for a so-called performance review.

Maudie didn't smile. *You may think I'm not being straight with you, Oscar, but you need to understand how different all this looks to me than it does to you. Whatever you may think of the president, he's the one who brought this country from colonial rule to self rule; he's still our national hero and revered by all of southern Africa. And he's still the one the rest of the world has to do business with.*

Understood, Maudie. No argument about that. I'm just trying to figure out—best I can—what's really going on, and how I can represent it back in Washington so they'll want to keep on supporting Zimbabwe. I don't have to tell you that even the world's richest nation is feeling a pretty big pinch these days. And there's a lot of pressure from conservatives to cut back on everything that doesn't directly benefit them. They're not too keen on newly independent African countries. It doesn't take much for them to abandon them to what they arrogantly regard as their own fate.

Maudie's eyes narrowed. Oscar had seen this before. He knew it meant he'd pushed Maudie as far as she would go. *Well, Oscar, you're a big boy, I know you'll find a way to respond to all that.*

The ride back to Oscar's apartment was mostly in silence, broken only to comment on the storm clouds and whether they would deliver the desperately needed rains to the nation in a decade-long drought. Maudie pulled up outside the apartment house; she stared straight ahead. Oscar sat for a moment, covered her hand with his. She sat motionless.

I'll call you when I get back, he said as he opened the door and straightened his long body, stepping up and out of the low sports car.

You do that, she replied. Oscar closed the door. Maudie drove off without looking back.

[*Is that the same woman I just made love with?*]

*   *   *

THINGS LOOK DIFFERENT NOW

Oscar slept fitfully on KLM flight 1339 from Amsterdam to Washington. He was grateful that McKinsey allowed him to travel Business Class, but even so, his long limbs were cramped on the seemingly endless flight. From Harare to Amsterdam the Air Zimbabwe flight had stopped in three places and he'd gotten little sleep.

From Amsterdam to Washington Oscar finally dropped into the sleep of the dead. And he dreamed. He dreamed he and Maudie were at the Philadelphia Zoo. They came to the monkey cage and Maudie calmly, without explanation, opened the cage door and walked into where the vervet monkeys were fretting and squabbling. She climbed into the crotch of the leafless tree where she perched herself as if she were one of the troop. The monkeys began gathering around her until there were 10 or 12 in the tree with her. Maudie was dressed in an ankle length skirt, a silk blouse and had a cashmere shawl draped over her shoulders. The monkeys were wearing morning coats, cutaway jackets, striped trousers. They all sat and stared at Oscar as he stood outside the cage. Maudie's face was expressionless. Oscar called to her, begging her to come out and be with him. She seemed not to hear him, not acknowledging him in any way.

Oscar waved his arms, desperate to get Maudie's attention. The largest, seemingly dominant monkey climbed into her lap, wrapping his arms around her neck. He extended his arm towards Oscar, showing his silk sleeve with its diamond cufflink. Oscar realized the monkey was pointing at him, at his pants. The monkey's lips were drawn back over his teeth in an exaggerated grin. Oscar looked down at himself. His khaki pants were shredded and his penis was exposed, drooping, misshapen, like a timepiece in a Salvador Dali painting.

Oscar woke; his blanket had slipped from his lap and the air nozzle overhead was directing cold air into his lap. He was cold and as stiff as if he had played five sets of tennis. His mouth had gone bone dry. The dream left him feeling uneasy and he wasn't able to pull back enough detail to quite remember why.

The pilot came on the intercom and announced they would be landing in Washington in 30 minutes. Oscar was grateful for McKinsey's no-business-for-24-hours-after-travel policy, but doubted, based on the way he felt right now, that he would be very sharp for the meeting Gretchen had scheduled for the following morning.

He dialed McKinsey from Dulles Airport to see where they had booked him, and was surprised, delighted, to learn from Gretchen's secretary that he was staying at the Hay Adams, across Lafayette Park from the White House. His suspicions rose again. Yes, it was close enough to walk to the meeting on K Street, but so were a dozen other, less expensive hotels.

When the taxi left him at the hotel the concierge took his bag and told him his room would be ready in an hour. Oscar hoped to keep himself awake for as long as possible and go to bed approximately on eastern U.S. time. He'd take a Melatonin and struggle to represent himself with some semblance of intelligence in the morning.

He'd always loved the walk around the White House and the Old Executive Office Building. The view of the Washington monument and down the mall from the south side of the White House, the flags fluttering at the base of the monument, made him proud to be an American, stirring his patriotism in ways he would usually have thought cheesy. Today, having spent the past six months in Africa, the walk was especially inspiring.

Oscar! He was day-dreaming, looking wistfully down the mall, and hadn't seen Syd Katz, a Wharton classmate who had come to Washington to work for AID. *I thought you were in Zimbabwe.*

Oscar recovered enough to call Syd by name. *In fact I am, Syd*, he acknowledged, *I'm just back for a couple of days for meetings.*

How's Maudie?

Great, last time I saw her. But you know she's been made deputy president and she's so damn busy I don't get to see much of her.

Yeah, I read that. From what you hear about what's going on in Zimbabwe, I'm not sure I'd want her job.

Yeah? Oscar was on guard. *What've you heard? I'm pretty out of touch with the way things over there are playing in our press.*

Well, Oscar, as you know, our press has always been almost totally clueless about Africa; mostly just ignores it. I rely more on the BBC and Reuters. Even our own in-house intelligence tends to have a gossipy Time/ Newsweek flavor. But mostly what I'm getting is a picture of chaos and corruption. What we seem to hear about every African country these days. I don't have to tell you how spooked western journalists are when an African country arrests reporters for writing stuff that pisses them off.

Well, maybe you can imagine, Syd, it all looks kind of different when you're in the middle of it. Oscar was surprised at how loyal, almost like a Zimbabwe patriot, he felt, portraying the country to Syd. *What looks like chaos and corruption to a visiting western journalist often turns out to be routine—or even smart business—over there. I have to keep re-examining everything I thought I was clear about, because none of my old assumptions seem to hold up over there any more.*

I know what you mean. I haven't been in country yet, but everyone tells me the lines get blurred between your allegiance to the U.S. and your excitement about your new country. It's kind of scary to think about how your loyalties can get screwed with.

Oscar felt himself drifting from the conversation with Syd, to the afternoon before he left Harare [*was that just yesterday, or a month ago, the way it feels?*] to his conversation with Maudie, as they drove back from their tryst in Borrowdale. He wondered what Syd would think if he could have known about that. [*Talk about being stretched between loyalties!*]

You know, Syd, just about everything I thought I knew and understood has been turned inside-out these past six months. It was as close to honest as Oscar would come in this encounter with Syd. Even as he said it Oscar on was on guard knowing fatigue and jet lag lowered his defenses. [*I better watch my ass, and get a good night's sleep before that meeting tomorrow.*] He knew it was more likely that he would toss most of the night.

You're not the first person to say that to me, Oscar. I hope I'm up to it when the time comes.

They exchanged a few more pleasantries and then both shifted uneasily from foot to foot as they looked for a polite way to disengage.

As he walked away from Syd, Oscar was relieved to have the conversation over, but more uneasy than ever at what it promised for the meeting tomorrow with Gretchen. Gretchen didn't give a damn about the peculiarities of Zimbabwe's politics and culture. [*But,*] Oscar thought, [*you didn't realize the extent of your own stake until that conversation you just had with Syd. You've been measuring everything you see in Zimbabwe through your American lens; suddenly it's like you've started seeing through Zimbabwe lenses, and you're feeling defensive about it. En garde, pal.*]

Looking across the south lawn to the Truman Balcony, Oscar wondered what the new President did to relax and keep his perspective. [*I never imagined,*] he thought, [*how different everything would seem when I was looking at it from a totally new perspective. What must it be like for that guy living in the White House? Maybe he's looking out at me right now, wishing he could be here, on the outside of this fence instead of inside looking out.*]

Oscar's legs felt like lead. His shoulders sagged. He knew he wasn't going to be able to stay awake much longer. He walked around the Treasury Building, turning left on H Street, crossed 16th Street and wearily climbed the marble steps to Henry Adams' old house, now the hotel address of choice for those who came to the capitol city to test themselves in power games. Heady as it was—just a year out of graduate school, rubbing elbows with the world's movers and shakers—Oscar felt exhausted, and more anxious than excited about what likely lay ahead.

*   *   *

TIGHTENING THE SCREWS

It wasn't Gretchen's huge New York office with the window overlooking the East River, but she quickly conveyed her power to Oscar and that she was in charge as he entered the meeting room in the nondescript glass-front office building on K Street. Before Oscar could take more than a single step into the room, Gretchen took several strides towards him and held out her hand in greeting. She looked rested and confident, neither of which could be said about how Oscar felt. Gretchen was dressed in her trademark green tweed suit. Her pageboy length brown hair flounced fetchingly as she approached him. Oscar knew he needed to be wary of Gretchen's appealing manner, not let it seduce him into making him forget this would be, as always, a heavy negotiating session. Oscar's lifelong wish for a smart, attractive woman to rescue him [*from what?*], combined with his being bone weary from travel, made him even more vulnerable than usual.

Oscar, how wonderful to see you! You look terrific; obviously life in Zimbabwe is agreeing with you. Oscar's guard was up. The schmooze was on. He'd checked himself in the mirror before leaving his hotel room; he looked as awful as he felt.

How about a cup of coffee? After the exotic coffees you've been enjoying in Africa, I'm afraid ours is going to seem tame and dull.

Gretchen, Oscar finally managed to get in a word, *I'm glad to see you, too. I'd love that cup of coffee.* He wished he could come up with something clever in response to her mock defensiveness about the coffee. [*Was that a test of how much my American identity and loyalties have been eroded?*] But his mind was a weary blank.

Gretchen walked over to the credenza where a plastic thermos was surrounded by styrofoam cups. Oscar marveled that she could, just by her presence, transform a generic Holiday Inn type meeting room into a place where you were unmistakably in the presence of corporate power. She poured two cups, turned toward Oscar and handed him his cup.

Oscar, something about the way she spoke his name cut through Oscar's fog; he came alert. ***In a couple of minutes we're going to be joined by two men who are interested in McKinsey's work in Zimbabwe. I'm not going to play games with you; Ethan Pinsky is CIA, not undercover, and Jim Newmark is with the IMF, responsible for servicing their Zimbabwe loans.***

[*Holy shit,*] Oscar thought, [*that didn't take long. No preliminaries. Let the games begin!*]

Gretchen stopped, eyeing Oscar as if she was waiting for a response. Oscar disciplined himself to stay silent. He knew any leverage he might have would disappear with the first words to come from his mouth. He wondered how long he could hold out, how long Gretchen could.

She went first.

Obviously you know a lot more than we do about what's going on in Mugabe's government right now, especially with the arrest of the two journalists. There's growing concern in this country about whether the president has taken some sort of irreversible step away from democratic rule.

[*Yeah?*] he thought [*And what might that have to do with my six-month review with McKinsey?*] Thanks to two years learning from Maudie, Oscar could maintain a poker face a lot longer than he used to, and that's what he showed Gretchen now.

I suppose you're wondering why these two would be coming to this meeting. First let me reassure you that we're not going to ask you to sign on as a spy. Oscar felt relieved. Gretchen had showed her hand before he had to and the previously unmentioned issue was now on the table. But he knew better than to think her apparent candor was reason to relax.

[*Watch your ass, Oscar Anderson.*]

You've no doubt heard that McKinsey has a relationship with various agencies of the U.S. Government. It's as much informal as contractual, but we try to be good citizens, especially in those areas where the government's limited resources make it difficult for them to get the information needed for making good decisions. And, God knows, our Africa intelligence is pitiful.

[*Right*]. Oscar was feeling testy. [*Don't let it show, Buddy! Now, there's some corporate arrogance; McKinsey has better access and deeper pockets than Uncle Sam? Give me a break, Gretchen.*]

So we simply pool information from time to time. Nothing very exciting, no nuclear secrets or identities of spies, just routine stuff. Crop numbers, health of key figures, relationships between political opponents, that sort of thing.

None of this was computing for Oscar, with his experience so far. [*What about our embassy, for Christ's sake? Tony Lane seems pretty plugged in.*]

You're probably wondering about our embassy, why we'd need to duplicate their efforts.

[*Jesus, did she plant a bug in my brain?*] He was feeling increasingly cautious.

We find we always get a little different slant, occasionally even different actual facts, from NGO people than we do from those on the government payroll. So it helps to look at all different sources from many different perspectives and see what dovetails and what takes a different tack.

[*I wonder if I'm going to be invited to be a part of this spy mission, or maybe told it is already in my contract?*]

Gretchen's voice lowered an octave to a warm, intimate tone, and she took a step toward him. **You're pretty exhausted from your long trip, and I wouldn't blame you if you were feeling a little uncomfortable about all this. I want you to know we aren't in the habit of sandbagging our consultants with clandestine assignments, and we aren't going to do that to you. All we're doing is asking you to listen to what they have to say, and then tell us whether you're comfortable taking a modest piece of the action. Most of all we want you to be clear that it musn't compromise the contract McKinsey has with the primary client, in this case the Zimbabwe Finance Ministry and Minister Baunda.**

Oscar's thoughts were racing: [*Oh, right, Gretchen. You're trying to tell me that there's some way I can sign on with the CIA and not sully my relationship with the people I'm supposedly working for, but really I'm spying on?*]

Not that I blame you, Oscar—you must be reeling—but you haven't said a word. Do you have any response to all this?

I confess I'm more than a little a little stunned, Gretchen. I really hadn't anticipated this. It doesn't feel much like a performance review.

Now look, Oscar, there's no need to freak out. This is all more mundane and routine than you likely yet understand. Gretchen sighed from somewhere deep within her. *Why don't we just ask Ethan and Jim to come in and you can hear them out?*

Fair enough. [*Fair, my ass.*]

* * *

OSCAR MEETS HIS HANDLERS

Their easy charm and surprisingly casual dress (Jim was in jeans and a sweat shirt with a Disneyland logo, and Ethan wore pleated khaki pants, sneakers and a Ralph Lauren polo shirt), made it seem as if they were meeting in San Diego rather than D.C. Oscar thought their look and manner returned the room to its Holiday Inn ambience. Ethan and Jim were type-cast, characters straight from a James Bond novel.

Look, Oscar, Jim was talking, the conversation had gone on, one-sided, for nearly a half-hour, and Oscar, after their initial greeting, had said nothing. *We aren't asking you to do anything more than cut us in on your regular weekly memos you prepare for Gretchen. We're already pretty tight with Minister Baunda, and we count on him to supplement our information, too.* Jim paused, checking for any response from Oscar. Oscar continued to hold himself tightly in check.

So you intend to tell Baunda that I'm working not only for McKinsey and for the Finance Ministry, but also for you? Oscar could feel himself getting dangerously close to the fatigue that he knew could make him start saying things he'd wish he hadn't.

Well, we don't have to rub his nose in it, or put him unnecessarily at risk in his own organization. He's a big boy; he doesn't need to have everything spelled out for him. He's been around the track a few times himself.

Oscar struggled to discipline his words, speaking slowly [*Was that meant to be a signal that Baunda's Ndebele identity means he's willing to compromise his loyalty to Mugabe? This is some serious shit!*] *You do understand that my memos to Gretchen are quite different from my memos to Baunda? Gretchen is my boss, so she hears about how I'm doing in my job. But the 'what' of my job—numbers, projections, potential politically sensitive stuff—that goes to Baunda to do with as he sees fit. It doesn't go to Gretchen because it's confidential to the client. I'm sure I don't have to remind you that those are the ethics of consulting.*

Oscar, we're all adults here. Ethan's tone had become patronizing, impatient. Oscar thought maybe Ethan was going to be the bad cop in this interrogation. *We'd never ask you to compromise those Boy Scout morals you learned when you were 10. It's just that in the grownup world, where billions of bucks and people's lives are constantly on the line, sometimes those precious values we hold so dear have to give way to some hard realities. Nothing illegal, just some economic and political realism, where people often—for their own understandable reasons—tend to blow a little smoke, providing cover for what must be done to protect everyone's interests. If we're going to do justice to the taxpayers who fund these deals, as well as to Zimbabwe's needs, we need ways to clear some that smoke.* ⟨of⟩

[*So this is how it begins. Is that what the intelligence guys said to Lyndon Johnson after they trumped up the Gulf of Tonkin incident? That Boy Scout values needed to yield to a little smoke? Is this where I become Henry Kissinger?*]

Gretchen had been silent through this exchange. *Maybe this is a good time for us to break for lunch. Ethan, why don't you and Jim go have a bite, and Oscar and I will go back to the Hay Adams, and then he can take a nap before we come back together again at, say, 3. Remember, he was traveling for nearly 24 hours straight.*

Jim smiled; Ethan scowled. Oscar felt he'd received a momentary reprieve.

* * *

GRETCHEN-OSCAR-MAUDIE

Look, Oscar, I have been aware all morning of how guarded you are, and I can't say I really blame you. But I want to reassure you that we're all on the same side. And we're playing straight with you on all this. No tricks up my sleeve.

Gretchen, it's taking me a little while to get used to those other two guys. It would have helped to give me some warning.

I do apologize, Oscar for springing them on you. I didn't know until yesterday that they wanted to be an actual part of our conversation. I knew they wanted me to talk with you about helping gather some information, but I thought I was going to do the asking on my own. I think the sense of urgency has been ratcheted up a lot because of the journalists' arrest coming right before the next installment of the IMF load comes due. That's got a lot of people spooked.

It's got a lot of people in Zimbabwe spooked, too, Gretchen. But let me be up front with you about how this is hitting me right now. When I was job hunting I interviewed with the CIA and they offered me a job. I decided I didn't want to do that kind of work. And I still don't.

And no one's going to ask you to, Oscar. You turned down undercover work; this is all on the up and up, out in the open. It's just that we'd much rather be straight with you on this one, and be sure you know who's going to be in the loop with the information. And of course we need to know too.

Look, Gretchen, I don't mean to be rude, but if you don't mind, I'd like to skip lunch and just go upstairs and catch a nap. I've got a nasty headache and I need a chance to get myself together. How about if I meet you back at the K Street office at 3? Oscar enjoyed feeling he had regained at least some small amount of control.

That's fine, Oscar, but why don't I come by and pick you up a few minutes before we reconvene, so you and I can talk about how you're going to respond about all this before we talk with Jim and Ethan?

[*So much for my taking back some control.*]

That'd be fine. Oscar's head was pounding now. He hadn't the energy to try to keep up this fencing match. He wondered if he'd be able to make it upstairs to his room before he collapsed.

Oscar paced the floor of his room on the third floor of the Hay Adams. The room looked out over the AFL/CIO building and that little gem of Latrobe architecture he'd always liked, the small, yellow domed, stucco, St. John's Church across 16th Street where he could see just the corner of the White House across Lafayette Park. Washington made him manic, as if he ought to be making frantic phone calls to important contacts. And the more urgency he felt about figuring how to respond to Gretchen and her goons the less clear he became about what he was going to do. Sleep, though it was what he needed more than anything, was clearly out of the question.

[*Wonder what time it is in Harare?*] He checked his watch. [*It's a little after eight. Wonder what Maudie's doing? Probably negotiating a treaty with the Chinese to redo Vic Falls. So what? God knows, she's got as big a stake in what I'm doing here as anyone.*]

Hello, Oscar. Oscar thrilled to hear her voice. She sounded close by. And not the least surprised to hear from him.

Maudie! I'm so happy to hear your voice. I really should be getting some sleep before my next meeting. But I need to run a few things by you.

Oscar? Where in the world are you? You're not calling me on my secure number from an open phone in Washington, I hope.

Don't be paranoid, Maudie. I'm not totally inept at this stuff. I'm calling from my room at the Hay Adams, using the scrambler phone. I'm so happy to hear your voice. I miss you. How are you?

I'm fine, Oscar, just a little busy with everything. Seems like this country still won't run itself.

Maudie, something's come up in these talks that I'm not sure I should be talking about with you, but I don't know who else I could bring it up with.

Like what? Maudie's voice took on a tentative tone that only increased Oscar's anxiety. [*Maybe this is a bad idea?*]

Well, like a couple of guys from government agencies showed up for my conversations with Gretchen, and it's turning out to be a little different from the six-month evaluation it was billed as.

Let me guess, Oscar; one is from the CIA and the other from either the World Bank, or maybe the IMF, right?

Jesus, Maudie, you always know. How'd you know that?

Oscar, I've been hanging around this crowd with my father since I was 16 years old. They're the same the world over, especially your guys in the U.S. They're so transparent. It's a wonder you ever won a war. By now I can just about always predict who's going to be at what meeting. I think the interesting thing is that they identified themselves, especially the CIA guy. At least that means he's not undercover.

Well, I can't say that has made me feel a lot better. I'm wondering what's in it for them to come right out in the open like that. I suppose I should prefer it to clandestine—and I guess I do—because at least I know who I'm dealing with, or I think I do. But I wonder what they want from me?

So what exactly are you asking me, Oscar?

I don't really know yet. We're taking a break and I begged off lunch with Gretchen to come take a nap. But I'm too keyed up to sleep, so I thought I'd call you. Try to get some perspective. I'm still a pretty raw recruit to all this.

It doesn't take a political scientist to predict what they're going to be asking you to do, Oscar. They know about you and me, and you're inside the Economics Ministry, the two things they're focused on; the president's political future and the Zimbabwe economy.

Well, Maudie, I feel like such a rube about this stuff. I can't figure out who owns my primary loyalty. [*This is all too fucking weird, talking with my sweetheart about whether I'm going to agree to spy on her.*]

I don't know this term 'Rube,' Oscar, but I think I can figure out what it must mean. I know how much you love thinking of yourself as pure, your integrity not up for grabs. And I must say, that's more true of you than about anyone I've ever known. But this is the real world, what you like to call the Big Leagues, and if you're going to do any good, be of any use, you're going to have to turn loose some of the picture you love to paint of yourself. Your loyalty now is to the best outcome, not necessarily to one country, or group. You're going to have to decide what you hope may come of your part in this and figure out how best to help that happen. Forget that Boy Scout loyalty oath. [*I wish I'd never told anyone about being an Eagle Scout.*] *With that in mind, I have a suggestion about what may work best, if you think you're up to it.*

I'm listening, Maudie. Though he was feeling increasingly shaky, Oscar *was* listening. [*Am I about to become a traitor? To which country? I mean, I work for a private company, or at least I used to think it was a private company. But those two spook goons show up and are clearly a lot more comfortable in that conference room than I am. What if they knew I was having this talk with Maudie? Or maybe they do know. Is this consorting with the enemy? But Zimbabwe is hardly an enemy of the United States. Shit! Wall Street and the big bucks look pretty inviting right now.*]

Oscar, what's the outcome we're all looking for? Your president, our president, the whole world? It's that President Mugabe's revolutionary agenda—freedom and prosperity for our people—be preserved and extended to even more people in Zimbabwe, right? Everyone on both sides can agree on that. So how can you act in this situation so you will best lend to that?

Oscar realized Maudie hadn't spoken for several seconds. Was she really asking him a question? [*I sure hope not, because I haven't the vaguest notion of how to answer.*]

Oscar, assuming for the moment they're going to ask you to pass along information to them, what comes across your desk at the Finance Ministry, what you pick up from hanging around with me, and just moving around Zimbabwe with you eyes open, how might you respond?

I'd tell them to buzz off, Oscar replied indignantly. *Let them hire their own fucking spooks to betray the people they're supposed to be loyal to.*

Oscar, remember? No Boy Scout stuff, OK? We're talking subtle nuance here, not principles. What would happen if you agreed? Said that, while you're not interested in being a full scale mole, in the interests of providing solid, useful information for smart decision-making, so they might feel better about extending the loans, you'd be willing to give them reasonable access to some of what you come across over here?

But why would I do that? For whom? [*I'm more confused about why you'd want me to do that.*]

Because, Oscar, you may be able to do them some good, and us some good at the same time. Win, win. Their problem is there's no one on the ground here with good enough contacts to give them information they can believe. Except for you. And our problem is that they don't trust us. They think we're doctoring our numbers. The reality is that we both need some way to break that impasse. Maybe you could provide that way.

But, Maudie, it's not really that simple, is it? I mean, what about when they ask me stuff about your father's business interests offshore, and Congo's diamond mines, and his arrest of the two journalists?

Well, maybe that's where your old pure ethics really do come in handy, Oscar. Have you and I ever talked about any of those matters?

No.

Well, then, what will your answer be?

I think I begin to see what you mean. [*Jesus, I don't think I'll ever get this Machiavellian stuff down. Does Maudie think about this stuff all the time, even when we're . . . ?*] Oscar's groin stirred.

Do you, Oscar? I hope so. Because when you go back into that meeting you're going to need to have your wits about you. They're looking for what we're all looking for—common interests. And I think there are some that are worth pursuing, and legitimate. But I promise you that your personal conflicts are going to be of zero concern to them. No one's going to look out for your interests in there except for you. They could give a shit about your precious principles. And that includes Gretchen. God knows who signs her paycheck.

Oscar shuddered involuntarily. These past six months had provided a life's worth of lessons for him. He realized increasingly that his image of himself—unfailingly decent and concerned for the other fellow—did nothing for him in the job he accepted from Gretchen back in what now seems a lifetime ago, except to make sure he could be bamboozled in every transaction.

The phone on the desk buzzed. *Hang on a second, Maudie, let me see who this is . . .*

Oscar, I've got the president waiting for me, and he'll be in here, steaming mad, any second if I don't go. So I better run.

Oscar, it's Gretchen. I'm downstairs in the lobby. We've got a few minutes before we're due at the meeting. May I come up?

The conversation with Gretchen was brief and to the point. *Oscar*—she had a whole new way about her now, straightforward, her gravitas degrees heavier than during the morning meeting—*let's not play any more games with each other. The stakes are too high. The IMF's due date for its next installment on the loan to Zimbabwe is right around the corner. But there's growing resistance in every quarter of the Fund and the State Department to paying it if things over there continue to deteriorate.*

[*'Over there'! Just putting it that way sets my teeth on edge. Six months and I already feel like an alien among my own people.*]

OK, Gretchen. Gretchen's change of mood made Oscar bolder. *I'm ready to talk turkey. But first, maybe you could explain something about the relationship between McKinsey and the CIA, not to mention the IMF, that I thought was supposed to be independent of any particular nation. I don't remember any of this coming up when I was being interviewed.*

Quite right, Oscar, it didn't. Gretchen betrayed her first hint of impatience, rolling her eyes, shifting in her chair. *But I had you figured for a grownup who would understand that our country has interests that would inevitably come into play in a job like the one you're in. No one's going to ask you to do anything clandestine, just provide another ear. For everyone's benefit.*

And as for the connection between McKinsey, the CIA and the IMF, there isn't one, at least not officially. But we are an American company, and we do what we can to help the country's legitimate interests. The IMF doesn't have a sufficiently sophisticated information gathering arm, and sometimes the CIA can help. McKinsey does business—government and private—in virtually every country in the world. When our interests coincide, legitimately, as they often do—and as I happen to think they do in this case we help each other out, legitimately. Does that come as a shock to you? I sure hope not, because if it does, I am a lousy recruiter and a poor judge of character.

Oscar chose to ignore Gretchen's not so subtle slight. *Who's paying my salary, Gretchen?*

McKinsey.

Do you work for the government?

No.

What if I refuse, say no?

We'll all be disappointed, and go looking for other ways to get the information that's needed to help us make good decisions about how best to help Zimbabwe. And perhaps have to rethink your usefulness, to Baunda and to McKinsey.

[*Oh my, crack some nuts, why don't you, sweet Gretchen.*]

And if I do agree and my cover is blown, what're the consequences for me down the road?

We learned a long time ago, the hard way—when those National Student Association kids were discovered to have been recruited by the CIA in the '60s—down the road that can do harm to a political career. You need to consider realistically that it could one day do the same to you. There is a limit to how much we can protect you. Not that we're asking you to betray atomic secrets. But political enemies are very skilled at making use of this sort of thing when they get hold of it. I can't pretend otherwise.

I have no political ambitions, Gretchen, but I do care what people think about my being trustworthy. About my word being good.

I understand, Oscar; so does everyone. Even Bill Clinton once did until Monica Lewinsky took that monkey off his back. Jimmy Carter, our most failed President, was the last and maybe the only one who refused everything he thought compromised his integrity. God spare us another like him. Well, almost every offer, until he made that futile attempt to save his presidency by a clandestine and insane attempt to rescue the hostages from the American embassy in Teheran.

The conversation back at the K Street conference room was short. Oscar figured out before they got underway what he was going to do. It was his earlier phone conversation with Maudie that had persuaded him, not his hardball exchange with Gretchen.

[*No need for her to know that, though. Now I'm beginning to think like one of them. Maybe I'm doing this to please Maudie. Shit, I have no idea what my real motive is. I just haven't the energy or any clear idea of why I might turn them down. Do I even want to?*]

Oscar's most uncomfortable moment was when Pinsky and Newmark, having obviously devised strategy during the break to weaken his resistance, put on a full court press . . . *Oscar*, Ethan Pinsky said, *maybe you should run this by Maudie. She's been around this scene longer than you have, and I know you trust her.*

[*Maudie?! Now this is bizarre. Basically you're trying to get me to spy on Maudie and her father, and you're suggesting I ask her advice about that. You really are a babe in the woods, Oscar.*] He decided to keep his counsel even though he'd already made his decision.

I hadn't thought of that, Oscar responded, trying to look thoughtful. [*I wonder if the scrambler on that phone works. This cat and mouse stuff can get pretty weird.*] *I'll give that serious thought when I return, and I'll get back to you within the week.*

In the meantime, Oscar, Ethan said, reaching into his briefcase, *take this back with you, and use it whenever you want to communicate with me. All you need to do is press send and it rings directly through to me. The signal is scrambled, secure, and I can patch you through to others if*

need be. He handed Oscar a tiny black phone that fit into the palm of his hand. It had no dial pad. "Qualcomm" was inscribed across the face.

[*Jesus Christ, this world is incestuous! Do you guys pay me off in Qualcomm stock? By the time I leave this job I'll have more phones than teeth.*] **I confess to being a little disappointed.** Oscar enjoyed letting that hang in the air, watching the three of them squirm. [*I wish they would squirm, just once.*] **I had half expected to be able to talk to you through the heel of my shoe, like Agent Smart.**

Their feeble laugh covered their relief that he wasn't backing out. And their uneasiness at having to depend on a dork like him. [*Guess they've never watched clips of that old show.*]

As if he felt the need for some other sign of their appreciation, Jim Newmark said, **Oscar, we recognize that you're doing extra work for us. And we're prepared to open an account for you with our Wells Fargo office here in Washington. We'll make a monthly deposit in your name. It's a good way to start saving for retirement.**

[*You guys leave no stone unturned. No bribe un-offered.*] Oscar didn't respond. He accepted the phone and put it into his jacket pocket. [*I suppose that makes it pretty clear, doesn't it? The price of my loyalty is a sexy little Qualcomm phone.*] It wasn't Oscar's most embarrassing thought so far that day, that he really did love having these spy-craft gadgets.

I'll give you a call by a week from tomorrow. That gives me five days after I return to get my thoughts together.

Gretchen offered to drive him to Dulles in the morning, but Oscar demurred, saying his plane left so early there was no point in both of them losing a night's sleep. In truth he'd had enough of all of them and was looking forward to the long flight where he could sleep and think and veg out, alone.

*   *   *

BACK (HOME?) IN HARARE

Maudie, it's me, Oscar.

Oscar, are you calling again from Washington? I don't think this calling all the time is a good idea. Even with scrambling, these international signals are pretty easy to pick up.

No, Maudie, I'm back. Got in early this morning. I've had a few hours' sleep and I really need to talk to you. I know how busy you are, but this is important, and it's going to be just as important to you, too.

Thinking about your coming back, Oscar, and all that has been happening, I've cleared my calendar for five days starting day after tomorrow. I've made reservations for us at Troutbeck Inn at Nyanga. God knows I need some time off myself, and I can't think of anyone I'd rather spend it with. So you better get your life together. The President has already spoken with Minister Baunda, so that's all set.

The pace at which this was all moving made Oscar's head spin. [*Do you suppose Maudie's been talking with Gretchen? Or wouldn't I love to think this is maybe because Maudie has missed our being together as much as I have. I'm not so sure Maudie works exactly the same as I do about what matters most to me? Skin. Hate to admit it, Oscar old boy, but it's a whole lot about skin. We'll do anything, our kind, to get a lot of our skin next to a lot of someone else's skin Or is it a guy thing?*] The thought made the hair on Oscar's neck prickle. His groin stirred. [*It's all pretty basic. God, I can't wait! But what if it's about something totally different for Maudie? Maybe I'm the lamb being led to the slaughter? I have no idea any more who's on what side.*] It was with

---

162

some shame—but certainly a manageable amount—that Oscar admitted to himself that right now he really didn't care what her motives were. If she was willing to spend five days with him, he would take it. [*If she turns out to be Mata Hari, well, as the man said, why not lie back and enjoy it?*]

*   *   *

A DREAM VACATION

Maudie picked up Oscar on the corner in front of his apartment early Wednesday morning before rush hour traffic snarled Samora Michel. Oscar was relieved to be getting away even though he'd only been back at work for one full day. He had a sense that Minister Baunda had been watching him out of the corner of his eye. Why else—besides knowing he was working a parallel, secret job—would a boss never mention the fact that he hardly ever showed up and was going on a five-day vacation the day after he returned?

[*What does he know? Is he in on all this? Those spooks in DC spoke as if they were on intimate terms with him. I never knew they had laid eyes on him. Am I the only one in this drama who isn't cozy with everyone else? Here I've been working away at these economic models on the computer as if I'd actually been hired to do this work. Probably all a cover. If it is, I'll be the last to know.*]

Maudie was dressed in a pair of pale green linen pants and bright print blouse. She'd wrapped her hair in a kerchief in the traditional headdress of Zimbabwean women. On her feet were those Italian loafers he loved that had belonged to her mother.

You look fabulous!

Thanks. Hop in.

Oscar tossed his backpack into the back seat of the Range Rover and slipped into the passenger seat beside Maudie. He was glad she wasn't driving the Mercedes. Too conspicuous, and low to the ground, nasty on those rural highland roads. He'd gotten used to seeing her dressed severely, for power meetings, and it excited him seeing her like this, apparently ready for some very different time away from her weighty life as deputy president. [*I sure am. I've been thinking about this for half a year.*]

They drove in silence for several minutes, Oscar was at a loss for words. Maudie always seemed more comfortable than he felt, being together in silence. But now there was the added confusion of whether they were going on this trip for business or for pleasure. And if for business, [*Just what is our business, Maudie? Maybe there isn't any difference between the two with us?*] Oscar wasn't sure which would be more emotionally demanding for him. They'd never really talked about how it was that Maudie became the initiator early in their relationship, in conversation, in choosing a movie, in making love.

[*I wonder if she'd like me to take the lead more? I always hold myself in check until I get a signal from her about where she wants it to go. It's really OK with me. I suppose this is another of those fucking residuals from growing up a preacher's kid. I watched my father take his cues from parishioners—and from Mom—before he would ever risk showing his own hand.*]

They'd cleared Harare's traffic and had the two lane tar road to themselves. Oscar's daydream was short-circuited suddenly when Maudie reached across and gently fondled Oscar's crotch. She was still looking straight ahead, not speaking a word. [*OK, Baby, I'm happy to have you take the lead!*]

OK. So, I guess we're going on a real vacation, huh Maudie?
Maudie smiled.

Disappointed? You looking for some high level government business? She continuing massaging his lap. Oscar felt himself begin to swell, pressing against her hand.

That answer your question? he asked. She smiled again.

It's just that there's so much confusing stuff about my trip back to Washington. Though I have to admit, I'm pretty confused about what I should be talking about with who.

Whom, Oscar. You're the English major, for goodness sake.

Oscar, you're so fickle. You complain that we never have time together, and now that we've stolen these five days at Troutbeck, you suddenly want to talk business. The business will be there when we get back. I've left word I'm not to be disturbed except for a real emergency. Even Father agreed he wouldn't bother me.

[*Cool, it's, "Father," not "the president," we're on our old ground.*] Oscar got a buzz, entertaining a colorful fantasy about the next five days.

*　　*　　*

COULD IT EVER REALLY BE LIKE THIS?

His fantasy was tame compared with the reality.

Troutbeck was a fresh-air activist's dream, the closest one could find to a piece of rural New England in southern Africa. It was as if they were a newly married couple on their honeymoon. They rode horseback through pine forest, hiked into the hills, played squash and badminton, fly fished in the cold stream, threw horseshoes, and talked about everything in their lives that mattered, except their work. They even exchanged whimsy about how their dreams and their passions might play out in a perfect world. Maudie had always been reluctant to talk about this with Oscar. Oscar understood she was totally focused on what she was preparing to do—what she was now doing—and he finally accepted it as the defining fact of their future, a future in which he knew he didn't figure. Now he was powerfully affected as she spoke about things she never had before.

Oscar, there are days when—if I have so much as 10 minutes to myself—I imagine living in some rural place in a three bedroom house with you and two little mocha babies. Oscar's heart raced at the thought. He knew better than to do more than smile and embrace her.

They rarely wore clothes when they were in their cabin, making love randomly through the days. And when they were exhausted, too spent even to read or talk, they lay naked on the bed, talking, laughing, unhurriedly exploring each other's dreams and bodies for hours, until they fell asleep.

In the two and a half years since they'd become lovers, their lives had been focused on their ambitions, busy with achieving, and their love-making had usually seemed hurried. He assumed that would always be the way it was with them, and he wasn't about to complain. Maudie was so at home in her body, and so expert at arousing his, that he would have been happy to keep it just as it was forever. For Oscar, Troutbeck was like beginning their affair over again, learning a whole new way of being together, a relaxed intimacy he wished he could believed might last forever.

[*I wonder if she finds this as wonderful as I do? I'm not about to break the spell by asking.*]

The second afternoon, after a ferocious squash match in which Oscar prevailed in a deuce fifth game, they returned to their room, hot, sweaty, spent. As Oscar closed the door behind them, Maudie stepped out of her shorts, then pulled her shirt over her head. Oscar watched her smooth belly stretch taut. She looked over at him staring, and smiled.

Save 7, she said, ***shower with your steady***. She pulled off her bikini briefs and twisted out of her sports bra, freeing her full bronze breasts. Oscar stood still, spellbound. He'd never stopped admiring her skin, the rich earth-color on every part of her body. A piece of exquisite sculpture. She walked away from him toward the bathroom, seemingly unaware of the effect she was having on him.

Oscar pulled his clothes off, catching a glimpse in the full-length mirror of his own body, its varying shades and hues, pig-pink groin and butt, farmer's-tan legs and arms. [*splotched Anglo pigment sure looks anemic next to those sumptuous hues on every inch of your beautiful body.*]

He followed her into the bathroom. She stepped into the large stall shower, leaving the glass door ajar. Self-conscious—his erection required him to turn full face toward her to get through the door—Oscar stepped into the warm, hard stream of water, and into Maudie's slippery embrace. He shuddered at the feel of her hard nipples against his chest, her coarse pubic hair on his thigh.

Maudie reached over and punched the soap dispenser, filling her palm. She reached behind him and rubbed his back, working the soap into lather. She scrubbed his buttocks and ran her fingernail along the tendon that joins the scrotum to the asshole. Bringing her soapy hands around in front of him, she began to lather his rigid prick, slowly stroking its full length, holding his balls for a moment, then running her hand down the shaft to the head of his penis. When her hand touched the glans, Oscar moaned, twitched.

Breathe in deeply, darling, don't rush. We're going to be at this for the rest of the afternoon.

Oh, God, Maudie! He reached down, and with his open palm between her legs, lifted her off the ground. She wrapped her legs around his waist, her arms around his neck, rolling her hips, rubbing her pubis across his stomach. Their tongues explored each other's mouths. Maudie dug her fingertips into Oscar's scalp. Oscar had a death grip on Maudie's buttocks. Oscar's penis began to throb.

Maudie, I can't last!

Maudie slid down the length of him until she was wrapped around his buttocks. Then she let herself down to the floor, holding his legs behind the knees, pulling him down on top of her. The shower drenched their faces, they were inhaling water, but neither noticed. Oscar fell onto her, breaking his fall with his hands. Maudie took him in her hand and slipped him inside her, and with her heels dug into the small of his back, thrust herself against him. Oscar convulsed into her.

Go! Maudie cried. Oscar pushed himself forward, shouting, *Oh, God, oh!* A primitive cry came from somewhere deep inside Maudie as her hips swung into his. The scream, an octave lower than any sound Oscar had ever heard from her, startled him. Maudie seemed to abandon herself, rolling her head from side to side, moaning, twitching, water splashing onto her face, eyes closed, and Oscar, too, lost all sense of himself, where he was, what was happening.

Oscar finally became aware of the water cascading down onto them, slowly returning to consciousness, returning from his stupor.

Jesus, Maudie, we could drown like this. [*This tile's hard; must be crunching Maudie.*]

Maudie began laughing uncontrollably, her breasts heaving as she lay on the shower floor beneath Oscar's large, inert body. Her laughter made her sex muscles contract, grasping Oscar inside her. Oscar jerked.

What's that about, Oscar? Hurting you?

No, Baby, not hurting, just so sensitive.

The shower continued pounding down on them. They sputtered and choked, spitting out water, laughing, holding onto each other.

Maybe we better get on with what we came here to do, Maudie said through her laughing. *I tell you what, you wash me and I'll wash you.*

Disentangling themselves proved challenging. *How did we ever get ourselves into this contortion?* Oscar asked as they cautiously pulled each other up together, gingerly, so neither knocked the other over. Only then did Oscar—half erect—slide out of her. When they were finally both upright, Oscar soaped his hands from the dispenser and, starting with Maudie's neck, scrubbed her the length of her lithesome, athletic body. They both became aroused again as he slowly, with his big, strong hands worked her wet flesh. When he had massaged every inch of her, pausing each time he sensed her take a deep breath, Maudie took her turn, working her limber fingers into each crevice in Oscar.

They must have been in the shower a half-hour before Oscar reached up and turned off the water. He pulled the big terry cloth towel from the back of the shower door and rubbed her dry. Then she did the same for him. They walked, wobbly-kneed, into the bedroom and slipped naked under the bedspread. Legs and arms entangled, they fell asleep. When they woke it was dark.

What time is it? Maudie's voice was thick from sleep. *How long have we been asleep?*

I think it's about eight o'clock, and I think we've been asleep almost three hours. I'm starved.

I hate getting dressed to go to dinner, Maudie said. *I could spend the rest of my life naked with you like this.* They ordered room service, Kudu pate, French Wine, sitting in the dark looking out at the moonlit woods.

For five days they savored the time and each other's bodies. Twice, Oscar started to bring up the subject of what he had been asked to do by Gretchen and the others. Both times Maudie responded in the same way.

Hush, my precious. Let's not let our other life and someone else's agenda wreck this time together. Oscar needed no persuading.

[*I had no idea she's missed our life together as much as I have. And it sounds like she's getting sick of all the bullshit her life is filled with now. Maybe, maybe . . .*]

The last night at dinner, Oscar proposed a toast. *To the happiest time I can ever remember. Ever. And may it last forever.*

Maudie's answering toast put Oscar back on his old familiar alert status. *To one of the happiest times I can remember. And to our finding the way to ensure a prosperous future for this great African nation.*

* * *

The Real World

Intrudes . . . Again

Their lovemaking the last night wasn't the long, unhurried coupling of the previous nights. This night it felt more urgent. And they both fell asleep immediately without talking.

At 2 am Oscar woke. The wind was whistling in the pine trees. His feet were cold. His head ached. He pumped up his pillow and turned over, looking for a position that would let him relax enough to sleep. Every time he moved, some new place itched, and when he reached down to scratch, he ended up in a more awkward position.

[*Fuck, this is all going to end in a few hours. Then what? I've got to call Gretchen today and respond. Maudie and I haven't even talked about it, and how can we? I'm supposed to ask Maudie her opinion of whether I should agree to spy on her father and on her for the CIA? What a fucking joke.*]

After rooting around for another half-hour, Oscar got out of bed and went over to the overstuffed chair by the window and sat. He tried to meditate but his mind wouldn't stay still. The itching migrated around his body.

[*I'm an American, so of course I'll do what my country asks. Bull shit! That's the Eichmann defense. Maybe Maudie'll marry me after these incredible days here and we can go live in Costa Rica. Bull shit! She's going to be president, if her father doesn't get bumped off. Or if she doesn't get caught in flagrante delicto with this white Yank. So what's the future for me in all this? Lose—lose. If I don't get caught for spying and get executed. Is it really spying? Where's Maudie's head right now? She couldn't be faking these entire five days; that'd*] *be the best acting since "When Harry Met Sally." I'd give anything to be able to turn off my goddamn mind; this is likely to be a full day and I'm going to be a basket case. Middle of the night mind games. Fuck!*]

So, what's the buzz, big guy? Oscar was startled. He'd been looking out the window at the moon bathing the trees in its light, and hadn't seen Maudie slip out of her side of the bed and cross the room. It always caught him off guard when she used one of those American slang expressions that tempted him to think she might have become fully Americanized.

I couldn't sleep. She was wearing her sheer nightie. Oscar considered running his hand up her thigh, but thought better of it. The storybook holiday was over. Maudie sat in the chair opposite him and pulled the throw from the back of the chair, covering herself from shoulder to foot.

I'm feeling pretty restless, too. Shall we talk?

May as well. [*Here it comes.*]

You want to talk about your meeting with Gretchen and the others in Washington?

[*Others? Did I tell her there were others? Oh yeah, in the phone call.*] **I really do need to talk about that, Maudie, but it feels incredibly awkward to me. I mean those other two guys in the room were from the CIA and the IMF. Just as you guessed. Like maybe you already knew.** Oscar waited, watching her for a reaction. Her face was impassive, Shona expressionless. He knew she could outwait him.

I mean, they didn't exactly give me a license to kill or anything, but just the fact that those two guys showed up at the meeting spooked the hell out of me.

Now Oscar, you're a grown man. Your father's in international affairs. And now so are you. When you signed on with McKinsey to do this job with Minister Baunda, did it never occur to you that they might want you to do something more complex than crunch numbers, something with a little more intrigue? Did it ever occur to you that there are countless Zimbabweans with accounting skills? And that you bring access you can't buy in a Zimbabwean? Did that never occur to you?

Never. Oscar felt foolish. [*I hate looking like an asshole, especially to Maudie.*]

Oh, Oscar, you really are an American puer aeternus. The real thing. That's just one of the things I love about you. You actually believe what people tell you, take them at their word. Not an ounce of guile in you.

—

173

What you see is what you get. It may not make you the world's most skilled negotiator, but it sure makes you a wonderful human being. And prized friend, like few others. And what a lover!

But I knew this would come along at some point. McKinsey and the various government agencies don't waste opportunities like this one. That's why they waited months from the time Baunda first approached them before filling the post; they wanted to make sure they knew who they were sending and that he would suit their purposes.

Jesus, Maudie, I hope to hell you're not suggesting I got this job just because our relationship made me easy pickings. Are you?

Oh no, Baby. They're not above using you to get at me, but that was by no means the only reason they tapped you. Now, I'm going to tell you something that's going to upset you when you first hear it, but try to stay calm and just listen. It's not what it may at first seem.

Oscar's head felt heavy, fuzzy. [*Fuck, Maudie, don't tell me you're Mata Hari, seducing me for some patriotic purpose.*] He eyed her warily, waiting for he didn't know what, only that he dreaded hearing it.

Though we never said anything concrete about it, when Baunda asked for someone to fill this post, the president and Baunda counted on it working out pretty much the way it has. I don't mean you specifically, but someone with your credentials and background.

[*What the shit?*] *You mean they went looking for someone to spy on you?*

Not exactly, Oscar. What we want—what we desperately need—is for accurate, reliable information to reach the people who make the decisions that may decide whether we succeed or fail as a country. Most of what the CIA and the IMF collect is from unreliable alcoholics, drug addicts, international fugitives, soldier of fortune wannabes. And it's not simply wrong, it's dangerous misinformation. For African nations to get western countries and agencies to actually believe what we tell them is nearly impossible. Between the almost total lack of firsthand Africa experience on the part of American decision makers, and the eager, unreliable people who pose as experts, the flow of information from here to there is sparse, and mostly wrong, if not deliberate disinformation.

[*Christ, I need more sleep to get my head around this*]. *Maudie, was I handpicked for this job? Was this a big setup?*

You mean are you the lamb led to the slaughter? Did I seduce you back at Wharton so we could use you?

[*I'm about to jump right out of my skin right now. Are you leveling with me now, Maudie? I'd just as soon kill myself as believe that you'd do that to me*]. It took every ounce of self-discipline to keep Oscar from denying he'd ever thought such a thing. He felt like he'd stopped breathing while he waited for her to go on. [*On man, I've been out of my league ever since the moment you and I first met*].

She got out of her chair, letting the throw fall to the floor, and walked over to Oscar, knelt in front of him, taking his face in her hands. Her breasts were exposed, her musty sleep-smell intoxicated him.

Please, Maudie, please don't. Let's just keep talking. I need to understand as much as I can about all this. Something about it makes me feel like my whole life's on the line. Like maybe I tried to step out of myself and become somebody I'm not, never could be. Like I let myself fall in love with this woman who is so much smarter and tougher than I am. The stakes are so much higher than I ever imagined. Like maybe nothing is the way I thought.

I know, Oscar. She backed into her chair, covering herself with the throw. *I'm a tough woman; I've had to be, especially since my mother died. And I know how to manipulate people when it suits me. But you're going to have to decide whether you trust your own body and your instincts enough to know whether what we have between us is real or contrived. So far I can honestly tell you I've never used my sex like that, though I wouldn't say I never would. In my world you learn never to say never.*

Maudie, I'm exhausted—only had a couple of hour's sleep—not as clear-headed as I'd like, but this is as big a deal as anything that's ever happened to me. Of course I've understood right from the start that you and I had different stakes in our relationship; you've been totally up front about that right along. No secret that my dream has been to marry you, have babies with you, and live happily ever after. You've never mislead me about your putting your country and your father ahead of everything. And that means no happy ending for the two of us.

I really do understand all that, even though I can't keep myself from wishing it could be otherwise. But if I thought that your ambition and your loyalty to your father and Zimbabwe was all there was for you in being with me, well, I really don't know what I'd do. That would be such a huge assault on the fragile image I already have of myself, I just don't know how I'd handle it.

She let that hang in the air between them. They sat perfectly still, staring at each other in the dim moonlight, neither speaking for what felt to Oscar like an eternity.

[*God almighty, I'm going to have a heart attack!*]

I want to say this carefully, Oscar, and I hope you listen just as carefully. Instead of answering your question the way I know you think you want me to, reassuring you that I really love you, that I'm not a whore for Africa, I'm going to tell you that you're going to have to answer that one for yourself. Everything I might tell you is going to come back to haunt you, as you smell double meanings and nuances that make you wonder if you've been a fool to trust me.

In the end there's only one gauge you can count on, and that's your own nerve endings. I know everything in your life has taught you to trust your own perceptions least and last, to believe your rational head even when it contradicts all your other senses. But if you're going to make your way through this scary moment without going crazy, you're going to have to make a completely different kind of judgment. And if you don't, then you'll have to live forever haunted by your doubts and fears.

Have you been making love with a whore these past two years? Have you been ignoring warnings coming from inside your own body, that you shouldn't trust this; it isn't real? Because what I'm about to suggest is going to make it a lot harder to sort that out, not easier. It's going to require you to go back inside yourself—to places you've been trained never to visit—and figure out, not what your country wants you to do, or whether your groin outvotes your good judgment. What you're going to have to do is figure out what it is you really do trust. What you can count on, build your life on. Not who you hope you can charm, so they'll like you, and believe in you, applaud you, and decide for you what they think you should want. But what you want. What you trust. I don't think you've ever done that.

[*Jesus Christ, Maudie, right now you seem like you're at least a generation older and more experienced than I am. What I want? Trust? I've never known what I want until someone I love or admire tells me. I'm so fucking weary. What I want right now is to have this over and done. Go to sleep.*]

Oscar looked across the room at the clock radio, 2:54. *Maudie, I don't think I can do any more of this hard work in the middle of the night like this. Maybe we need to sleep on it and talk more on the drive back in the morning.* [*She's not going to buy it. Neither do I. I couldn't sleep now if my life depended on it. I'd sure like to put this off. Forever. I'm so tired*].

Maudie laughed. *Wouldn't that be nice? Snooze away while life gets put on hold. Good luck sleeping now, Oscar. We're into it; we may as well plow ahead. It won't be any easier or clearer in the morning. I don't want to over dramatize, but nothing between us, or about how we each go on from here, is ever going to matter more than what it is we're talking about right now. So, first question—do you think you've been duped? Not what I want to hear, but what you feel. Not even what you think, what you feel. Get it? Feel? Nerve endings. You know about nerve endings?*

Fuck off, Maudie, you don't need to speak to me as if I'm an ignorant child. I know all that bullshit about how you Africans live close to the soil, and you're all so in touch with your feelings. Maybe I'm an over-intellectualizing whitey, but I also happen to be a poet, in case you don't remember. Not some Wall Street pig. I get sick of all this shit about your authentic full-body responses versus my head responses. Yes, I do have feelings. And you know what, Maudie; thinking counts, too, you know.

[*Fuck off? I just told Maudie to fuck off. Man, this whole thing may be going right down the tubes here. I brought up the Africa thing. Maybe I really am a racist. Never done that before. Shit, this isn't how I pictured we'd end our happy holiday. Or our relationship. If that's what we're doing. That romp in the shower seems like a dream I once had.*]

Maudie looked calm, impassive. *Quite aside from all that hysteria, the question stands, Oscar. Have it on your own terms; what do you think? I'm not even asking you what you might think my motives might be; just what your instincts tell you about your own part.*

[*Am I really going to say it? Out loud? What's it going to cost me to hear myself admit this? Probably everything.*] *Maudie, you want to hear it straight? I think I'd probably have gone ahead with our relationship even if I thought you were totally, cynically using me. If what you're asking me is; would my pride have kept me from a reckless affair with you if I thought you were using me, I'm embarrassed to say the answer is no, probably not. I have no pride. No integrity. OK? I would have sold my soul for one fuck with you. Does that answer your fucking question?*

It's your question, Oscar, not mine. No, that wasn't my question, but it does answer your question, at least in one way. If you're saying—I don't want to put words in your mouth—that whatever it is that our being together does for you matters enough so you were willing to risk everything, even being betrayed by me. Even having to swallow your pride.

[*Do you have to put it like that?*] **Yeah, that comes pretty close, though it makes me feel even more like a hopeless asshole when you put it like that. Like I'm some pathetic guy so needy and totally lacking in self-respect that I don't even expect the relationship to be reciprocal. Which I've just admitted to you I am.**

You are such a dear man, Oscar. I'm not teasing, I promise. You are like no one I've ever known. It makes me sad that you always trash yourself. Because not only are you about the emotionally strongest, most mature man I've ever known, but I honestly don't think you're at risk here in the way you fear. But maybe that is about all we can manage for the moment. I'd say we've pushed this about as hard as we can in one conversation. I think we both need to step back and consider all this for a while. If you can sleep on it, great. I'm going to try and get a couple of hours in before we head out. By my lights the most important issue you were pressing for has been settled. On the ride back to Harare we can talk about the details, where it takes us. But they'll be a footnote to what we got settled here.

The basic issue has been settled? Not for me, Maudie. Not so I noticed. Easy for you to make pronouncements about me. What about for you? What are your issues? Or am I the only one with issues here? Oscar felt like his head weighed a ton, he knew he was beginning to unravel. He knew his anger was about to take hold of him.

Maudie, on the other hand, though weary, remained calm. **All fair questions, Oscar, and I promise to come as clean as I can on the drive back. But I'm spent. I can't think straight. I'm going to try to get a little sleep before we get tackle all that. And I really hope you'll think about what you've just said, because now that you've owned up to the reality of what I know you have feared above all else, you're going to have a chance to be clearer than you've ever been, maybe about anything in your whole life, when we have that next conversation.**

Just one more thing before I collapse, Oscar. I know you feel like you just exposed yourself as a hopelessly weak, admitting what you did. I really meant it when I said I don't think I have ever known a stronger, braver man than you just were in coming totally out in the open like that. Not trying to hide or even defend yourself. I have no idea where this will all come out—likely not as either of us might choose—but you have just proved to me that I have been right about you all along. Why I love you. Despite what I know you think right now, you've just proved to me that you have as high a regard for yourself as I have of you. And you do know

*yourself. You do know how to take good care of yourself, no matter how
intense the situation becomes.*

[*I think I nodded off. What did she just say? Did she say she loves me?*]

Maudie rose from her chair and slipped back into bed, pulling the
covers up to her chin. Oscar climbed into his side. Maudie reached across
with her leg, hooking it between his, and pulled him toward her until
their legs were entwined. In seconds they both dropped into numbing
sleep. Maudie knew Oscar dreamed because she woke twice to his
mumbling, but she couldn't make out what he said, and she was awake
only long enough to roll over. When she woke it was 9:13, and she heard
the shower running.

*   *   *

THE LONG DRIVE HOME

————

Mind if I drive, Oscar? I just feel like it. Oscar was happy to have her drive. He wanted to be able to watch her face as they talked. She wore sunglasses, but despite her intimidating Shona ability to keep her facial expressions neutral, never betraying her feelings, Oscar had learned—mostly by the way she held her mouth, the angle of her head—to read her pretty accurately. Sometimes. And he understood that she wanted to be able to look straight ahead for what she had already promised him would be a loaded conversation. They had just turned out of the Troutbeck drive when she waded right in.

So, Oscar, today must be the day. You ready to respond to Gretchen's request?

I think I will be by this afternoon. But I'd sure like to know what you know about my conversation with her and the other two. And how you know?

Honestly, only what you've told me and what I can put together from having been around that scene for many years. It gets pretty predictable after a while.

How about you tell me what you think went on? And maybe I'll tell you how close you come.

Why not? I bet they asked you to be their ears in Zimbabwe. Not to spy, but just help them gather accurate information so they can make good decisions. Is that about right?

On target so far. Anything else you think might have gone on? Oscar found this fascinating, and not a little unnerving.

Oh, I'd guess the arrest of the journalists has thrown the IMF people into a panic. They're trying to figure out if this is a signal that the

————

president is going to drift further and further right, until he's effectively a dictator.

And what about that, Maudie? How would you respond to that concern if you were asked?

We're getting a little ahead of ourselves, Oscar. Before we get into that, I'd like to know what your answer is going to be to them. Will you be their eyes and ears in Zimbabwe?

If I believed their motives were pretty much as they portrayed them to me, and if I thought I could do it without betraying the trust I have with Baunda, and of course with you, yes, I think I would. I wish I could be more clear about my own motives, stop worrying that I might be rationalizing all this just to make it easier on myself. I'd love to be able to come up with some noble reason for agreeing. But why should this be any different from every other decision I've ever faced? I never trust my own motives. But yes, I think I'm inclined to do it.

And do you believe what they said about their motives? And do you think you could do it without betraying us?

No and yes, in that order.

You're not as naïve as you like to picture yourself, Oscar. So what's your answer going to be?

You have a stake in what my answer will be, Maudie?

Matter of fact I do.

And it is?

I would hope you would agree to do it.

Just like that? No reservations? Oscar's suspicions were on the rise again.

He saw the tiny, nearly imperceptible twitch in the corner of Maudie's mouth. He figured they were getting close to whatever it was Maudie was pushing him so hard about last night.

It's never that simple, is it Oscar? She smiled a wide sunny smile. Despite Oscar's trying every way he knew how to elicit that smile, this time it didn't make him feel better. *Oscar,* her tone made him feel suddenly solemn, he sat motionless, preparing himself. *I'm about to ask you to do something, not because of your feelings for me, but because of the justice of Zimbabwe's revolution, and what you believe about how the world would work if people of conscience ran it. Maybe I have no right to ask that; you didn't suffer through generations of colonial rule. But I am asking. And everything I know about you, Oscar, makes me believe you might actually be able to.* She let that hang in the air between them for so long that Oscar wondered if she was waiting for him to make some sort of response, even before she told him what she was asking. He had to hang onto himself to keep from to blurting out *Of course!,* not because he was suddenly a patriotic Zimbabwean [*ugly truth be known, I don't give a rat's ass about the frigging revolution*] but because of his feelings for her. [*Christ, is there anything I wouldn't do for Maudie*]*?* Oscar was relieved when Maudie finally broke the silence.

My request is pretty much the same as theirs, kind of parallel to theirs. Not contrary to or in conflict with theirs. Equally benign. I hope your eyes and ears might be tuned in two directions, toward us, as they asked, and toward the American government and agencies, too, since they are so important to our being able to carry on our work in this country.

[*Counter spy. Maudie's asking me to be a counter spy for Zimbabwe against my own country. Holy shit! Oh my sweet Christ! What have I gotten myself into?*] Oscar waited for her to say more, but he realized she was waiting for his reaction before she spoke again.

Have I got this right, Maudie? Oscar's tone was a combination of sarcasm and outrage, with a sprinkling of terror. *You want me to be a counter spy, to turn against my own country? That's called espionage; in wartime it's punishable by firing squad.*

Come on, Oscar, no need to play the drama card. I'm sure Gretchen and her friends didn't ask you to be a spy, and I'm certainly not asking you to be a counter spy. Their request is reasonable and prudent; they haven't got any other access to good information, certainly not remotely as good as you can provide. The same is true for us. And the reason we both want it is not to take advantage of each other, but so we can be better, more responsible partners. It's what is sometimes called a marriage of convenience. Not romantic maybe, but often very healthy. And productive for both.

You're in a unique position, Oscar. As things have worked out there's just no one else in quite the spot you're in, at least not since Zimbabwe's independence, and neither we nor Gretchen, nor the IMF, wants to squander the opportunity. There are so many ways all this could go wrong unless there is reliable, good information flowing in both directions.

[*No wonder she pushed me so hard last night about whether I trust myself with her. Am I ready to be Julius Rosenberg?*]

You're pretty unique yourself, Maudie. I mean I have to admit, you're the first lover I've ever had who's asked me for anything quite like this.

He'd meant to make a joke, but as soon as he heard his own words, he knew he'd only darkened things. Oscar's stomach tightened. [*Every time I open my mouth I make things worse.*]

Maybe we need to revisit last night's conversation, Oscar. Her tan knuckles whitened as she gripped the wheel. Oscar felt the car speed up. *I'm not trying to be coy with you. The reality is that under the right conditions anyone is capable of betraying anyone. You know my passion for this country and my commitment to the goals that drove our revolution. I hope I'd never ask you to betray your own country, but you know as well as I do that it's not beyond imagining. To my mind this is not asking you to betray anyone. This looks to me more like a smart business deal, a win-win agreement between enlightened people. For many perfectly legitimate reasons neither party can be totally candid with the other. It's clearly not a betrayal in my eyes, but you have your own issues. So you're going to have to decide if what I'm asking seems a betrayal to you.*

You could at least do me the kindness of telling me it's not. Or that I'm not just some naïve white American you've been setting up for the past two years.

I just did, Oscar, if you could clear out all that anxiety and listen. This isn't about betrayal; the United States, Zimbabwe, the IMF, all have a common interest in there being an exchange of accurate, dependable information. But right now that common interest is being derailed by events none of us can control and that can sometimes seem as if they divide us. At its heart, I don't believe our interests differ in these matters. But right now you have become the indispensible man. With suspicions running high on both sides, the only way we can make sure the channels critical to us both are kept open, so miscommunications don't screw everything up, is with your help. Unfair as it may seem, you turn out to be in a unique spot here, Oscar.

[*Christ, she's not even smiling. Guess it didn't come out like a joke.*] *OK, Maudie, OK. Look, It may be a suicide mission, but I'm not the least hesitant about you and me. Despite my question, I do trust you. Whether stupidly or not, I surrendered that worry a long time ago. The part that still feels murky to me is about me, not you. It's whether I'm smart or disciplined enough to keep clear where the boundaries in all this are, what should be shared and what should not. To trust myself to be able to do what you and Gretchen are asking. Whether I even really get exactly what it is that's being asked of me.*

Which brings me to another thing I feel like I need to know; the extent to which you and Gretchen are in on this together? Are you two talking?

No, Oscar, absolutely not. Not that we wouldn't love to be, if only we could. But it just isn't possible; it would lead to situations that could quickly spin out of control. That's the way this world works. We have a pretty good idea, and even some inside information provided by the likes of your Mr. Pinsky, about what's going on with each other. There are people undercover on both sides. But Gretchen and I don't talk. We can't. Which is another reason we have each asked you to do this.

OK, Maudie so what's to keep you, or Gretchen, from feeding me disinformation when it suits your interests? I mean I may not have any integrity, but I'm not wildly enthusiastic about being the drone, the diplomatic cuckold in this. How am I to know when, or if, either of you is using me like that? I mean it's one thing for me to be willing to be of help to the two of you, and our two countries, as your collaborator. Quite another as your stooge.

How do you know you can trust this conversation we're having right now, Oscar? What's to keep me from being the whore for the revolution you keep being afraid I might be? How would you ever know?

[*It all just keeps getting murkier! I'm miles above my pay grade here.*] **OK, Maudie, there are a few more things I need to know before I'm ready to sign on.** [*She knows I'm bullshitting. She knows I'd turn Jesus Christ over to her for a lot less than 30 pieces of silver if it pleased her. How did James Bond keep his cool with all those sexy women? He must never have fallen in love with any of them.*]

Who besides you and I will know about this arrangement? Does the president know? Besides those other paragons of virtue, Baunda? And Gretchen? And Pinsky and Newmark? Is this just a cozy arrangement between you and me?

Hey, Oscar, you've got a perfect right to ask these things, but it's not going to help get clearer for you to hide behind sarcasm. It's tricky enough trying to work this complicated puzzle out when we're being straight with each other. So how about dropping the victim thing, and let's finish the conversation?

[*Fuck you, Maudie! Who's playing games with who? Whom?*] **I'll do my best, Maudie, but I don't find it very convincing that now you resent my screwing around with you after the way I've been left to dangle. Pun intended. I'm just trying to make some sense of whether this is some bad** *dream, the stupidest thing I've ever done, or a maybe an essential and legitimate piece of this job I've signed on for. I'm not playing games with you. I haven't exactly hidden that I'm wildly in love with you. And you haven't been a big help in my figuring out how reciprocal that is. I'm still trying to sort out how much weight that carries for me in all this. It's kind of an old cliché that history is littered with the remains of men who made stupid, suicidal decisions because they fell in love with a tough, ambitious woman. And let her agenda become his.*

Maudie didn't respond. Oscar waited. She looked straight ahead. Nothing. Oscar was determined to let the silence hang as long as it took. But he couldn't. He caved.

Right, Maudie? I mean you acknowledge that my anxiety about all this isn't just my paranoia, right?

Oscar, remember what we talked about last night? Now maybe you can understand what I was driving at, why I pushed you so hard. We're right back at that hard place where there's nothing I can do to help you. Only you can decide whether I'm playing Delilah to your Sampson. I understand that you want me to reassure you, to take away your dilemma, but I can't. You've got to work that one out for yourself. And this is where all that intellect has to give way to something I think much more dependable, but much less precise.

OK, OK. You can at least answer my question about who else is in on this with you.

No one, Oscar, at least not at this point. I'm not saying I'd never share any of the stuff you tell me with anyone else; I just can't quite anticipate how that might play out in some hypothetical future. But what I'm asking of you is totally my own idea, and as yet I haven't mentioned it to anyone else.

Well, can you at least promise to always tell me who else you might talk with about what it is we talk about?

In a perfect world, I'd gladly do that, Oscar, because I know it seems only fair. Sitting next you in this car right now, I can't imagine a scenario in which I wouldn't do that. But I keep bumping into situations I never anticipated, couldn't have imagined. This world is turning out to be so much messier than I ever imagined. So I'm not prepared to make any solemn agreements at this point. There just isn't room in this for absolutes.

You're not exactly cutting me a lot of slack here, Maudie.

—

I'm being a hell of a lot more candid with you than I would with anyone else I might talk with about this. And that includes the president.

Oscar restrained himself from asking, "You mean your father?" He felt what Maudie had just said might be—if it was true—the weightiest piece of the entire conversation, and counted for more with him than anything else she had said before. Maudie shifted in her seat. Oscar thought maybe her self-assurance seemed just the tiniest bit dented. It made his spirits lift, a little. He didn't like himself any better for wishing Maudie would lose some of her normally awesome self-confidence. But he hoped it might mean he could take a little better care of his own interests. [*Maybe I haven't surrendered both my balls. Yet.*]

You know, Maudie, I don't think I'm exactly straining at gnats here. We're talking about international agreements, diplomatic back channels, and what little may be left of my integrity.

Maudie exploded. *Oh for Christ's sweet sakes Oscar, what we're discussing is routine for people in the diplomatic business. Get used to it. Or go home. Your integrity is for sale just like anyone else's. But I'm not asking you to sell your integrity, just give us some plain, non-classified help. I'd hope it's more than just your sex drive that made you to take the job consulting with our Finance Ministry.*

Maudie, don't.

Sorry, Oscar, that was out of bounds. But listen to yourself. What kind of purity are you looking for? Because you won't find it in this line of work. Maybe back in Wharton's ivory tower, or in your father's holy work with God. But here in the real world things don't fall so neatly into place. My suggestion is that we drop this conversation now, and you do your soul-searching after you get back. Maybe there's someone you need to talk with, though I doubt anyone else can do this work for you any more than I can. That's the key, Oscar. It's your work.

Oscar was in despair. [*Maudie's right. This is going to kill me. If I can't talk with Maudie about this, who the fuck can I talk with? That's her whole point, isn't it? That all this talking just confuses things, makes me crazier.*]

They rode mostly in silence for the next hour and a half. Maudie pointed out the color of the rondavels, the round mud huts in which many of the villagers lived, how it changed to a deeper crimson color as they left the eastern highlands and drove closer to Harare. Oscar was too preoccupied to respond. His sadness deepened as the distance from Troutbeck grew. Familiar landmarks as they approached Harare only deepened his despair.

*   *   *

No Hiding Places

Maudie dropped him off a block from his apartment. [*As if your goons don't know where we've been the past five days.*] His loneliness enveloped him as he walked into his living room, musty and hot from being closed up,. When he had felt this way in Philadelphia he used to call up Maudie, but he knew better than to try that now. He wandered down the hall to the kitchen, opened the refrigerator, considering the jar of Mazoe orange; the little plastic pouch with the milk that was inevitably sour, and the three lonely bottles of Lion beer. He could feel the depression creeping in like a rising tide. He checked his watch. [*7 pm. Let's see, it's around noon in New York? Don't do this, Oscar; it's only going to make it worse.*] Oscar dialed the international code and the familiar local number. He knew the comfort he was looking for would be at best fleeting. Self-defeating. [*You're like an alcoholic picking up a drink.*]

Hello. His father's voice sounded thick with sleep, there was an echo, as if he was speaking through a big pipe.

Hey, Dad, it's Oscar.

Oscar! Are you back in the States?

Nope, Dad, I'm calling from Harare.

Harare? Everything all right, son?

Everything's fine, Dad, Oscar lied, **I was just missing you and Mom, wanted to hear your voices.**

Your mother is sound asleep. I can wake her. I know she'll want to talk. But it is 4 in the morning. Everything OK?

[*Shit. Got the time wrong, again.*] **So sorry, Dad, I always get the time difference screwed up. Don't wake Mom; it's not a crisis.** [*Except for me.*] **Yeah, everything's good, thanks. I did have something I wanted to run by**

—
188

you, a sort of dilemma. But nothing urgent; nothing important enough for 4 am . . . CLICK. The line went dead for a couple of seconds, then Oscar heard his father's voice again.

. . . we must have been interrupted, Oscar. Don't worry about waking me; I never sleep much anymore, and I'd much rather talk with you, anytime. Your mom wears earplugs and sleeps the sound sleep of the innocent. But I missed the last thing you were saying. I heard 'but I did have something' and then there was a lot of static and a dead spot.

[*These Zimbabwe spooks can't even bug a cell phone without giving themselves away.*]

I just wondered whether you'd used Chloroquine or Mephloquine for malaria prophylaxis when you traveled in malaria areas?

I can never remember, Oscar, but I'll check with our travel people and let you know. You don't want to fool around with malaria. I figured McKinsey would have sorted all that out for you.

They mostly have, [*You asshole, Oscar, you thought Daddy could fix it?*] *but there seem to be some differences about which is the better drug over here.*

[*Idiot! You knew calling your father for advice was a dumb idea. Now you've got to back yourself out of this conversation without the spook who's listening in understanding you were about to blow your cover.*]

Well there's really nothing urgent about it. Nobody in Harare is much at risk, and I seem to be spending just about all my time here.

I'm relieved to know that, Oscar. You sure don't want malaria. Seems you never really get rid of it. But I'm so proud of you for risking it, instead of doing the Wall Street thing, to go do that great work you're doing. You know, I've spent my life preaching about what you're actually doing. You're making a difference, teaching them to fish rather than giving them a fish. I was proud of you when you graduated Summa, but this is more than I ever dreamed. I preach about it; you do it.

Thanks, Dad; that's nice to hear. Very kind. [*You'd die if you knew what I was really calling about. You've preached against the CIA and I'm working for them. You've ragged on the IMF for gouging the poor to keep the ruling plutocrats in charge, and I may be about to deliver these people into their hands.*] *But you sell yourself short. Where do you think I learned to care about justice?*

Probably from your mother whose hard work and ambition have funded all of it.

Don't beat yourself up, Dad. [*That's probably exactly right. You've never had to wrestle with whether playing ball with those bogeymen in the CIA and IMF might actually end up doing more good than marching in demonstrations and shouting slogans. Or if you have, I sure never knew.*]

I'm so happy to hear from you, Oscar, but I'm getting nervous about how much this call is going to cost you.

You're right, Dad. Just wanted to hear your voice. Give a big hug to Mom and I'll look for you on email.

Great! Now be sure you've got the right Malaria drug. Love you so much. Bye, Oscar.

*   *   *

THE SPOOKS WANT MORE

As he hung up the phone Oscar's stomach felt as if he were in an airplane that had just hit an air pocket. For a moment he wondered if he was going to throw up. He started down the hall to the bathroom when the phone rang. [*Maudie!*] His forgot about his nausea as he rushed for the phone.

Hello, Oscar, this is Gretchen. [*Oh God, I'd almost forgotten about you. You're at work at 4 am? Give me a break.*] **I'm going to be in and out all day today so I thought I'd try to get hold of you in case you called while I was out of the office.**

Great, nice to hear from you, Gretchen. I was going to call you later today to talk about what you're asking me to do. [*I'm getting pretty comfortable with these half truths. Maybe being a spy isn't as hard as I thought*]. **You beat me to it. What're you doing up at 4 in the morning?**

Oh, it's routine when most of your business is international. Oscar, before you give us your response, I'm afraid we're going to need to have one more face-to-face conversation to clear up a couple of things we left hanging when you were here last week. I apologize for jerking you around like this, asking you to do these huge flights back to back, but things have suddenly really heated up, both in Zimbabwe and at the IMF. I just checked with KLM and they have a connection through London that leaves Harare tomorrow morning at 8, gets into London at noon their time, leaves London at 6 pm and gets you to Dulles in time for you to get a night's sleep before we meet the next morning. I've taken the liberty of booking a seat for you in Business and gotten a room at the Jefferson. Hope that all works for you.

[*The Jefferson? What happened to the good old Hay Adams? Guess you're not wooing me any more. Feels like my leash is tightening.*]

Sure, I can do that, Gretchen, though I'm a little concerned that I haven't put in much time over at Finance lately. I've just walked in the door from being away for five days. McKinsey's going to have to return the consulting fee if I don't start showing up.

We'll cover for you on all that, Oscar. Everyone understands you have more than one master. Baunda's in the loop.

[*I'll bet. I'm the only one who doesn't know who all my masters are, or which ones are talking with who, or what about. I'm like the promiscuous man who thinks his lovers don't know about each other, only to discover they are all in it together and he's been set up.*]

So who is going to be at the meeting, Gretchen? Oscar wondered if the question sounded as casual as he tried to make it.

Oh, the usual suspects. No surprises. Have a safe trip, Oscar, and we'll look forward to seeing you at 9 that next morning.

And I look forward to seeing you, Gretchen. [*The usual? Last time the usual had expanded by two pretty significant people. I guess we've given up any pretenses about this being McKinsey business. Wonder if that big-ass office Gretchen first met me in for the interviews in New York is a dummy? Everything since has been in a motel shit-hole in Washington.*]

Oscar hung up. The sun had set, and Oscar hadn't turned on any lights. The city sparkled beyond his window. He remembered how beautiful Samora Michel Avenue looked the first time he'd stood at this window. The Jacaranda trees lining the street created a filmy lavender shadow against the amber street lights.

Oscar knew he was utterly alone. Beyond his love for his girlfriend, he'd lost all track of what his own interest in this drama might be. All he was sure of was that his appetite for Maudie was turning out to be a meal perhaps too rich for him to digest. [*And this flying back and forth across the planet every other week. For what? Sure as hell not for anything noble. No suffering peasants will be lifted out of poverty thanks to these meetings. Maybe I'm just propping up another avaricious African dictator for a while so he can fatten his Swiss bank accounts. This isn't exactly what I pictured myself doing. But you've already rolled over for this one, pal. You'd rape Mother Teresa if Maudie told you it was for the good of the country. I want so much to believe her, she wouldn't have to stretch the truth much. Do you really think that's what*] *she's doing, Oscar? No. So what's in it for Maudie, besides a conduit to the IMF? How many times are you going to torture yourself wondering that?*]

Exhausted, Oscar walked to the fridge, opened one of the bottles of Lion beer, went and sat in the dark living room and drank it while he watched the traffic below. When he finished the beer he had just enough energy to walk down the hall to his bedroom, throw a few things into his overnight bag, drop his clothes on the chair in the corner and slip into bed. He set the alarm for 5:30, hoping he'd sleep until it woke him. He knew he would not.

*   *   *

Squeeze Play

After rolling over to look at the lighted digital dial every couple of minutes for the last hour, hoping maybe he'd slept a little, Oscar threw back the covers at 5, showered, went down to the street and found a man asleep in his cab a half block from his apartment. The driver agreed to drive him to the airport for half the fare the last time he'd gone. [*Something to be said for negotiating with a sleepy man.*]

Which is what Oscar was as he walked up 16th Street to the K Street meeting the following morning. [*Or was it two days following; who can keep track?*] He tried to collect his thoughts, hoping he might at least come across as if he had some sense of himself this time, not like the deer in the headlights he thought he was in their last meeting. But he was, once again, jet-lagged, hung-over, fuzzy-headed. [*At least I'm too whacked out to even feel anxious.*] As he climbed the steps his legs burned. [*I feel like I just ran a marathon*]. He'd shaved, but his face still felt coarse to his touch. [*God, I've already grown stubble.*] Even though it was a cool morning the ten-minute walk had left him with clammy armpits. His undershorts stuck to him. He reached behind him to free his wedgie.

Hello Oscar. How was your trip? Ellen startled him. He wondered if she had seen him picking at his butt. Ellen, Gretchen's front woman, greeted Oscar like an old friend.

Fine, Ellen, and how have you been? [*You look like such a wonderful, easy-going woman, Ellen. I bet you go home to Arlington every night and cook dinner for your adoring husband and child. Maybe I could fall in love with someone like you.*]

Gretchen's expecting you, said to tell you to come right in.

194

Oscar, so good to see you! You're great to come on such short notice. You must be exhausted from all the traveling. Gretchen, as always, looked totally put together, in a tailored dark blue suit with a pin stripe. The blouse had a ruffle at the neck, a reminder that this power person was also, under there somewhere, female. Seeing her so turned-out made Oscar feel, by contrast, like an unmade bed.

[*You hope I'm exhausted. Thank God she's alone. I haven't got the energy to deal with three people this morning*].

No, I'm really fine, thanks, Gretchen. I'm starting to get used to this international travel. [*She used to at least come around from behind the table and greet me. Uh oh, don't start getting sensitive, Oscar. You better be ready to take care of yourself, not look to her to give you strokes. Gretchen's not your mommy. These corporate/CIA style bullshit throwaway lies come easier and easier.*] Oscar couldn't stifle a huge yawn. [*That jaw-breaking yawn must be pretty convincing evidence of how alert I am.*]

Ethan Pinsky and Jim Newmark will be along about 9:45, but I thought it'd be good if we had a few minutes before they joined us. How's Maudie?

Fine, so far as I know. Her life's crazy busy since becoming deputy president, and I don't see that much of her. I don't suppose I'm exactly what you'd call her greatest political asset. [*Easy, Oscar, let's not drop too much information right away. You're tired and you guard's down; keep your counsel. No time for candor.*]

Did you ever have a chance to talk with her about our last conversation?

[*Keep your wits; this is a minefield.*] *We did have one brief conversation in which I mentioned that I'd met with you and Jim and Ethan. She seemed to know who they were.*

I was sure she would. Did she have any opinion about your being a source of solid information for us?

[*Jesus, is this a bad dream? Didn't Maudie tell me she doesn't talk with you? Is this a test to see how much I'll reveal to Maudie about our conversation, and how much of her conversation I'll tell you? And what's a passing grade for this test? Candor or secrecy?*]

Well, as I'm sure you can understand, I was pretty cautious how we talked about it. I mean, in a sense, it was almost as if I was asking her how she felt about me spying on her. But she seemed to take it all pretty much in stride, the way you do. Like good information is so important and so hard to come by, that any way it can flow through is more important than all the usual loyalties and protocol.

Did she want any reassurances in return, Oscar? I mean like wanting you to keep an open channel to her about what you were passing on to us?

[*Damn, Gretchen, you really are going to squeeze me through this knothole, aren't you*]?

Well, we didn't try to pin that piece down too precisely, Gretchen. We both acknowledged that for it to be a really useful channel, the flow needed to go at least somewhat in both directions. But we left it pretty vague just how the information would flow back and forth. But if she knows who Jim and Ethan are and who they work for, especially Ethan, I guess she must understand how these things work.

Sorry if I seem like I'm pushing you on this point, Oscar, but Ethan and Jim are going to want to know who, besides them, is going to have access to the information you give us. It makes all the difference in how they can use it. Gretchen stared at Oscar.

[*You'd like to know if I'll sell Maudie out. Or is it that you already know what Maudie and I have talked about and you're testing me to find out whether I'm playing straight with you? Man, I don't think I'm cut out for this, even at the top of my game. Today, I'm feeling so beat-up, I may vomit all over myself.*]

You're not pushing me, Gretchen. [*Like hell, you're not.*] *It's just that I'm not always sure exactly what it is you're asking. If I understand your question, I think the answer is 'no'. Maudie didn't ask me to make any prior agreements. But it's pretty clear she's hoping she'll be in the loop unless there are strategic national interests on either side that make that impossible.* [*Man, Oscar, you make Bill Clinton sound like a straight shooter*].

Just so you know, this is certain to come up when Jim and Ethan join us. You might want to think about where you mean to draw your boundaries, because they'll want to be clear about that in their own minds.

[*And you? Are you the good cop in this game of charades? Am I supposed to believe you and Ethan aren't joined at the hip in this?*]

The intercom buzzed. Ellen announced Ethan and Jim, who came through the door, cheerfully with a burst of energy, as if they were joining old friends for a day of fun. Oscar's exhaustion deepened. And with it his despair and sense of doom. The walls were closing in. He decided his only hope to hold his own was to wade right in, not wait for them to take the initiative. Before they even greeted each other, he began.

—

***I've decided I'm willing to do this information deal with you, but there
are a couple of understandings that I need to be clear about.*** Oscar meant
to head them off for a few minutes, take the offensive and give them the
good news first. [*That was a strategic mistake, to say I'd do it, before getting
anything settled about the conditions. I'm such an eager beaver. Now they know
they've got me. Now all they're going to care about is the conditions. And they're
going to wait me out on those, let me hang myself*].

No one spoke for an uncomfortably long time. Oscar wondered if he
might have nodded off. He looked at Gretchen. She was expressionless,
looking at him. All three of them were looking at him. [*How did I let
myself get on this side of the table with the three of them on the other side? Oh
God, I really might just slide off this chair into a deep sleep.*]

***Naïve and pious as it may sound, I actually have come to feel some
personal stake in Zimbabwe's success,*** he began, wishing he could sound
more casual, less earnest. ***And it seems pretty clear that the U.S. has a
compelling interest in that, too.*** [*Here goes your Eagle Scout routine again.*]
***And I don't think I could do anything that felt to me like I was selling
them out. I choose to believe that you and I share that same concern*** [*How
about just a hint of response from you ghouls?*] ***or we wouldn't be spending
all this time and energy figuring out how to help that small country. But
it all looks kind of different when you're right in the middle of it. I mean,
I don't feel any differently about my loyalty to the States, but I have to
admit I have a different picture of a lot of things than I did before I spent
these past six months in Zimbabwe.***

No response.

***And I have a question for you: I'd like to know just what your
relationship is to Maudie Mugabe. Or maybe what you perceive mine to
be. Because she's not my main source,*** [*liar, liar, pants on fire*] ***but I'm not
going to lie to you about this.*** [*I just did.*] ***I'm not interested in using my
relationship with her for anything except the personal friendship it is.
The deal I'm making is between the two countries.*** [You guys laughing
at me?]

You know Maudie far better than we do, Ethan Pinsky finally broke
the silence on their side. ***And I'd guess you know better than we can what
would be appropriate and inappropriate in your exchanges with her.***

Oscar knew he'd cooked his own goose now. He already said he was
going to do what they wanted, they knew he was out-of-control in love

with Maudie, so why should they bother to negotiate with him about any of it?

What we're asking is really pretty straightforward Oscar, [*Pinsky, closing in for the kill*] *just a clear understanding about who you're working for and who gets what information. And in what order. Of course we understand the subtleties and the chances for misunderstanding, but the clearer we can be now, the less chance for that happening down the road.*

Oscar felt a drop of sweat escape his armpit and roll down his side. *I've always understood I was working for McKinsey, and I see no reason that this changes anything about that. He looked over at Gretchen for agreement.* She smiled enigmatically. [*And what am I supposed to make of that, Mona Lisa?*]

That's been our understanding all along also, Oscar, Gretchen finally spoke. *This isn't the sort of thing we normally get involved in, but this case is different in almost every respect from our usual contracts. McKinsey would like to contribute to the welfare both of our own country and of course Zimbabwe's, so long as we aren't compromising the integrity and independence of our company.*

[*McKinsey's independence? Nice speech, Gretchen; should give you a shot at your Eagle Scout badge. Notice that neither Jim nor Ethan has spoken or even hinted that they give a shit about McKinsey's precious integrity? Or, for that matter Zimbabwe's. Sure as shit, not mine.*]

We understand—Pinsky again—*that it would be awkward for this to be widely known. Not because there's anything illegal about it, but because it's murky enough that it could be a political liability for some of those involved. Here and in Zimbabwe. So since we have to be circumspect not only about the information, but also about the money flow as we discussed before, we're prepared to set up an account for you back in this country—could be an IRA or maybe a Keogh—and we'll make deposits monthly. No problem there. But one thing we really do have to be clear about is who else will be included in what you're telling us. Like, will Maudie?*

[*OK Oscar, it's jump—off-the-cliff time.*]

What I tell you will remain between us. If there's something I think could be damaging to Maudie, or a betrayal of my contract with Minister Baunda and the Economics Ministry, I will consider pretty carefully whether I really need to pass it on to you. If there is a conflict that I can't resolve in my own mind, I will resign.

Pinsky and Newmark remained impassive—no expression, no comment.

[*You could give a shit. You just want what you want. And you figure you've already got that.*]

I don't see all that much of Maudie. [*How much do you goons know about us, about when we're together?*] *I'm not in the habit of talking with her about what I send back to Gretchen, but neither am I about to tell you I never have or never will.* He paused, checking for some reaction; there was none. *I figure I work for McKinsey, and Gretchen's my boss. What Gretchen chooses to do with the stuff I send back to her is beyond my control.*

I should be straight with you about how I view Minister Baunda. He's McKinsey's client, which means that, except under some extraordinary circumstance I can't imagine, he's paid for the information I generate and it, technically—and legally—belongs to him.

Jim Newmark spoke for the first time. *We've got no problem with Baunda being in the loop. In fact we prefer it.*

[*That's because he's your mole in the government, right? Does the president—or Maudie—know that? Is that because he's Ndebele and can provide information about the political opposition?*]

That settles pretty much everything except the issue of Maudie Mugabe. Pinsky wasn't to be diverted. *What can we assume about her vis-à-vis the reports you send back to Gretchen?*

Oscar felt his annoyance growing as his fatigue deepened. *As I told you earlier, my relationship with Maudie is personal. Yes, she is deputy president, and I won't be so disingenuous as to tell you we never discuss anything to do with politics. I'm not about to make any commitments to you about where I'll draw the lines in my talking with Maudie, because I can't envision or predict the future.* [*Thanks, Maudie, for giving me this one.*] *So if that's a deal-breaker for what you're trying to set up with me, then maybe you'd better find yourself another pigeon.* [*You're losing it, Oscar.*]

It doesn't wreck anything, Oscar. I'm sure Ethan agrees. Gretchen's voice had dropped an octave, clearly intending to calm Oscar.

Absolutely. Neither Pinsky's voice, nor his expression had changed at any point in the conversation. *We just need to understand what information is secure, coming only to us. And what information may be shared more widely. No surprises, that's our goal.*

Gretchen was in summing-up mode. *I sense we're all on the same page on this one, and now we're into splitting hairs. Not that the hairs don't matter, but none of them is significant enough to get in the way of what we have agreed to.* Gretchen was the peacemaker in today's meeting. Oscar was fading fast. He wanted to get out of the room before he did something stupid.

Oscar, we'd like you to take this back with you. Pinsky reached into his attaché case pulling out a small black plastic holder that looked like it might hold a pen or a tiny paint brush. He pulled the ends apart revealing a numerical pad and screen that glowed green. [*This meeting's prize. Fly half way round the world; get a new toy.*] *This is our latest secure phone, just delivered. It runs off our own satellite and uses our scrambler. When you enter your code and press this button it activates and goes through to only one receiver. Either I or my assistant will be on the other end no matter what time you call day or night. The phones we gave you earlier will continue to work fine. For our usual communications, feel free to use them. But for anything perhaps more sensitive, we'd prefer you use this.*

Oscar looked at Gretchen. [*So, is this how I keep clear that I'm a McKinsey employee, not a spy for the CIA? You guys are like a sinister cell phone company; every time we renegotiate my contract I get a new phone. Well, I'm not signing up for another two years for this one.*]

It's all on the up and up, Oscar.—Gretchen speaking—*We have an open, largely informal, contract with the U.S. government that has been approved by Congress, so we can do this without putting you or me in the position of being inadvertent spies. This information is, despite the secure channels, declassified. There's a difference between classified and confidential, and this is confidential. Because of our international contacts, we do this with clients frequently, not only with the government.*

[*Seems like we're splitting some pretty fine hairs here. Good job, Oscar; you wanted to do good in the third world, and you're ending up spying on the guys you want to help, working for the guys you used to trash.*]

He reached across the table and accepted the phone from Ethan Pinsky. *Can I use this to call my Mom? Sure could save on the long distance charge*s.

It can be used for nothing except communicating with me; it recognizes only your voice on your end and mine or my assistant's on the other. Pinsky's expression tightened.

[*You could do with some 3-in-1 oil on that sense of humor, pal.*]

Consider yourself on a 'need-to-know' basis, Oscar, Pinsky added. *We're particularly interested in gaining accurate stats on the Zimbabwe economy, and some indication of what the government may intend to do on matters that will impact the economy going forward. Like the status of the troops and materiel in the Congo, and the government's intentions about maintaining a price ceiling on mealies. But there's no reason for you to tie yourself in knots about our motives, or whether we have sinister reasons for asking you to do this. Baunda entered into this contract with McKinsey hoping it would improve the accuracy and speed of the information flow between us. This can only help that. And so long as Baunda and Maudie are the only ones who may know what you're sending to us, we have no concerns about the integrity of this information.*

[*Integrity? Get real. We're in Orwell country. This deal was drained dry of any hint of integrity a long time ago. I always knew I could be bought, but I never thought it would be for such a vague price. I still have no idea who's in on this or whether Maudie is my lover or my handler.*]

You guys do understand, I hope [*watch the sarcasm, Oscar*] *that I'm not usually consulted about sending troops to the Congo. And I see the production numbers that are sent in from the field, with no mechanism for verifying their accuracy. I am asked to calculate the impact after the price of mealies has been set, not before.*

We understand you're not privy to a lot of the numbers, Oscar. All we're asking is that you help us get better information than we have in the past. The reality is, even what you pick up in informal conversation over there is likely more accurate than what we have been able to come up with on our end.

We'll also communicate with you on this phone when we are passing along confidential information, Jim Newmark said. *It's fitted out with a holster that fits comfortably under your belt so you can feel it vibrate when we ring you. If you're in a situation that makes talking inappropriate, just push that red button on the bottom of the case and we'll know to leave you a message that it will store until you can get back to us. But normally, unless it's something really pressing, we won't be contacting you on this phone. In fact I'd say there's a good chance neither the IMF nor the CIA will ever feel the need to use it.*

[*So much for the IMF operating independently of the CIA. Jesus, does anyone do business as advertised any more?*]

I'll guard it with my life, Oscar said, with theatrical solemnity, confident these guys wouldn't recognize irony if it kissed their sorry asses.

Well, Oscar, that takes care of what we came here for. Anything else you're concerned about before we take off? Oscar thought he heard almost a softness in Pinsky's voice. [*Or did I dream that? I'm not even sure any more whether I'm asleep or awake.*]

Oscar knew he shouldn't be taken in by the change in tone, and that he should drop everything and leave before he lost it completely; **Only that I'd like to know what you're looking for, and how you're going to use this information. You know, Zimbabwe is really a pretty wonderful country, and it's having tough growing problems. I can imagine how it must look from over here, but it's just the sort of situation the United States could lend a big hand to, or screw up royally, depending on how we move over the next few months.**

I know the arrest of the journalists has everyone pretty upset, but I haven't heard you say whether you think it could be a deal breaker for the IMF. I think they'd love me to come back with some sense of whether this puts the next installment of their loan in jeopardy. I mean, I know what it must look like from back here, but they don't have the fetish we do about an independent press. Not that we always do either, in practice. [*Time to bail, Oscar, before you step in deep shit.*]

We're grunts, not policy makers, Oscar, just information gatherers. Pinsky's voice didn't harden. **Our stance towards these matters is neutral until and unless we get orders to take on a partisan position. So I'm afraid you'll have to be just like us—in the dark about a lot of this stuff right now. I know that's hard, but in fact I think it'll make your job less complicated. I do want to reassure you every way I can that while this may be a departure from the usual consulting contract McKinsey makes, there is nothing politically underhanded about it. There's no Iran-Contra scandal lurking here. What we are asking is in a sense no different from what would be asked of any consultant trying to manage a tricky merger between two corporations. I think it's fair to say that the IMF is eager to play a constructive role in helping Zimbabwe resolve its economic**

problems. But the specifics of the policy are being made by people above my pay grade.

Right. [*Back off, Oscar, they're not going to give you anything, even if they do know themselves, which they probably don't.*]

The two men left and Oscar and Gretchen remained behind for a few more minutes. He felt suddenly relieved, almost close to Gretchen, as if he and she were allies against the other two.

[*On alert, Oscar. Danger lurks.*]

I hope you're feeling comfortable with this, Oscar. I know it isn't how you pictured things when you took this job. And in fact neither did I. But events often outstrip what we can anticipate, and we have to use the resources we have. Who could have know you'd become about the most important resource on the ground as you certainly have?, The realities press in and we're all flying a little by the seat of our pants on this one. I hope you can find some satisfaction in what an indispensible role you're playing. For both countries.

Comfortable? No, that's too strong a word for what I'm feeling, Gretchen. But I guess I'd have to say I've taken every step along the way with my eyes open. So far. Or as open as I know how. No, It doesn't exactly match the picture I had of myself when I began this work, but I'm not a child, and I know job descriptions are written to be thrown away.

There is one thing I have been wondering about and wanted to ask, but haven't felt entirely comfortable bringing up with Newmark and Pinsky. It's about Tony Lane, our political attaché in Harare. I've gotten to know him pretty well and have found him a useful sounding board. But I don't really get the relationship between the State Department and the CIA. Hell, I can't figure out what the IMF is doing in this cozy arrangement with the CIA. But what I wonder is, how openly should I be talking with Tony?

You know, Oscar, it's a valid question; an important question. I've lived abroad, and I know how lonely it can be trying to find friends. I can appreciate how comforting it is to find someone like Tony with whom you're simpatico. But based on the conversation the four of us just had, I'd have to say 'not terribly open with Tony.' I really think you set the proper boundaries in this conversation today for who might be in the information loop and you'd be better off sticking to them.

Oscar had known before he asked what her answer was going to be, but as he walked back to his hotel, the terrible and increasingly familiar loneliness swamped him. He was headed back to Harare on his own, unclear not only about who he was working for and why, but also about whether Maudie was his lover or was cultivating him as a useful contact. Or both. Gretchen and Newmark and Pinsky all but told Oscar to talk with Maudie about all this. He guessed that meant she was in some way in on what they talked about. But did that explain her entire motivation, finding Oscar a valuable source and conduit? Or could she maybe also still be attracted to him, young woman to young man?

[*Come on, Oscar, you just got back from those five fantastic days with Maudie at Troutbeck. And she's right; if you don't believe what your senses tell you about those five days, you'll never be able to trust anything. Ever.*]

As for Minister Baunda and President Mugabe, Oscar could only assume they pretty much viewed him as an American spy with whom they would use appropriate caution, and who they might find useful for sending whatever signals they thought would give them an advantage.

He couldn't remember ever feeling so alone. His parents thought he was an Albert Schweitzer look-alike that made them so proud of him. [*Man, Dad would really flip . . . the CIA! Mom? She'd probably laugh at all my shaking around.*] Gretchen had hired him to work as an economist in an emerging economy, maybe. [*You should have known. Shit, Oscar, you knew. There were a dozen sharper economists in your MBA class. As for Minister Baunda, well, who the hell knows? And then there's Maudie. OK, so I already admitted I'd pretty much do anything if I thought it would help me with Maudie. But is this—whatever this turns out to be—going to help me with her? Hell no. What am I thinking? She's never once wavered about her future, and it has never included me. No matter which way all this goes, it's going to end up with me losing my relationship with her. Jesus, sometimes I wish I could back all this up and start again, not that I have any idea what I'd do differently.*]

[*I'm dead tired all the time, and I know it's not just because of all this travel and hard work. Sometimes I feel like I'm really going to lose it. I wonder if I could ever pick up some of those spiritual disciplines—prayer, meditation, all that—I keep telling myself I'm going to do someday? Right now I'd latch onto anything that could give me a little peace. Who gives a shit about whether you really believe it?*]

*　　*　　*

204

All I Ever Do Is Dream, Dream, Dream

When Oscar fell asleep that night he dreamed he and Maudie were getting married in a cathedral. He couldn't make out if it was the Anglican Cathedral in Harare, a building he'd come to love with the two feet deep walk-in font decorated with the huge fish mosaic in bright tiles directly in your path as you enter the building. Or Washington Cathedral with its great aisle and high-backed, carved-wood choir stalls. He knew it was a cathedral because of the way the priest's voice echoed as he gave them their vows, like the anesthesiologist's voice as you're going under anesthesia.

To love, honor and obey . . . *Obey* echoed off every surface in the building in a haunting reverb. The priest and Maudie both looked at Oscar, waiting for him to respond, Oscar heard the word—*obey*—echoing over and over. He looked at Maudie for some hint of what she expected. He noticed that around her neck, instead of a necklace she dangled the little spy phone that Pinsky had given Oscar in that afternoon's meeting. The metal case was pulled apart and the green lighted dial was pulsating. Maudie's face was blank, Shona expressionless. Oscar wanted to ask her if she knew the phone was on, live and whatever they said would be broadcast back to the CIA. But how could he do that in the middle of the wedding with everyone—his parents, President Mugabe, hell, probably the president of the USA—in the congregation? And all of them listening in?

Oscar, we're waiting for you to answer, Maudie chided in monotone. Oscar felt desperate; maybe she didn't realize about the phone. Maybe it had been planted on her. He stared at her throat trying to get her to look down. Finally she did.

Oh that; is that what's worrying you, Oscar? You've really got to give up this purity thing, dear boy. This is real life, not one of your feel-good movies, with heroes and villains.

Oscar woke before he could respond, *Obey* ringing in his ears. He was dripping sweat. He looked at the clock, 3:30. His limo was picking him up in two hours. He knew he'd never get back to sleep. He turned on the light, sat up, and began reading the figures projected for this year's tobacco and maize crops.

*   *   *

TUMULTUOUS RETURN (HOME?) TO ZIMBABWE

Oscar woke, choking, as the plane was making its descent into Harare. He'd asked the attendant to wake him before they started spraying that miserable insecticide they used to disinfect the plane. But she hadn't. Oscar had packed a surgical mask in his overnight bag for just this moment but there was no point in putting it on now.

[*Mom worries that I'm going to get macheted and eaten by cannibals over here, but I'm more likely to die of liver disease from this Malathion they're spraying around the plane, or the drugs I'm taking to keep me from dying of malaria.*]

The plane broke through the clouds in its descent and he could see the green fields of maize and the villages of huts on the riverbanks. Oscar felt a rush of pleasure. He knew his affection for this country, rooted in his love for the fertile earth, so emotionally tugging, even having been here such a short time, was entwined with his feelings for Maudie. On this return the terrain itself felt disarmingly reassuring, as he looked down onto what was feeling more and more familiar, almost as if he were coming home.

[*If Maudie wasn't here, or if she would have nothing more to do with me, would I still want to be here? It is a beautiful country. Maybe I'll become one of those men without a country, an ex-pat.*]

Seeing the long line snaking its way out of customs as he walked from the plane to the terminal, Oscar wished he'd accepted Gretchen's suggestion that he carry a diplomatic passport. Certainly Gretchen's goons would have gladly gotten him one. Those spy-masters made it clear in yesterday's meetings that they would have preferred that he travel diplomatically, removing any lingering ambiguity—to them and to him—where his patriotic obligations lay.

Which was a big reason Oscar didn't want one. He preferred to travel as a private citizen, preserving what little he could, for as long as he could, of his original understanding of his role. But this was a huge, long line, and it didn't appear to be moving. When he finally inched close enough to the door, he saw the soldiers with their Uzis at ready. Four of them.

[*This is something new. Wonder what's up]?*

Passport! the young soldier demanded gruffly.

Oscar fished around in his shoulder bag nervously while the man watched impatiently, his hand resting on the trigger of his weapon.

I hadn't expected to be asked for this until I got inside. Oscar meant it as an apology, or explanation for why it was taking him so long to produce it, but the abrupt way the man poked the Uzi into his face without replying made Oscar realize the man thought he was being challenged.

Passport! He demanded again, this time he shouted it.

Oscar was relieved to feel the passport in his bag. He handed it to the man.

[*He can't be 18 years old. Hope he's had some training in using that weapon.*]

The soldier cradled his rifle in his arm as he flipped through the pages of the document. **U.S.?**

Yes, U.S.

Journalist?

No, businessman. Oscar reached for the passport to show him where it listed his occupation.

No! The boy-soldier yanked back the passport and poked Oscar in the shoulder with his Uzi. **You have camera?**

No. Oscar was being extra cautious now, wondering what could be going on. [*These guys are really jumpy about something*].

I look. The soldier motioned for Oscar to open his shoulder bag so he could look inside. Oscar took it off his shoulder slowly, seeking to reassure the man that he was no threat. He held it open so he could see inside. Holding the passport and rifle in one hand, the nervous young soldier fumbled through the bag with his other hand.

[*Hope I got the fastener on that trail-mix tight. I'll be until the end of time picking the raisins out of my bag*].

The man pulled his secure phone from the bag. Oscar's heart thumped. [*No one said I should hide it*].

What is it?

Better play it straight now. **It's a phone, a cell phone. May I show you?** Oscar was careful not to reach for it, but gently gestured toward it with his hand. The soldier handed the phone back to Oscar and watched intently while he pulled the case back revealing the number pad. When the soldier saw the screen he smiled broadly.

Very Nice, he said, handing back Oscar's passport, gesturing with his Uzi toward the door. **Pass through**.

Oscar felt his blood pressure return gradually to normal. He walked through the door into total chaos. As his eyes adjusted to the dull, yellow light, he saw uniformed people lined up across a counter. Passengers on the opposite side of the counter looked harried, their luggage was open, its contents strewn around while the inspectors questioned them belligerently. Behind each passenger a long line waited.

[*Jesus, you don't suppose someone's tried to assassinate Mugabe? No, I'd have heard. But I've been on the plane the past nine hours.*] He couldn't think what else might have caused such uproar. [*Looks like I'm going to be here a while. God, I'm tired.*]

Mr. Anderson! It took him several seconds to locate the person calling him. Elias, Minister Baunda's driver and bodyguard, was shouting his name above the din, motioning for him to come to the side door. Oscar, his brow furrowed, nervously considered each armed man he had to pass on his way through the mob to the door.

Elias! Oscar greeted him enthusiastically. **Am I glad to see you! What are you doing here?**

Welcome home, Boss. Elias used the old colonial, deferential title. **We knew it was going to be like this out here, so Minister Baunda sent me to escort you through.** He said something in Shona to the man guarding the door, showed him a pass, and Elias and Oscar walked through the door into the main terminal, which was even more crowded and chaotic than customs had been.

Elias, what's happened?

We go to the car first, Boss. Then I explain. You have checked bags?

No, thank God, just the overnight case I'm carrying.

The two of them slalomed through the crowd of people who were sitting on bags, some sleeping on the floor. Finally they emerged into the hot, sticky day where the familiar black Mercedes with the low number government plate was parked at the curb.

Traffic. The traffic in Harare between the airport and downtown was of a different order from Washington or any other American city. Oscar was terrified every time he got behind the wheel, and he was glad Elias was driving now. Oscar never could have carried on a conversation without running over someone on a bicycle or motor scooter, or a dog or chicken or child. Not to mention the near head-ons with motor bikes scooting around oncoming vehicles and into their lane. The numbers of children, many half naked, running loose in the streets of Harare had grown alarmingly just in the six months since Oscar arrived.

Elias seemed unflapped by it all, swerving without looking, glancing over at Oscar, smiling his toothy, reassuring grin, engaging him in conversation as if they were sitting quietly in someone's living room.

What's up, Elias? Oscar was struggling to sound casual. The frantic airport scene, the tension and fear he saw in the young soldier with the Uzi made him feel anything but casual. *Seems like something big has changed since I left just a few days ago, like everyone's suddenly on red alert. So what's happening?* Big grin from Elias. [*Sometimes that beguiling smile pisses me off, but it's all I've got right now, so better go with it.*]

Well, Boss, some excitement around here has everyone a little on edge. A couple of journalists wrote some bad shit about our troops in the Congo, and the president's reasons for sending them. The president believed the reporters were trying to subvert his government, so he had them arrested. Now Elias went silent as if he'd told Oscar all there was to say, though Oscar knew he'd gotten less than even the bare bones. [*Old information. The meat—whatever has escalated all this—is likely to be harder to come by.*]

Journalists? Anyone I might know? Oscar decided playing dumb was his best chance to get the information. [*No need to tell him that I've just come from a meeting in Washington in which these these very arrests were at the top of the agenda.*]

Maybe, Boss. John Masuko used to write for the Herald before he went on his own, and Booker Muchaya has been free lance for many years now. Oscar recognized the journalists' names, thought he might have met Muchaya once at a press conference at the Finance Ministry.

No more information was going to come unless Oscar extracted it, one tiny piece at a time. He found the cluttered streets distracting. [*Glad Elias doesn't seems able to drive without distraction.*] **So what sort of things did they write?** Long silence. Elias' face relaxed, his smile dropped, he appeared thoughtful, as if he needed to choose his words carefully. Oscar tried to look like he wasn't concerned about whether Elias gave him a straight answer. He was thinking about his conversation with the group in Washington and wondered whether they had stiffed him on some information that Elias might provide, information that would have come in handy here.

Well, Boss. Elias sighed. [*I don't think I've ever heard Elias sigh.*] Oscar remembered a psychiatrist once saying that when his patient sighed, she paid close attention because something that had been tightly held, deep down inside, was about to emerge. **The journalists wrote bad things about the president, things they shouldn't have written.** Oscar wondered whether Elias was emotionally capable of saying what they'd written, as if by repeating it he might become their accomplice?

Was it about the president personally? Oscar hoped he could dance around, play 20 questions until Elias might give him the information without saying the offending words, **or was it about the government's policies?**

Both, Boss. Elias seemed to be concentrating on his driving now, even though they'd left the congested road near the airport and were on a larger, more open road, where the danger wasn't so much congestion as livestock, and erratic drivers going at breakneck speed, **Well,** Oscar decided to probe in the safer areas first. **What did they say about the government's policies?** [*This is going to take longer than the ride to town.*]

They said the government didn't humanely notify the families of soldiers who had been killed. They didn't tell them in a timely fashion. Elias looked uncomfortable delivering this news, but Oscar knew they still hadn't gotten to the really heavy stuff.

How many people have we lost, Elias? Oscar thought maybe the "we" in that question would soften up Elias, make him let down the guard Oscar knew was raised. Even though Elias and Oscar had developed what seemed to Oscar a real friendship, Elias was talking with an American.

The number is unknown, Boss; information comes slowly from the remote fighting places. Maybe 200? Oscar new he was meant to understand the number as a question, not as Elias reporting it as fact.

And what would ever have made the journalists write that the families haven't been properly notified? Oscar had learned a higher order of patience these past six months. Any sign of impatience now could prove fatal for the rest of the conversation. He hoped he'd succeeded in maintaining a measured, almost disinterested monotone.

Maybe—Elias shrugged as if he was merely the conduit for all this hearsay—*some of the families talked to them, Boss?* Again a question, not Elias' concurring.

[*We haven't gotten there yet,*] Oscar knew. Nothing, so far, to get under even Mugabe's super-thin skin enough to react the way he had, aware, as he had to have been, it would piss off the whole world. *Did they accuse anyone in particular of being behind this failure, any government ministers?* Oscar knew he was getting close to the bone here. He held himself in check, willing to wait through the uncomfortable silence.

Maybe the president, Boss? Elias finally said, his voice rising at the end, again asking Oscar a question rather than answering one.

President Mugabe? Oscar knew he'd let too much feeling creep into his voice, but thought maybe it was all right since his surprise was on the proper side. *They think the president should be notifying the families when our soldiers are killed?* ['*our,*' *good work, Oscar*]

I don't know, Boss, there are many accusations, like they receive back an arm or a leg with no assurance it's the limb of their relative.

[*Ooh, that's pretty gnarly. I think we're getting to the nub.*] Oscar sensed the minefield growing more dangerous. He knew about the ancient taboo among both Shona and Ndebele about burying the body with all its parts, in a proper grave and ceremony. [*Maybe we're ready to make the turn into whatever was directed personally at the president.*] *Elias, in what way possible did they connect the president to the war?* Oscar saw Elias' face stiffen. [*Was that question too direct?*] Silence, then on a different tack. *I hope they didn't accuse him of anything hurtful, anything that might cause Miss Maudie to feel sad.*

Boss, Booker Muchaya wrote that the president had sent Zimbabwe troops to the DRC to protect his personal wealth, his mining interests there, diamonds.

[*Oh man, where did these guys get the guts to write this stuff? And what must this be like for Maudie?*] *Oh, Elias, that must have hurt the president deeply and made him very unhappy.*

Maybe. I think so, Boss.

And who's made a fuss about it so far, Elias, anyone from the U.S.? [*Minefield.*]

I think the IMF, Boss. [Not precisely the U.S., but everyone knows the U.S. calls the shots with the IMF.] *They say they may not pay the next loan installment.* Now Oscar understood where all this news really pinched—the Finance Ministry. *And maybe Amnesty International.*

[*Jesus! Amnesty International, there must be a lot more to this than I've heard so far. Thanks, but no thanks to Pinsky and Newmark for stiffing me when I asked about this.*]

Boss, you know that attorney who made the big noise when the Army broke up the demonstrations in Bulawayo two years ago, the white man [*wonder whether he notices my pale skin?*] *who used to be with Barclays Bank? Well he went to the Supreme Court and persuaded Justice Hatendi to issue an order to have the journalists released.* It was all building like a tsunami in Oscar's mind.

And did they release them?

Well no, because they were being held by the Army and the president said this wasn't a civil matter, but a military matter, because the journalists were endangering the war effort and undermining the international interests of the nation. [*Oh shit, now we've got a full blown constitutional crisis, just like the U.S. 200 years ago, testing the powers of the different branches of the government. John Jay and the banks. Or maybe Nixon and the Watergate tapes. Or, get real, Oscar, how about the 2000 election?*] *So what happened then, Elias?* Oscar knew he was looking too invested, too interested, pressing, which could scare Elias into silence, but he was beyond subtle games now; this was major league.

[*What I wouldn't give to talk to Maudie right now*]. As the wish entered Oscar's mind, so did the realization of how conflicted that conversation was likely to be. [*Oh God, I'm more on my own than ever on this one.*] *Elias, how about dropping me in front of my apartment and I'll leave my bag and walk to the Ministry? I need the walk after sitting the past 24 hours on the plane.*

Sure, Boss. If Elias found anything untoward about Oscar's request, his inscrutable African facade provided no clue.

Oscar unfolded his weary, outsized frame from the Mercedes onto crowded Samora Michel Avenue, breathing in what he guessed, for the foreseeable future would be his last moment of anonymity. His travel valise was slung over his right shoulder. He'd begun sweating the moment he stepped from the air conditioned car, but he had much more on his mind than either dropping his things off or staying cool. He reached into the small pocket of his bag, pulled out the Zimbabwe secure phone—phone number 1—and dialed the number only Maudie answered.

* * *

WHAT NOW?

Deputy President Maudie Mugabe, please give positive ID. He realized she'd lost trust even in her caller ID on her own encrypted phone. [*She's freaked.*] He could hear the weariness and anxiety in her voice. He dialed his code. ***Maudie, it's me, Oscar.***

Where are you, Oscar? Anyone else with you, are you calling from a secure phone; are you in the Ministry, you're not calling from the plane are you?

Whoa, hang on a minute, Maudie, this is Oscar. My code, your encryption. Remember me, the guy who loves you, who's on your side?

Where are you, Oscar? Maudie wasn't falling for Oscar's charm assault today.

I'm standing in the park across from my apartment, out in the open with people milling around. I'm talking on the secure phone only you ever answer.

I got news for you, Oscar; that phone is secured by the people who gave it to you, but don't you think for one minute that necessarily means it's secure for you or for me, especially since I can see on my screen that you didn't hit the scrambler button before you dialed me. Might be a good idea to try to keep in mind who it was who gave you that phone.

[*I've still got a shitload to learn.*] He had forgotten to push the scrambler button which, as Maudie pointed out—struggling to keep from betraying the contempt she felt for him for this oversight—would not even necessarily have prevented the call from being monitored. He mashed down the button hard, as if that might make up for not having done it before. Not only the folks back at Langley CIA—who likely wanted him to use this phone precisely so they *could* listen in—but anyone in Harare who happened to be monitoring cell phone traffic. His conversation with Elias, and now Maudie's tone, suggested there were likely to be scores of eavesdroppers on all points of the political compass given the shape of political life in Zimbabwe—and in the U.S. at the moment.

[*Slow it down, Oscar; seems like the wheels may be coming off.*]

Maudie, I'm sorry; this is just a friendly check-in call. I'm just back, just stepped off the plane, and wanted to hear your voice and ask when I might see you.

Oscar, life's too frantic right now for just friendly talks. If you've got something helpful to talk about, then I'd be eager to see you. But otherwise I'm afraid I can't spare a moment for anything but getting us through this. It's hour to hour right now. Oscar felt a chill at hearing the distance—was it fear?—in her voice, the abrupt way she put him off. He was as awed by her steeliness, as he was put off. He was immediately back in that shaky place where he could end up feeling sorry for himself because Maudie didn't respond with the warmth he always hoped for. He'd never get used to how cool and calculating she could seem. [*Not as if she never warned you. Get a grip, man. Sounds like the whole country may be falling apart. Your hurt feelings may have to take a back seat here.*] He knew the trouble feeling sorry for himself always got him into, especially when—like Maudie—he most needed to be tough and calculating.

I think it'd be good if you and I talked, Maudie. I've just been in some pretty important conversations with some friends of yours in Washington, and it might be useful for you to hear what went on. She was quiet; he had her ear.

I'll pick you up on the corner by your apartment in 45 minutes, Oscar.

I'll be waiting, but make it an hour. I smell like a goat after all that time on the plane, and I'd like to take a shower.

An hour it is. Just don't lie down because, if you do you won't pick up your head again for 36 hours. Oscar knew she was right. He suddenly felt as if he'd put on 100 pounds. Walking across the street to his apartment and getting on the elevator was like running a marathon.

*   *   *

The Fat's In The Fire
Maudie And Oscar
Confront The President

An hour later, showered, shaved, a couple of Ibuprofen and an energy drink in him—none of which curbed his exhaustion—Oscar struggled to keep his excitement—and dread—in check as the Mercedes roadster pulled up to the curb. He leaned down, opened the door, slid his rear end in first, then pulling in his long legs, he leaned across to kiss Maudie. **Buckle up**, she commanded, as she pulled into traffic, ignoring his pursed lips. [*Shit, get a grip, buddy. How do I always let myself hope she's going to greet me with the same enthusiasm I feel greeting her?*] But he was still so happy to see her. As he stuffed his too-large frame into the low leather seat, Maudie flashed him the smile that he now knew, without a doubt, he'd commit treason for. [*Fuck you, Pinsky and Newmark. Shoot me.*]

Good trip? she asked.

Exhausting, but good, I suppose. Plane didn't crash. Discussed our conspiracy with the co-conspirators. I pretty much signed onto going undercover for, not one but two countries. I guess that's the meaning of double agent. Never thought I'd fit the job description. But guess what?

[*Shut your mouth, Oscar, before you make a total ass of yourself. Maudie didn't pick you up to reassure you.*]

How's Gretchen? He was grateful she ignored his sarcasm. And Oscar wondered, again, how well Maudie and Gretchen knew each other, whether no matter what she said, they did in fact talk, whether he was once again last into the loop, [*Or maybe I'm the errand boy who has unwitting safe passage, goes back and forth across the battle lines, and people slip messages into my sleeves when I'm not looking.*]

Well, she's fine, so far as I could tell. We really didn't have much time for pleasantries; just enough for me to say I'd sign onto what they were asking. And exactly what did they ask? If I've got it straight, that I give them a heads-up on how good the numbers are they're getting from here, so they could make good decisions.

Did they say anything about the next payment on our IMF loan? Oscar knew he was in that deep water again, the place he dreaded, wondering who knew what, and where people's real loyalties lay.

No, that never really came up in the conversation.

Never really came up, Oscar? The scorn in Maudie's question made Oscar squirm. *Or never at all? Because we need to know exactly what they intend about paying the money we're due. Look,*—Oscar's anxiety spiked—*even the American papers are reporting the stuff about the two journalists who've been arrested. No surprise. We know the American preoccupation with the press, about their much vaunted independence, so we expected that. We're not too concerned about what's in the papers; that's all posturing. We're much more interested in how the IMF is viewing it. And what their intentions are.*

Hey, Maudie, you do understand that the IMF is an international body, not a branch of the U.S. government?

Get off it, Oscar, you and I are way beyond playing these little games with each other. Not only does everyone know the IMF does your country's bidding, but one of those people in that room with you when you and Gretchen were doing this deal was Jim Newmark, Zimbabwe's handler at IMF.

You seem to know a whole lot about what went on, Maudie, maybe more than I do. Maybe you can fill in some of the gaps I'm troubled by, that everybody seems to understand except me.

Come on, Oscar, this innocence dance is cute, but unconvincing. Let's dispense with the pretenses. McKinsey is the CIA, is the IMF. We don't begrudge that, it's the same the world over. It was ever thus. We're just trying to work out a very tricky piece here, and you've become the pivotal player, working both sides of the street. We understand. We're grateful. We don't find that a big problem. Apparently they don't either. But I'd appreciate it if we could jump over all the posturing and cut to the chase.

OK, Maudie, I'll grant you everything you just said. I'm doing my level best to be straight with you, but I'm not going to pretend to you either that I really understand where everyone is in all this or that I'm not more than a little uneasy passing along information when I don't really know where the lines are drawn. I know you think it's about my being pure, but it's really about trying to figure out whether I'm doing what I think I'm doing or being totally duped. I've given up any hope of hanging onto anything resembling integrity, but I'm still hoping I might figure out just a little about who's on what side? Call it covering my own ass, self-preservation. I may have signed on for more than I knew, but I'm still hoping it might stop short of treason.

Fair enough, Oscar. I think you understand where I am. I'm the deputy president of this country. I trust you have no doubt, none at all. When I consider my options, the well-being of the nation and its people is my first priority. Before everything else. That clear enough for you?

[*How I wish I could be that clear about anything. If Maudie turns out to be Mata Hari, I'll end up in front of a firing squad. And I'll gladly give the order to fire.*] He suddenly was so tired his eyelids drooped. *Maudie*—he reached for her hand resting on the steering wheel, she didn't remove it—*just about the only thing I'm not confused about is how I feel about you. I haven't quite been able to totally erase my dream of spending my life with you. I know better, and I've accepted the reality. But surely you understand how big a part that plays in how I sort all this out. The truth is that I honestly don't have the answers to your questions. Newmark and Pinsky know my priorities, too, and they're not about to risk any information with me that they wouldn't want to come out if you tie me up and pull out my fingernails. Or maybe bribe me with sex.*

He was crestfallen to see his little trick to lighten things up, even for a moment, had fallen flat. *Oscar, I don't know how to put this any more clearly: things are falling apart in this country right now, at this very moment. We're looking at a disaster. And I have no idea what—if anything—is going to stop things from getting a lot worse. The president made a strategic, stupid mistake arresting those journalists, even though they're assholes who deserve it. And he won't admit that or do anything to correct it. He's not listening, even to me, which means he's all alone, listening to nobody. We've run out of options. The time has come when we have to make some scary, dangerous moves, not just to save his political skin, but maybe his life. And to give ourselves any chance at all of an orderly, non-violent change in the country. Events have probably already forced us into a choice between some sort of non-violent coup, succession, or something much worse. Much scarier. Nathan Pinsky knows that I've been in touch with some of the ZAPU leaders, and we've begun talking about what needs to happen now. One of the key people who've agreed to help is Minister Baunda.*

Oscar was stunned. He tried to hide from Maudie how unprepared he was for this news. [*So you do talk with those guys. My boss? And Pinsky? Thanks for cluing me in.*] *And how much does your father know about all this?* As both of them kept their eyes straight ahead he saw her knuckles whiten as she gripped the wheel.

Sweet Jesus!

I know how self-serving this must seem to you, Oscar, but my part in this is every bit as much out of concern for my father as it is for Zimbabwe. If we don't make a very decisive move soon, I fear not for his presidency, but for his life.

I believe that, Oscar reassured her, *but I'm not sure your father would.*

I'm absolutely certain he would not. But this most recent event, the arrest of the journalists, as obnoxious as they were, has taken away all our remaining options. And we're fast running out of time. Our CIO is so conflicted that we're having to rely on your CIA for what's likely going to happen. They're convinced there's going to be a coup unless there's some pretty clear signal from me in the next 48 hours that I'm willing to help find a way through this. And if there's an armed coup, the president will sure as hell dig in his heels and refuse to budge—Maudie drew in a long, deep breath before finishing her sentence—*until they kill him.*

What about you, Maud?

I'm not concerned about me. I'm doing what I must. But I do have concerns about you, Oscar. And you ought to have some about yourself. You're all of a sudden directly in the line of fire, thanks to your friend Gretchen and her cronies. Minister Baunda is going to be a key player when this plays out. He's our chief Ndebele operative. I'm not sure how much he knows about all you've been up to, but he certainly knows you are key in our chances of getting our hands on the money we need so badly from your guys. Right now you're the man on center stage, the critical piece in interpreting to the U.S what's happening here. And in being able to speak to the IMF about why, even though it may look as if the wheels have come off in Zimbabwe, it's imperative—for their interests as well as ours—that they make that next installment.

Very sweet of you to be concerned about me, Maudie but I'd say we're way beyond personal issues now. Not that we haven't been the whole time I've been here, for God's sake. Seems like a long time ago we sat in Rubenstein's class at Wharton. I don't think I really want to hear it, but maybe you better fill me in. Give me a heads—up on what's coming down.

And where you see me in the midst of all this.

I know it must seem unfair, Oscar. This isn't exactly what you signed on for, but I see you filling a role in our next move no one else can. When I tell the president I believe his only choice is to resign, his shock will be so great he will be unable to see me in that moment as anything other than another person, the worst possible person, to have joined the conspiracy against him. Not as his beloved daughter. He respects you. I think he may even have come to like you. And though I hate to admit this to you—and he never would—he fears you, because he fears and respects the United States. With you in the room he will think your CIA has a hand in this. And as angry as that will make him, it is probably about the only thing that could intimidate him enough to make him think he has no choice.

Oscar's mind was racing. [*What in God's name have I gotten myself into?*]

[*And Maudie? Is this what she has been setting me up for all along? Now I am up to my eyeballs in whatever it is that's going down here? And the CIA is involved; maybe I am the CIA. Holy shit! What was it I went to Wharton for again? And how about falling for Maudie? What was that about? Well, Oscar, you always wanted to be in the thick of it—not some abstract theorist like Dad. Looks like that silly saying of his may hit home: "Careful what you pray for."*]

They drove on in silence for several moments before Maudie picked up the thread.

Oscar, we're heading for the Presidential Palace. The confrontation with the president can't wait another day.

Right now, Maudie? The embarrassing squeak was back in Oscar's voice. *Don't you think we need to do a little planning before we just jump right in and ask the president of the country to resign?*

There are a whole lot of things we need, Oscar, but what we have is a crisis that's ripening as we speak. What we don't have is time. We've run out.

OK, assuming that's right, what about your relationship with your father? Are you prepared to junk that? I've never known a father and daughter who were closer than you two. Are you sure you can live with whatever happens about that?

Oscar—Maudie's voice was hoarse, exhaustion etched in her face—*there is no time any longer for luxuries like sentiment. The future of this nation and the president's life quite literally both hang in the balance.*

Right, I understand Maudie, of course; but we're talking about your own father . . .

God damn it, Oscar! The president can be protected only if he willingly steps aside. If he refuses he'll be assassinated. That's the reality we have to face right now. No matter whose father he is.

Oscar marveled as he had so often at Maudie's resolve, her determination, her focus. Despite the frightening conversation her voice remained low and even. She seemed to be giving rapt attention to navigating around the taxis and bicycles changing lanes without warning, all the while carrying on her end of this terrifying conversation, never missing a beat.

Oscar, on the other hand, was the picture of distraction. [*Maybe it's true that women can do more than one thing at a time; I'd have had a wreck by now if I was driving.*] *So how do you suggest we talk to him? Just walk in and say, Mr. President, your daughter and I think you should resign, and, by the way, your daughter would like your job?* [*Ooh, that didn't come out very well, Oscar. Better keep the lid on that sarcasm. Anxiety makes you say weird, inappropriate things. You need to play this one dead-on straight.*]

Being a smart-ass doesn't help, Oscar. You and I will be the only ones in the room with him, because anyone else would make him embarrassed, ashamed, and then he will get his back up and refuse to listen or think rationally. I intend to tell him what I know and what I think, as clearly and dispassionately as possible. He's going to be incredulous when he hears it. He'll certainly turn to you at some point and ask you what you think. And by the way, before we get in there, you better decide what you do think. And how you might describe it to him. I realize you haven't volunteered for this, and if I was more honorable, or less desperate, this is when I would ask you if you want out. But the weird way the president has taken to you, and the role you have assumed—not to mention the 800 pound gorilla nation you represent—means you're the only person who can help me with this.

Oh God, Maudie, you want to know what I think? I don't have even a remote idea what I think. I totally agree with you that this country looks like it's about to blow up. And unless something happens fast to break the stalemate between the government and what appears to be a growing insistence that there has to be a dramatic change—not to mention whatever those goons in Washington are cooking up—there's likely to be some scary shit coming down. But I've never played for stakes this high. How to figure what needs to be done feels like it's way above my pay grade. Not to mention any legal right I have to be where you're taking me.

OK. I get all that. Put it all away now because there's no ducking it. First thing I need to know is if you do understand what it is you and I are going to propose to the president?

I think so. You're going to ask him to step aside, to surrender the power he won in a bitter war, and all the perks of his high office. And what is it, exactly, you're offering in it's place?

Oscar was relieved that Maudie didn't jump on him for the anxious sarcasm he seemed unable to curb. [*She's using me as a sounding board, rehearsing what's likely to happen when we face her father.*]

First of all, I'm saying that if he'll agree to step aside, I'll be able to guarantee him immunity from prosecution, and protection from having his personal assets threatened in any way. We're proposing a coalition government with ministers drawn from among the three major parties. I—his daughter, the present deputy president, Zanu-PF—will be president. So Zanu-PF—and a Mugabe—will remain the principal parties in power.

Oscar resisted telling Maudie that when she listed all those honorific titles after her own name she sounded uncharacteristically tentative, as if she were trying to convince herself as much as her father.

I know you understand, probably better than anyone, Maudie, that as recently as last year's election, Zanu PF won all but five seats in Parliament? What if the president doesn't think he's in any danger of prosecution, or even of being brought down by his political adversaries? This may seem to him more like an old-fashioned coup than a compromise he needs to accept to save his own ass. I mean, look at it from his point of view. Why the hell should he step aside? He won a huge majority in the last election; he is still the only southern African leader to have driven a white regime out of his country, and he is the only president this country has had in its 30-year history. He remains a legendary hero in the eyes of most of black Africa. I'm not so sure I'd step down if I were him.

They drove on for several moments in silence. Maudie brooded over what Oscar had said. [*This sucks; why do I have to be the one to point out the mess? And what's in it for me? Besides maybe a choice between prison in Zimbabwe or prison in the States? Or a bullet in the brain. So this is how it plays out, my noble life and my scheme to persuade Maudie to hook up with me for life. Maudie as president or me as executed spy, isn't exactly a neat fit with our living happily ever after.*]

The Presidential Palace was dead ahead. Oscar's dread was like a vise tightening around his chest, making his breathing labored. Maudie slowed as she turned in, stopping by the guard house as the soldier in brightly colored ceremonial garb stepped forward and leaned down to speak. Just inside the closed gate was a tank, one of the leftover N. Korean models from the decades-ago revolution. Its weird pointed nose gave it the look of a monster in a horror movie. It was positioned so it blocked one lane of the driveway. A soldier in battle fatigues sat on the turret behind a machine gun. The guard at the gate, who normally carried a sidearm in a holster, today had an Uzi slung over his shoulder. Oscar could see that the clip was in.

Ms. Deputy President, the guard greeted her—not his usual cheery smile, but a solemn expression. *And Mr. Anderson.* Oscar was usually pleased when he was recognized by the palace guards, but today it didn't seem reassuring. *You'll find security especially tight today; please be patien*t. *And cautious.*

And we will, John. Thank you.

[*No wonder they all like Maudie; she knows every one of them by name, as well as the names of most of their wives and children.*]

The huge iron gate swung open slowly, and the soldier jumped down from the tank, stationing himself directly in front of the car. Maudie looked at the guard inquisitively.

There will be several more roadblocks before you go inside, I'm afraid, Ms. Deputy President. Don't worry, we're all following orders—no exceptions, no matter who—and be assured everyone knows who you are.

Please state your business and display your ID and pass, the soldier at the next check point demanded in a flat voice. He cradled an automatic weapon in his left arm as he examined the Palace passes they both handed to him through the driver's side window, as if he had no idea who they were.

We're here for a meeting called by the president, Maudie explained, hoping the guard didn't have a daily schedule. Again Oscar marveled at her matter-of-fact tone. [*I'm sure glad I didn't have to answer; my voice would have come out an octave higher than normal.*]

The soldier handed back their credentials and held up a clipboard hanging from his belt. He checked the top page and then looked at his watch. [*Jesus, they're not fooling around; you'd think they had no idea who this is driving in, as if they'd never seen her.*]

Drive on, slowly, the soldier ordered, **and be extremely cautious as you proceed. Do not leave your vehicle until you're told to.** [*Are you kidding? I'm not breathing in this place without permission.*]

Right, Maudie acknowledged. Oscar could see another tank parked just in front of the entrance to the palace. [*You don't suppose there's already been a coup, and we're walking into a trap?*]

Nervous, Oscar? You look like you're about to vomit. Try to relax. You're going to need every ounce of energy for our meeting with the president. I know what you're thinking. No, these guys are all loyal to the president; I know them. There hasn't been a coup.

As Maudie drove slowly up the driveway, another soldier stepped out from behind the tank and gestured to them to stop. When they pulled alongside him, Maudie stopped the car and waited for the soldier to quiz her. They went through the same routine twice more as they entered the building. A uniformed soldier instead of the woman who usually sat at the desk outside the president's office, a handgun lying on the desk in front of him. Though Maudie greeted him by name and Oscar knew him as a member of the president's honor guard, he insisted on checking their credentials. He pressed the intercom, announcing, **The Deputy President and Minister Baunda's aide.** The president was alone, sitting behind his mahogany partners desk on the far side of the room in front of a wall of ceiling-to-floor French doors. [*Incredible how U.S. power icons have proliferated throughout the world. This room could be the Oval Office in the White House. Everybody wants to be President of the United States. They may hate us, but everyone still has POTUS envy.*]

Maudie, Oscar. President Mugabe remained in his chair, signaling his superior status. His greeting was cordial, warm. **I'm glad you've come; we've got much to talk about. Tell me how you think things are going out**

there. That's one of the drawbacks of this office; I can't get out among the people often enough to get a good sense their mood.

Oscar sensed Maudie tense. He heard her draw in a big breath.

Mr. President, I've come to ask for your resignation. For the good of the nation and for your own safety and welfare, I believe it is imperative that you resign. Immediately.

[*If someone lighted a match right now, this room would explode.*]

The president placed his hands palm down on his desk and pushed himself to a standing position. His deep black skin seemed to Oscar as if it had darkened from some inner rage, to another shade, purple. He was staring at Maudie, as if he was trying to make sense of what she'd just said. For a moment he looked defeated, like he might cry. Then he inhaled a long deep breath and squared his shoulders. [*I wonder if this is what it was like when Barry Goldwater told Nixon he ought to resign? The silence filling this room feels like a poisonous gas, choking off all the oxygen.*]

So you think I should resign? Mugabe's voice was strong, clear, ringing with indignation. **And on whose authority do you make such a bold suggestion to the lawfully elected president of this country?**

On my own authority, Mr. President. The authority you yourself entrusted to me.

[*Jesus Christ, these two are cut from the same cloth. Ice water in their veins. But at this moment no one would guess they're even related, much less father and daughter, except maybe for their mutual brass gonads.*] Through the window behind Mugabe Oscar saw yet another tank taking up position in the drive on the far side of the Palace. If Maudie or her father saw it they gave no hint.

You have given birth to this nation as surely as George Washington birthed the United States, or Lenin the Soviet Union. You will always be celebrated as the founding hero—father of Zimbabwe, the first and only warrior to drive the white colonialists from African soil. But as you yourself have said to me many times, nothing—and no one—is forever. And the moment has come for you to leave this office with the honor your achievements have so justly earned you.

[*Jesus, did she stay up all night memorizing that?*]

Has anyone besides Oscar come here with you to make this shameful suggestion? [*Holy shit. He's noticed me.*]

We have come alone. But I have spoken this morning with the leaders of the two opposition parties, and they have agreed to lend to an orderly

transition, signing on to a coalition government, with power sharing by the three major parties.

And—if I may ask—who do you and your treasonous comrades envision as the person deemed worthy to assume the office I alone have held since Zimbabwe's founding?

[*Here it comes!*]

We all thought it would send the most reassuring signal to the country and the rest of the world if the deputy president became acting president.

[*My God, she said it without flinching. She's got his African mojo down to her toenails.*]

What is this 'Deputy President'? Don't you have the courage to say 'me'? My own daughter! You are leading a coup against your own father? And are you prepared to shoot me if I refuse? President Mugabe was shouting. He thrust his head forward menacingly.

[*Is there's anyone near enough to hear all this? Surely, the room must be bugged?*]

Oscar was dumfounded that—to appearances—Maudie seems unfazed by her father's outburst. She looked at him as she spoke again:

Me, Sir. Painful as this is for us both, it is an affirmation of your long and distinguished rule, not a repudiation. A Mugabe remains as president. Your legacy is assured. You will be revered as an elder statesman. Your retirement will be celebrated as the culmination—and affirmation—of our glorious revolution, and of your unique role as our founding hero.

[*Don't lay it on too thick, Maudie.*] Oscar fought to keep himself from looking over his shoulder to see if anyone was behind him. He watched President Mugabe's hands. Maudie had told him he kept a loaded revolver in his desk drawer.

I beg you, Sir, to set aside your personal pain and disappointment and consider the terrible alternative—civil war and bloodshed, the destruction of everything you've given your life for.

The President turned away from the two of them and looked out the windows across the manicured lawn where there were now two tanks and a squad of soldiers in battle gear standing at parade rest.

And are they there to see that I do what you ask? He gestured toward the window, his voice bitter.

No Sir, Maudie answered, **they're there to protect you against any attempt to overthrow you or do you harm. They know, as everyone in our**

government knows, that your enemies have become impatient and may mount a coup at any moment. Those troops you see are loyal to you. But they are human, too, and if it should become clear that your cause is lost, I am afraid the time may not be far off when they could become what you feared they already were.

For the first time the president turned his angry look on Oscar. He studied him for a long moment without speaking; his eyes narrowed to slits. Oscar's knees felt like rubber. He'd seen the president turn that withering stare on others who dared to so much as raise a question about something he said.

And you, Oscar, do you agree with my daughter that this . . . this insurrection, is inevitable? And just?

Well, Sir, Oscar struggled to keep his voice from cracking, *as an American, I think it would be presumptuous of me to advise you about the affairs of your own country. But in addition to holding a deep affection and respect for the deputy president—as I hope you know I do for you as well, Sir—I have the highest regard for her judgment. I can only imagine how difficult this must be for you both. But I also know she is utterly loyal to you and would never do anything that did not have your best interest—as well as the interests of Zimbabwe—at its heart.*

My best interest? Zimbabwe's best interests? He was shouting again, *My best interest is to submit to an illegal coup? Have you two gone mad? I should have known. I never wanted her to go to an American university. Your McKinsey, your IMF, the criminals from your CIA. I should have known. You came to our country to do this. I was a fool to agree for her American spy-lover to have access to my government. You have poisoned my daughter's mind with all that capitalist nonsense that exploits people like us. Now she is no longer my daughter. You two have been plotting against me from the start. I will call an emergency meeting of the cabinet. We will name a new deputy president.* President Mugabe pulled himself up to his full height (which at this moment Oscar was grateful was significantly shorter than either his or Maudie's.) He glared at them. *Oscar Anderson, you are hereby dismissed as aide to the Minister of Finance. And you*—he turned to Maudie, his eyes fiery with anger—*may consider yourself impeached as deputy resident. Nor do I consider you my daughter any longer.*

[*Son of a bitch, now what?*]

Sir, Maudie's voice remained calm; her words came out in measured cadence; *every member but two of your Cabinet is aware of the proposal I have just made to you. The two deputy presidents who have agreed to stand alongside me in the coalition are the Minister of Culture and the Minister of Finance.* [*Christ, Baunda's in the thick of this! Have I been asleep over there at Finance!*] *As you know, they represent the other two major parties and are prepared to cooperate in forming the new government.*

You've been a very busy young woman. Mugabe's smile was not a friendly one. *Is there anyone in Zimbabwe besides me who doesn't already know about all this?*

Maudie ignored his sarcasm just as she had Oscar's earlier. *Mr. President, I promised the Cabinet I would give them your response by tomorrow morning at 11. I assured them that once you recovered from the shock and had a chance to consider it, you would see its wisdom. We all retain full confidence in your sound judgment and your ability to read the reality.*

For a moment Mugabe's defiance seemed to wilt into sadness. He turned away from the two of them, pacing behind his desk, looking down at his feet. *If only your mother were alive,* he mumbled. The president seemed to be drifting off, losing the thread. *She would never have allowed such a thing to happen. She would find it even more appalling than I do. Our own daughter.* He walked toward the French doors, away from Maudie and Oscar, his mumbling too soft for them to make out his words.

Mr. President, Maudie called him back to the conversation, *I don't have an indefinite period before matters will be taken out of my hands. I am far from the master of events now.*

No—the energy and rage had returned, his voice strident—*not at this moment. I will not respond at this moment. You have had time to scheme and plan all this. I will take the night to consider it, and I will give you my response tomorrow morning by 9. Now I would like to be left alone. In my worst nightmares I never imagined I would be faced with such treason, led by my own daughter, who was taught from birth to honor her father and mother. I have nurtured you for becoming president when I decided to leave office, not when you decided. Since you were a little girl . . .*

Once more, Maudie didn't take the bait. Oscar was incredulous at her steeliness.

Father, neither of us could have imagined such a thing. But please understand how urgent this matter is. I would never have agreed to such a thing if I thought there was any other way. I fear the most drastic consequences if this plan fails. And I sincerely doubt whether you or I could be confident of the physical safety of either of us.

He turned toward Maudie, eyes again narrowed to a slit. *So now you add a personal threat. Is that yet another political trick you learned in America, bargaining by intimidation and fear? There are apparently no limits to what you will do. I understand your position perfectly, and I will consider what you have said and will not fail to offer my response by 9 am tomorrow at the latest. Now I would be grateful if you would leave me.*

Oh, Father! [*Finally, she's let herself feel it.*] Maudie took a step towards her father, her arms outstretched.

Please leave me. His body stiffened and he turned his back on her.

Maudie pivoted in a smart military about-face, and walked towards the door. Oscar hurried after her.

As they passed through the door the guard came to attention, eyes straight ahead.

[*Does that guy know what just went on in there? What's his job now—to guard the president against his plotting daughter or to hold the president under house arrest? Sweet Jesus, I thought this stuff only happened in movies.*]

Neither of them spoke until they had turned the corner and were alone in the long corridor leading from the office wing to the garage, where the guards had parked Maudie's Mercedes.

Jesus, Maudie, that was brutal!

Maudie in full stride, eyes straight ahead: *It went better than I expected.*

Are you shitting me? What the hell did you think was going to happen?

I thought he might order his people to arrest us both on the spot.

Thanks awfully for telling me that now. Did you bring me along so you wouldn't be thrown into a cell alone?

I brought you because I know he respects you and he fears the people he thinks you report to. And I figured he'd think your overblown conscience wouldn't permit you to take part in a coup if it was driven only by my hunger for power. And despite all his brave talk, you represent the only country that, no matter how much he rails against it, he truly fears.

[*So Oscar, old boy, in the end you do turn out to be useful to your lover. Pretty sweet ad for a Wharton MBA!*]

And suppose he had believed that I really am the one who persuaded you to do this, that it was an American plot, cooked up by the CIA? As he said in there?

That occurred to me, but I figured he knows which one of us initiates and which supports. So even though he may yet try to portray it as a CIA plot to unseat him, I didn't think he'd try very hard to pin that on you in this meeting.

Thanks for the reassurance and the vote of no confidence in my leadership.

You can skip the dramatics, Oscar. This isn't about you and me and who's the alpha wolf. These are the highest stakes you or I—or just about anyone else in the world—will ever play for.

And what do you think he's going to do?

The president has always been able to scare the shit out of anyone who opposes him. It's virtually always worked, gotten him what he wanted. But, above everything else he's a realist, a pragmatist, (though he hates that word because it's associated with American business.) He's a world class bluffer, but he didn't defeat Ian Smith and the Selous Scouts, and get himself elected president by making bets he wasn't sure he could win. I think he'll rage around and feel sorry for himself, and then he'll consider all the options, and realize the one we offered is the only one that actually can work.

And—don't misunderstand me in this Oscar, because I could be saying it about myself—he really doesn't want to give up the good life he risked so much for. He's spent enough of his life just struggling to stay alive. He doesn't want to have to do that again.

I hope to hell you're right, Maudie; I can't imagine where we'll be if he decides to fight you on this. Is there anyone he can talk to now? What must it be like to face something like this alone?

That's the piece of all this that really worries me, Oscar, there's no one. Since my mother died he's had no close confidante. Only me, and me not much lately. I'm of another generation, I was a baby during the war, and it was fighting that war that formed him and his generation. All his old comrades are either dead or have become potential or actual political rivals.

They arrived at the door to the garage where another armed guard stood at attention, saluted, then opened the door. Neither of them spoke again until after they had finally cleared the final checkpoint and driven off the grounds of the palace.

Maudie, what do those armed guards—many of whom have been members of his honor guard for decades—know about all this?

I wish I knew, Oscar. The defense minister and the minister for domestic order have joint command of those forces, and both of them have been an ongoing part of our negotiations. But how far down the chain of command the knowledge of all this goes, I really can't say.

And if the President chooses to resist? Could we be facing the business end of those Uzis this time tomorrow?

I'm not even going to think about that, Oscar. I'm going to assume he's too smart, and cares too much about this country, and about me, to let such a terrible thing happen. If it does . . . she hesitated and, for just a moment—the only time other than when she had reached for her father in his office—Oscar thought he saw all the starch go out of her, *if it does, well, then, we're . . . fucked.*

Oscar looked straight ahead, watching Maudie in his peripheral vision. [*She almost never uses my favorite swear. Hard to imagine any other word that works as well here.*]

Maudie dropped Oscar a couple of blocks from his apartment. *Not that either of us is going to get any sleep, Oscar, but I'll plan to pick you up at 8 sharp. If you have any belief left in you, you may want to pray that the president will begin to understand why we have done what we have. If not . . .*

Oscar leaned across and gave Maudie a light kiss on her cheek. *I love you, Maudie. I already admired you more than anyone I have ever known, but at this moment my awe is boundless.*

If only awe and admiration could change minds and influence events, Maudie said, looking straight ahead. *I'll see you at 8.*

*　　*　　*

OH MY GOD!

He wasn't sure if he had even dozed off when his secure phone buzzed. *Oscar!* Maudie's voice sounded odd, strained. Oscar looked at the clock next to his bed. 5:45. The morning gray, pre-dawn light baleful, like an ominous scene from a movie shot in sepia tone. *Meet me at the palace as soon as you can get there. No, second thought, I'll swing by and pick you up in 20 minutes.*

What's up?

Not sure, but something incredibly urgent; we'll talk when I get there. He heard the hang-up click before he could say goodbye. [*That was fear in Maudie's voice. Never hear that. She's really scared.*]

Inchoate fear churned Oscar's stomach. Felt like his balls sucked up into his gut as he pulled on his clothes, brushed his teeth, splashed water in his face. He hated the fear, hated feeling so at-risk before he was even wide-awake. Everything felt menacing these days. [*I've always known I'm not cut out for this life. Kind of late now, Buddy. Put a preppie in Africa and watch his save-the-world heart turn to mush—right after it seizes up from fright.*] His reflection in the bathroom mirror stared back at him, his eyes looked like he had been on a three-day bender. [*I really need a shave but I'm afraid I'd cut my throat if I tried it now.*] The idea kind of appealed to him. The sound of a Mercedes horn startled him back to reality. Oscar left all the lights burning—[*Conserve energy? Why bother? The electricity's never on for more than an hour any more in this God-forsaken city*]—as he bounded out the door of his apartment.

Maudie honked again just as Oscar bolted through the front door of the building.

Sorry; I got down here as fast as I could. You sure made it here in a hurry.

Maudie ignored his apology and his comment, pressing the accelerator to the floor as soon as Oscar's rear end touched the seat. He hadn't fully closed the door, the momentum of the car lurching forward slammed it, nearly catching his fingers. He reached over his shoulder for the seat belt, then saw Maudie didn't have hers on and decided to let his go, too.

[*Wishy-washy wimp to the end; is this supposed to be some sort of heroic gesture of chivalric love, putting your life at risk alongside Maudie's? Just shut up, over-anxious mind.*]

Without speaking, Maudie drove wildly through the mostly deserted streets. Oscar looked over at her a few times, hoping his glances might provoke some sort of conversation, but he wasn't about to initiate one himself. The sun was just coming up, the gray dawn sky turning a billowy pink. Oscar held fast to the strap above the door as they turned a corner, the roadster leaning heavily into the turn, feeling as if it might roll onto its side.

Whoa, Maudie! How about we get there alive?

Maudie continued driving recklessly, still not responding to Oscar. With a mixture of relief and foreboding, Oscar saw the gates of the Presidential Palace at the end of the next block.

[*What's gonna be waiting for us in there?*]

The blinding klieg lights were still on, and there seemed to be even more guards than when they left the night before. Several plainclothes security men milled around the front gate. [*I don't recognize those guys. They weren't here last night.*]

We're supposed to go round to the service delivery entrance. It was the first time Oscar had heard Maudie's voice since she phoned him. Its unfamiliar metallic quality—as if she were speaking through a scrambling device—startled him. The guards acknowledged her, but aside from a few nods of their heads made no move to check them. Nothing like the heavy security of the previous night. She pulled the car into a space reserved for deliveries at the foot of the ramp. A security light came on above the corrugated overhead door, blinding them. The door slid up.

In the glare they made out Gretchen Mallory, Ethan Pinsky and Jim Newmark, standing on the loading dock with Minister Baunda and Minister David Mutara, the sole remaining government minister who could be said to remain even remotely in President Mugabe's increasingly paranoid confidence.

Oscar was disoriented. [*Wasn't it just two days ago I was meeting with that group in Washington? What the fuck are they doing here?*]

Oscar saw Maudie stiffen. She sat motionless, silent, making no move to get out of the car. The group on the loading dock stared down at the two of them. No one moved or spoke. [*Surreal. Whose move?*] Finally Oscar opened his door and slowly unwound his full height, walked around the back of the car, not looking up at the puzzling group gathered on the dock above him, wondering what it might take to extract Maudie from the car. She looked catatonic. Dread crawled up Oscar's legs, turning them to stone, slowing his progress around the car to Maudie's door. His empty stomach growled audibly.

[*What the hell? How could they have even gotten here this fast? Has it even been 24 hours since I got back?*]

Oscar leaned down and opened Maudie's door. She looked straight ahead, as if she was unaware of him next to her. He touched her elbow, cautiously.

Maudie, Oscar's whispered voice sounded strained even to him, *let me help you out*. Maudie still didn't respond, but she didn't resist as he took her elbow and gently helped lift her from the car. She seemed in a daze, as if she had suffered a blow to her head. *Maudie, are you all right?* No answer. Her face was expressionless, shades paler than normal. Oscar guided her up the ramp by her arm, as if she was old and infirm. *I'm right beside you, Maudie. I won't leave you. It's going to be OK.*

Gretchen was the first to speak. *Maudie, Oscar, thank God you're here!* She opened her arms in a gesture that looked to Oscar like an offer to embrace Maudie. But Maudie continued to stare straight ahead. Oscar stifled his impulse to say something about how startled he was to see the three of them. He waited while they all stood, silently, awkwardly. For what seemed an eternity no one said or did anything, the seven of them standing uncomfortably in uneven formation, no one seeming prepared to take the initiative. At last Gretchen spoke again, directing a question to Maudie.

Have you spoken to anyone since I called you, Maudie? Has anyone given you any information about the president? About your father? Gretchen's voice dropped to whisper as she said, *your father.*

Oscar was shocked as he watched Maudie's face, considering Gretchen's question as if she had been asked to solve a complex problem. [*My God, this is what Maudie's going to look like when she's an old lady.*]

Her face was blank, impassive, as if she was suffering from Parkinson's disease.

What about my father? What information? she responded to Gretchen's questions with her own. *No, I haven't spoken with anyone else since your call, except for Oscar.* She pivoted, suddenly toward Oscar, addressing him in an accusing tone. *Oscar, are you in on this? Are you holding out on me? Are you and your American friends a part of something you're not telling me?*

No, I swear not, Maudie. I'm just as much in the dark as you are. All I know is the phone call from you saying you were coming to pick me up. Can someone please tell us what's going on?

We need to go inside the palace, Gretchen said, *We can talk as we go.*

Pinsky and Newmark flanked Gretchen as she turned and led them through the loading area, down a long corridor that Oscar had never been in. Ministers Baunda and Mutara followed a step behind.

Oscar's mind raced: [*How does Gretchen Mallory get to be in charge of a group of government ministers in the Zimbabwe Presidential Palace? If Maudie ever had any doubts about CIA-McKinsey conspiracies and me, this will sure as hell erase them.*]

Gretchen turned back to Maudie as if to say something, then seemed to think better of it. Oscar put his arm around Maudie's shoulder and she leaned into him. [*She's in a bad way. She's never let me touch her in an intimate way unless we were alone, sure as hell never when we were in the Palace.*]

Oscar gripped Maudie's shoulder tighter as they neared the end of the corridor. Before they went through what Oscar finally recognized as the secure door to the presidential office, the one never to be used except for a hasty escape, Gretchen began speaking. *I've got some terrible news, Maudie.* Oscar felt her go rigid. *I'm afraid your father is dead.*

No! Dead? No. Can't be. Oh no, who? Assassinated him. How? Maudie slumped against Oscar, her full weight against him, knocking him back a step.

No, he wasn't assassinated. He was alone. William was the bodyguard on duty this morning. He thought he heard something. He went in and found your father in his bed. He used his old service revolver, with a silencer. One shot through the heart. He must have died instantly. No pain.

Maudie staggered against Oscar, nearly causing them both to fall. She began to wail, the mournful wail of an African woman for the death of someone precious to her. The five of them stopped walking. Maudie leaned down, holding her face in her hands, bending at the waist, her body rocking back and forth.

Oh God, oh Father, she choked between sobs, then suddenly turned angrily toward Oscar. *This would never have happened if you and I hadn't had that conversation with him last night.*

Oscar mumbled something unintelligible, desperate to come up with a response. [*Oh Christ, Maudie. Honestly, I think you're probably right.*]

Maudie, Nathan Pinsky was speaking, *I can only imagine what you must be feeling about this terrible news. And about what we're doing here. I apologize for intruding on such a personal, horrible moment. The reason the three of us are here is because we received an intelligence report yesterday morning in Washington that left no doubt that the next move, within days, if not hours, was an assassination of you and your father. And Oscar. And a coup. Though we don't know what you may have said to the president last night; if you were encouraging him to resign and have you assume the office, that was the most responsible scenario we had heard mentioned that could possibly head off a bloody coup. We flew all night on a chartered flight to make that case to you today. Horrible as this moment is, and trying not to seem any more callous or mercenary than we already must, we still want to make that case to you. We still believe it is the last best hope for keeping your father's dreams for your country from being destroyed in a civil war.*

I'm afraid it's a little late now, wouldn't you say? Maudie's grief seemed to give way to eerie calm. Her voice was cold, distant. Dripping sarcasm.

We don't think that's necessarily so, Pinsky answered. *But if you're going to have any chance of heading off a disaster that could plunge this country into anarchy, or something maybe a lot worse, you're going to have to move fast. And be smart. And very lucky.*

Oscar looked over at the two government ministers. Attentive, but no affect that Oscar could read. [*Jesus! This is beyond bizarre. The two ministers and Maudie, outnumbered by four Americans, in the president's palace . . . he's dead, Maudie's maybe already effectively the new president. Maybe we're all about to be assassinated. The CIA is here, McKinsey's here. What the fuck?*]

You Americans. You really don't give a shit about anything except your own self-interest, do you? Maudie's eyes had turned steely. *Imagine the rest of the world's response; our president is dead. And the CIA, the IMF and McKinsey Global Institute, show up on the palace doorstep. How neat! How convenient! And you even have a script for me, so we need never miss a beat. I become your surrogate on the ground in Zimbabwe, another step forward in your running the world. My father's in there, dead, you cold-hearted bastards! What more do you want from me?* She began sobbing uncontrollably. Oscar, despite being implicated in her anti-American rant, put his arms around Maudie. She didn't resist, again leaning heavily against him.

Oscar's mind was a madhouse. [*Who am I here? Maudie's lover? McKinsey's flunky? CIA undercover? Jesus fucking Christ! President Mugabe shot himself because Maudie and I told him it was time for him to resign. Maybe it was, but . . .*]

Maudie, Gretchen's voice was low, solemn, like a mother speaking to her distraught daughter, *no one could blame you for any of what you're feeling. Any of us in your position would feel all you just said. But I'm afraid the situation is so volatile now that you're either going to have to decide to trust us and believe we may be able to help you, or you're going to face some pretty dire circumstances. In which case we're prepared to leave the country within the hour. And we'll have to insist that Oscar go with us. And if you choose not to go forward with what we think is your only possible way through this, we would strongly advise you to fly back to the States with us for your personal safety. The State Department has indicated it will grant you political asylum. If you refuse that, then I'm afraid we leave you here to face an uncertain fate. We don't know how widespread the coup plans may have already gone, and we don't know how they might be changed by your father's death. But we are encouraging you—with Minister Baunda and Minister Mutara, and the others with whom you have been meeting—to carry though with the plan you have been working on, and we think has the best chance to rescue the situation. If you decide you can trust us, and if you will hear us out.*

Maudie had stopped crying. She seemed to be listening to Gretchen. She wiped her eyes with her sleeve. She stepped out of Oscar's grasp and away from the four of them, standing stock-still, ramrod-straight, alongside the two Zimbabwe ministers, looking over the four white Americans as if they were cattle she was considering bidding on at auction.

—

Four white Americans and three Africans who have been lackeys of western interests here in Zimbabwe, and I'm supposed to believe you have a plan that is for our good, and not your own? Oscar watched Maudie, fascinated by the abrupt shifts in her mood, seemingly back in control of her will. And her rage.

We'd like to believe, Pinsky answered, *it would be for the good for all of us. That we do have shared interests here, if not identical interests.*

Yes, I'll bet you do, Maudie laughed scornfully, giving Oscar his first glimmer of hope that she might be able to put on her old crafty self and enter into this high-stakes negotiation.

But before we try to discuss anything more, Gretchen said, *I think you need to go to your father's chamber and do the terrible hard work of seeing his body, so you can understand the awful reality, that he really is dead. Then, if you're able, and if you're willing, we're here to talk.*

Who besides us knows of his death? Maudie asked. [*There's the old Maudie, beginning to collect information, figuring the angles. I think she may have a go at this. Wonder how I'll fare?*]

Only the seven of us, and William who found him and the head of the Presidential Guard, whom William called right away.

And, if I may ask, Maudie now sounded cold, sarcastic, menacing, further reassuring Oscar that she was getting engaged, *how might the three of you have gotten in on the act so quickly? Even before any of his own ministers? Or me? And getting to Baunda and Mutara, my main confidantes in our supposedly confidential conversations? You want me to set aside my paranoia? How about unpacking all that for me, if I'm not asking too much.*

Gretchen didn't seem intimidated by Maudie's gathering rage. *I'm prepared to answer any of your questions. I don't expect you to let go of your suspicions until and unless you're satisfied with what we have to say. I don't think we can begin to settle this while you are in what must be total shock. But I can tell you that because of his concern for your safety, your father didn't tell you everything, Maudie. He had left instructions with the head of the Guard that if anything was ever to happen to him, he should immediately notify one of the three of us, even before notifying you. The reason was, I'm afraid, that he didn't trust anyone around him. No one in this country. I can't soften the reality that he was in touch with our CIA. He was never sure how far he could trust your own CIO, and was afraid any assassination attempt would also come against you. We had pledged to him that we would use Marines from our Embassy, if necessary, to protect you. We were in flight—having been alerted by the head of the guard that he sensed the coup was imminent—less than an hour from here, when we received word that he was dead.*

The conversation stopped as they reached the end of the long corridor and went through the concealed door into the palace living quarters. They were approaching the door to her father's parlor and bedroom. Two guards in fancy dress stood at attention outside the door. They clicked their heels in salute as Maudie entered the ante-room.

I wish you would all wait out here. I want to go in alone, Maudie said, her voice now calm, controlled. She reached for the doorknob and let herself in. She walked through the ornate outer room, paused, took a deep breath, straightened her spine, and strode resolutely into her father's bedroom.

Except for being so eerily still, he looked peacefully asleep, not dead. He was propped up by several pillows, his head and face unmarked, his arms along his sides. Maudie stopped, standing still a few feet from the bed, waiting, fully expecting him to look up at her and speak. The bed covers were pulled up almost to his throat. Maudie walked to the bedside and pulled the covers away from his chest. A small bullet wound had shredded his silk pajamas over his heart. Though he had been cleaned up, a crust of dried blood stuck his pajamas to his smooth black skin.

Oh Ba! she cried, calling him the name she seldom used since her mother died, *you shot yourself through your heart. Oh God, poor dear man, you died of a broken heart. Oh, Daddy, I'm so sorry Oh Ba, it didn't have to be like this.* She flung herself across his body, tipping him onto his left side. She was shocked to feel his stiff, cold body against her own warm flesh. She lay on top of him for several minutes, wailing, keening. Then she abruptly sat bolt upright. She propped him back up, pulling his body into the position in which she had found him. [*Now you look the dignified hero of the Zimbabwe revolution.*]

OK, Mr. President, you've given your all. Now it's time to hear what these American Machiavellians have in mind for the daughter you have worked so hard to prepare for this moment.

Maudie went into his private bathroom—she hadn't ventured here since she was a young girl—washed her face and hands, straightened her jacket and blouse, while she considered herself in her father's magnifying mirror, taking several long, deep breaths.

You look a little beat-up, she said to her reflection, *but I don't suppose anyone's really going to notice that this morning.*

She walked back through the bedroom, past the bed holding the remains of her father, the first and so-far only president of the independent nation of Zimbabwe. Without so much as one backward glance at his body, Maudie, his chosen heir—president apparent Maudie Mugabe—walked through the door to the outer office where Oscar and Gretchen, the other American plotters, and her two government ministers waited for her.

Oscar became increasingly and uncomfortably aware that neither Minister Mutara nor Baunda had spoken a single word since he and Maudie had arrived. [*Is this more of that African deference, even in a moment like this? What's up with their silence? I could spend the rest of my life among these people and never learn to read them. That includes Maudie. Jesus, look at her. Two minutes ago I thought she would collapse in a nervous breakdown. Right now she looks like she's ready to face down the world and the four of us.*]

*   *   *

In Charge

Oh Maudie, I'm so sorry. Oscar rushed toward her as she emerged from the presidential suite, his arms extended to embrace her. [*Jesus, I think I'm gonna cry. Get a grip, man.*]

Maudie turned sideways, fending off Oscar's gesture. Clearly she wasn't looking for solace now. She addressed Gretchen:

So, let's hear what you have in mind. The steely resolve in her voice frightened and thrilled Oscar.

Nothing about this tragedy changes our original conviction that you are the key to whatever possibility there may be for an orderly transition. But it's unquestionably a good deal more problematic today than it was yesterday. Gretchen was reading Maudie perfectly, disciplining herself to be as controlled and matter-of-fact as Maudie was now clearly determined to be. *There are a few conditions that, if we can provide them, may up the chances of your pulling this off. How about we go downstairs to the Presidential Office? I don't think we've got a lot of time before the rumors begin to fly, and word may get out and then things are likely to speed up dramatically. And the faster things go, the more your options narrow.*

Maudie led the group around the corner to the secure elevator, greeted the operator by name and directed him to take them to the first floor. They rode down in silence. When the door opened on the first floor, Maudie walked out first and led them along the short, red-carpeted corridor lined with photographs—of her father with leaders from around the world. As they approached the door to the president's office, the guards on either side of the door clicked their heels as they came to attention, saluted and greeted Maudie:

242

Good morning, Deputy President. One leaned forward, opened the door and stood aside.

These people have been cleared and may proceed under my personal recognition, Maudie said to the guards [*very presidential,*] Oscar thought as she gestured to the six of them.

Very good, one guard responded.

They entered the large room with its one oval end. [*Yes, Pinsky and Newmark; yet another presidential office fashioned after ours.*] The guard pulled the door shut behind them.

This room is sealed when that door is shut. There's a scrambler on the phone and in every vent or place where sound could escape. Maudie was unquestionably in charge. She went around to her father's huge partner's desk, leaned under the knee-hole and flicked a switch. ***He often left the recording system on voice activation so he wouldn't have to turn it on when someone came into the room. I don't think we need to record this conversation. But I would appreciate it if someone—how about you, Oscar—would keep some notes of what gets said here. Just in case we need to refer back to them at some future time.***

[*Man, there's no question who's running this show*]. ***Sure, be happy to.*** He was grateful to have a task.

Why don't you two, Maudie gestured to the two ministers, ***sit on that sofa, while Gretchen and I sit here. And you two***—this to Pinsky and Newmark—***please take those two ladder-back chairs along the wall.*** She pointed to the sofa in front of which she was standing, and Gretchen immediately sat. [*How cool is this? She lets the two American spies know they're on the sidelines, spectators, not major players.*] ***Oscar, you'll need a surface to write on, so you can pull out the slot from this side of the president's desk and sit there.*** When they were all seated, Maudie turned to Gretchen on her left.

OK, Gretchen, let's hear it.

Gretchen never hesitated, acceding to Maudie's direction. [*sounds like Gretchen has memorized a script*] ***First we suggest you have the president's press secretary put out the word that the president has had a serious stroke and his condition is grave.***

Oscar, Maudie looked to her right where Oscar had begun writing on a yellow legal pad, ***destroy what you've just written, and don't begin taking notes until I tell you to.*** Oscar tore the paper into shreds as he nodded.

And you and Minister Baunda were meeting with him. It was a half hour before he lost consciousness. In that half hour he directed you to put into place the emergency plan for when the president becomes incapacitated.

I have never been certain who knows about the plan, Maudie said.

The Minister for Internal Affairs and The Foreign Minister both have copies in their safes. The president talked with them about this within the past year. Now, of course, Ministers Baunda and Mutara know. Neither man gave any indication they had heard what she said. [*What planet are these guys from?*]

[*How the hell does Gretchen know everything about what goes on inside Zimbabwe's government? Seems like more than even Maudie. If Maudie wonders, she's not asking.*]

What about any of the leaders of parliament? The opposition leaders, any of them know about it? [*How nuts is this? Maudie's already running things in Zimbabwe, but she's getting her information from Gretchen. I knew the world's power leaders were a pretty incestuous bunch, but this . . .*]

We're not sure; we know the president had some conversation with the leaders of the parliament, but things have been so bitter and partisan the past few months, we're not sure. We have no proof either way.

But we do know what, thank God, you have kept us abreast of; that for the past several months you and other leaders of your father's party and the opposition have been meeting to discuss various options. And the one they and you agreed to was the one you apparently proposed to your father last night, that he would step down and you would succeed him in a coalition government.

[*Do they have the place bugged? Did Maudie know?*]

Maudie seemed unruffled by Gretchen's having spoken about the inside information; it didn't seem to surprise her. [*Or is it that she's not about to show what she's feeling?*] *And do you have any reason to think that might have changed? That any of the opposition leaders believe they no longer have to support such a plan? That they can achieve power now without having to agree to this plan?*

If word should leak out that the president is dead before you put the transition plan in place, I'm afraid none of us can predict what chaos that might provoke. That is the reason we think you must act quickly, immediately, announcing that before he became incapacitated and lapsed into unconsciousness, he appointed you acting president. And then soon, maybe tonight, announce that he has died. It may be that your having already assumed the office will provide enough immediate legitimacy in the eyes of the country for them to support your becoming de jure president. As well as de facto. Our polls show continuing strong support for you as potential president. And your father's death should give you a cushion of at least the mourning period.

OK Oscar, Maudie turned to Oscar, *I want you to start keeping track now of what goes on from this point.*

Yes, Madam President, Oscar was trying out the title on her, and on himself, not sure whether he meant for it to be taken seriously or to provide some release of the tension. But Maudie didn't react, and neither did anyone else in the room. [*Jesus Christ; what're the chances of a white American boy being the president's lover? At-a-way, Oscar; always in character; there's a thought that brings new meaning to inappropriate.*]

I want the document that outlines the succession of power faxed to the press, both the government paper and the opposition paper. The president's press secretary needs to call an immediate press conference and announce to the world that the president has suffered a massive stroke, and that just before he lost consciousness he signed the appropriate papers to name me interim president. Minister Baunda, I want you to call Nkomo and tell him I need to see him as soon as he can be here. Assure him that although I intend to carry out my father's agenda, I also intend to work with him and ZAPU, fully and transparently.

[*Jesus, how long has she been getting herself ready for this moment? She hasn't faltered once yet.*]

Oscar, you need to get yourself back to the Finance Ministry and collect all your papers. I want anything potentially embarrassing shredded by this afternoon. You, Gretchen and Ethan and Jim are going to have to disappear, fast. I intend to keep you informed and I will count on you for many things in the future. But if anyone gets wind of your role—you're having been here through all this—no one will ever believe this wasn't some sort of sinister CIA coup. I'm having a little trouble not seeing it that way myself. It would be a good thing for you to leave the country before nightfall. But not through the airport. The best way would be for you to drive down south through the Lowveld and across the South Africa border at Beitbridge. We'll be sure they know at the border that you're coming, and let you right through. I want you to drive a car from the Zambian embassy, on whose business you were here. Minister Mutara can secure the car and driver through their embassy.

Maudie stopped talking, looking pensive. The four of them waited, wondering what she was thinking, what was coming next.

I want you to understand something, because this is likely the last time we'll ever be able to have a conversation this candid. I am grateful for all you have done; I think Zimbabwe might have been pitched into civil war or even tribal genocide without your help. It may yet, but if it doesn't, it's thanks in no small part to you.

But I expect you to understand that the role my father had you play is now over. I intend to run the country. I am president, and I have to be president in fact. That means weaning this government from its dependence on the United States. We will continue to be a friend of your country and will certainly continue to depend on you for resources we lack. But my father became far too enmeshed with you and your secret power brokers. That was part of the reason he lost touch with this nation and the needs and wants of our people. His fear of losing power caused him to give you more access to our government than was proper or in our interests. I don't intend to do that. From now on I expect you to communicate with me through proper channels. Having this country and this government learn to run and rely on itself rather than selling itself in return for special protection will be one standard I will hold myself to when I make decisions. I do not fear losing personal power nearly so much as I do Zimbabwe's losing what may be her last chance to become a nation in her own right. I hope you understand and will honor what I have said.

For several seconds no one spoke. [*Wonder what this means for me? That wasn't just a rehearsed speech, I don't think. But it must be how every new leader thinks it's going to be now. Even supreme leaders need a little diversion; maybe I can become her gigolo. But shit, she'll probably have to have a more politically correct playmate, an African. Oscar, this isn't about you, Buddy. Better get that straight, and get it now.*]

Madam President, Gretchen's first use of Maudie's new title startled Oscar out his daydream, *you can be assured we understand and respect the position you have just laid out as your nation's agenda. Though it would be presumptuous of me to try to speak for the American government, I feel confident in saying that the president and the American people would be comfortable, even enthusiastic, in aiding Zimbabwe in becoming a truly independent, autonomous nation. It's how we ourselves began, and what we wish for every nation on earth. I hope you will always regard us as a friend on whom you can count for all you wish for your nation.*

Gretchen, I am grateful for your response, and I will look forward to hearing it directly from your president. But lest we start off with naiveté that could quickly lead us to places neither of us wish to go, I want to be clear that, while we regard the United States as a valued friend and ally, our interests are not, and cannot be, always precisely the same. Our history, our culture, our beliefs, all lead us to pursue goals that are not identical to yours. I know how tempting it is for your nation to judge the actions of other countries by your own agenda. I understand that when you are the world's only remaining super power it is difficult to seriously honor the interests of smaller countries. But I will insist on putting the needs of my people ahead of all other matters, even when it may mean causing discomfort for your government. And—please don't write this, Oscar—unlike my father the past few years, I am not willing to accede to your wishes simply to maintain myself in this office.

Understood, Madam President. We thank you for your candor, which we will communicate to our president who I know will admire as much as we do your determination to serve your people's legitimate interests.

Please do that. Oscar thought Maudie suddenly looked exhausted. [*I sure am.*] *And now I wish you would all leave me alone. You may make the calls you need to make; we will see that your calls are secure and unmonitored. I need to spend some final time with my father before he becomes the property of the world. I know you'll understand.*

[*I suppose she means me, too.*] Oscar looked up from the paper on which he had been writing, hoping for a signal from Maudie about whether he was now being included in her formal dealings with this retinue, or was he different, her confidante, her lover. She made no eye contact with him. She rose from her chair and without a backward glance disappeared through the door into the presidential quarters.

Oscar watched her straight back, that gait, her profile, so familiar that he could pick her out in a crowd from a great distance. He knew that the sight of her, even on TV news, would always release a shower of emotions in him. He wished he could capture that sight of her as she disappeared through the door. He'd like to bottle the endorphins it triggered in him.

[*My halcyon days with Maudie just ended.*]

* * *

Oscar's Book

None of us knew then what was going to happen next. I went back to my apartment to pack up, preparing for the worst, though what the worst might be I was afraid to even guess. As I packed, I kept alert for assassins to break down my door. Gretchen, Pinsky and Newmark [*I still can't bring myself to call them by their given names, as if they were friends, or even human*], suggested I be ready to leave with them. I tried to stall, wanting to be around if there turned out to be anything I could do to help Maudie. Or even just see her.

There wasn't.

And I never did see her again. Well, never spoke with her. I did see her from a distance when she was sworn in as president and addressed The Parliament. Minister Baunda, who had been named first deputy president, left a message on my secure phone (I hadn't known he was aware I had that phone) saying President Mugabe had invited me to sit with foreign diplomats during the ceremony and speech. I assumed that meant she had negotiated her way through at least the first round and wasn't nervous about my being there.

Startling: **She hopes you will be able to attend**, Baunda's message said. President Mugabe, she!

I had a fantasy that she might somehow contact me surreptitiously, soliciting my help in writing her speech. Maudie had always praised my command of language, and while much of the speech would likely be largely in Shona, in deference to the considerable numbers of her countrymen who were not Shona, she would no doubt follow the usual custom of leaders addressing a national gathering, sprinkling large parts with English.

I knew it was fantasy. I never was sure whether Baunda's invitation was on his own initiative or hers. I tried not to dwell on the layers of potential trouble I could cause her if the story ever got out about how the president died and about the meeting Maudie and I had with him the previous night. I was sure someday it would come out but it's been more than 20 years, Maudie has long left the presidency, so except for its personal interest, I can't imagine it matters much now.

I interpreted the invitation to mean that I had not become persona-non-grata in Zimbabwe—at least not yet—and I let Gretchen's group leave without me. *Please make an appointment to see me as soon after you return as possible, Oscar,* Gretchen said when I called to say goodbye. *McKinsey will be eager to debrief you and consider how and whether your role in all this was a good fit with McKinsey's mission.*

I'll certainly do that, Gretchen. Safe trip.

I hoped McKinsey might be sobered by all that happened and rethink these contracts that could lead them into international intrigue. But my guess is it more likely whet appetites for the adrenaline rush that comes from insinuating one's self into the intrigue and power-scheming. Even though there's been a sea-change in international politics since then, human beings haven't changed that much. As old Henry Kissinger famously said back in the twentieth century, *Power is the ultimate aphrodisiac.*

I am embarrassed to admit how much that adrenaline rush motivated me in those days. I sat in that crowded parliament chamber feeling the electricity in the room. All eyes were glued to the new young president, wondering what she would say to them. How would the power her father had held so closely, so jealously, shake out now? I couldn't deny that I got a charge thinking about all the secrets between the beautiful young president and me. Even though I had learned enough to know more people than I like to think were probably in on them.

My comrades, this is a sad day for our great nation. Zimbabwe has lost a brave patriot and the only president we have ever known. I can report to you that his final concern was, as it had always been, for you and for our nation.

Comrade Baunda and I were meeting with him when he suffered the stroke. He remained conscious and alert for a full half hour, and he immediately recognized that he might become incapacitated or die. While he could still speak he asked us to continue the revolution he led, and to express his love and gratitude to the people of this nation who trusted him with their support.

She had needed no help from me. The speech was masterful. It went on for almost two hours, leading those anxious politicians on a circuitous course from grieving, to reassurance, to anticipation, to excitement for the future. Somehow she managed to lionize her father as the nation's founding hero, and distance herself from the policies that in recent years had made Zimbabwe an outlaw nation in much of the world.

When the Zimbabwe stock market re-opened after three days of mourning it scored its greatest gain ever. The IMF announced that same week that it would make good on the next installment of its loan. That the new President Mugabe did not promise to restore white privileges in farming or commerce was a disappointment to the white farmers whose land had been confiscated. But she did work hard to put more land into the hands of competent black farmers rather than political cronies, which had the virtue of continuing the basic shape of her father's agenda to move the nation's economy from dependence on western aid into indigenous hands. And at the same time she began the slow, essential job of restoring the nation's farms to productivity.

It provided an early signal to some of the most corrupt members of her father's regime—things were now different.

And perhaps simply because the old bogeyman was gone, and because Maudie proved to be a skilled and crafty negotiator, western business—including white business—re-opened their wallets to Zimbabwe.

I followed her and the nation she led—and I had once briefly served—with rapt attention from Portland, Oregon, where I was a professor of classics at Portland State University. Maudie had teased me about what she called my "brief soiree into political economics." She was right. It didn't take me long to return to my first love—language, especially poetry. I published a couple of books of my verse—one strongly influenced by my time in Zimbabwe and my romance with their president, whose identity I disguised, though nosy critics of course quickly figured it out.

Maudie was also right when she said I would fall in love again and marry. At the time she said it I resisted the thought. I'm happy now she was right. Allison grew up in a preacher's house, as I did. But everything else about our upbringings was as different as, well, as chalk and cheese.

Allison's father was pastor of a huge AME Zion congregation in St. Louis. A black church.

Happily for me, Allison wasn't the jealous type. When she'd look over my shoulder and see me reading a Reuters story about Zimbabwe or Maudie, she'd laugh. She was director of small business development for Mercy Corps and traveled the world, including, occasionally, Africa, and Zimbabwe. After the first time she met Maudie, she texted me: *Hey, Oscar, for a white boy, you got good taste in women!*

Though Allison never seemed jealous of the relationship Maudie and I once had, I was aware that she kept a close eye on me (the way my mother had my father) around attractive women, especially women who, like Maudie, and like Allison, were black and beautiful. And strong.

What is it about you and tough, turfy, black women, Oscar?

Good question.

I think she wondered if I was trying to reincarnate—in her or some other woman—what I had with Maudie. I revisited those tumultuous times a lot in my memory, it's true. But it was so clearly a once-in-a-lifetime lightning strike that I was never tempted to try. Thrilling as my time with Maudie was, it felt clear by a year or so after I left Zimbabwe that it was totally about that time and that place.

And I adored Allison. I guess it's in my DNA to find a woman I could adore. Emotionally, Allison was a different woman from Maudie. Never hesitated from the get-go—even before I had figured out the depth of my caring for her—to tell me how much she loved me. She had her own, very successful career, though after our two kids, Sandra and Alex, were born, she cut herself back to three-quarters time until they started school. I was a good enough house-husband—teaching gave me flexibility—that I was able and happy to take my share of all that.

In the years since that moment my dear Allison contracted malaria on one of her Africa trips. Back then malaria remained an unsolved plague. Hers quickly evolved into cerebral malaria, causing her brain to swell and she lost consciousness. She was deep in the Botswana bush and by the time they got her to a hospital she was brain-dead. When they finally got hold of me it was to decide whether to cremate her body over there or go through the horror of bringing it back to the States.

Sandra and Alex were bricks. Despite having to deal with their own grief, they nursed me through mine. I wonder if Maudie ever knew. She and Allison had met a few times and, maybe either because of or despite having me in common, they hit it off. I didn't try to contact Maudie after Allison died. Too much history had gone by.

*   *   *

MAUDIE'S BOOK

I love reading Oscar's account of those years.

It was a long time ago now, but remains vivid in my memory.

I am especially taken with his choosing to put it into fiction form (and not only because of those steamy sex scenes). He made it fun, if a little hyperbolic by my lights. I suppose one could argue that it would be impossible to exaggerate those stormy days. I am being more truthful than modest when I say his portrayal of the fictional me makes me more clever, beautiful and high-minded than the Maudie he actually knew. But then the beauty of fiction is the novelist's license. And it was clear to me—and unsettling—that from the earliest days of our relationship Oscar had made me into some wonder-woman of his dreams. I suppose we all idealize, though my father disciplined me from an early age to turn away from illusions and projections and stay focused on reality no matter how hard. That discipline served me—and the nation, and even, finally the world—well, I think.

But I know Oscar often found it frustrating. And his book is his chance to tell it his way.

It was horrible for me that Father wasn't able to follow his own counsel in the end. Watching that brave, wise man stumble and fall over an impediment he put in his own way was a lesson about the seduction of power I hoped never to forget. It ended tragically for him, which I still believe it needn't have. That made it all harder—and sadder—for me. I still believe what Oscar and I did that night was what Father on his best days would have understood. But his best days were behind him. His brilliance and judgment were clouded by old age and having been too long in power. My broken heart has never fully mended from his believing what I did was a betrayal of him.

That piece of Oscar's book—about my father's end—feels to me the most faithful to what it was like. Perhaps because it was a time when it was hardest for me to keep my emotions in check. Oscar's perspective was often filtered more through his emotions than his reason. It always was a difference between us. But in that awful moment when I learned Father had killed himself, my emotions threatened to take me over. I wasn't sure my inner discipline could hold up.

That was when I called on Oscar's inner strength. I think he had kept that reservoir of iron under wraps in deference to my need to build my own. I was more grateful than he will likely ever know as he stood next to me that day in the palace and held me, reassured me. Although he always deferred to me, never had outward the self-confidence I did, I knew his core was rock solid.

I was aware almost from the outset that my focus on my vocation and the realities it dictated could seem heartless to Oscar. It might have been kinder had I never become his lover. Before we ever slept together I seriously considered breaking it off. Maybe I was selfish. But I tried to be scrupulous about my future. And Oscar seemed willing to take his chances.

I don't think he ever knew how much I did adore him. Not, perhaps, as he would have liked, but as it had to be. It was so hard for him to believe that I could love him—become his most intimate companion—and not bend in staying faithful to my vocation.

Reading his account, despite it's being fiction, I get an even more poignant picture of what it was like for him than I understood at the time. I'm grateful he wrote it now, in old age, when time and events have softened the disappointments. How nice that he married Allison and had those children. He always wanted that. Allison was perfect, the woman I might have chosen for Oscar. He deserved the best and from the few times I met her, I think he got that in Allison.

Oscar's doesn't stress the political intrigue as much as I would. Maybe because he seems never to have doubted that I would prevail, make things come out as I wished. I didn't always share his confidence.

His presumed boss was Ndebele. (Presumed because Oscar never knew for certain to whom he owed primary loyalty) Minister Baunda had signed the contract with McKinsey [*Did he know he was going into business with the IMF and the American CIA?*] Though apparently Oscar never had an in-depth conversation with Baunda about Ndebele versus Shona, he knew our history and he must have wondered—as we all did. What did Baunda's loyalty to Zanu-PF and Father cost him? If I were writing the story, Baunda would come off as a bigger hero than I was. He put his hope for a prosperous, unified Zimbabwe ahead of everything—his family, tribe, and, I suppose, his personal feelings.

But it's Oscar's story and Baunda wasn't his lover. That story wouldn't have had those juicy love scenes.

Baunda nor Oscar nor I could have imagined the way my father would meet his end. If there is anything I sometimes let myself wish I could go back and relive, it is that. But rewriting history is an luxury unavailable to those faced with acting in the moment. I overestimated my father's will to live and underestimated his attachment to power. I suppose I idealized him as much as Oscar did me. I believed his years in prison and in the bush as a guerilla fighting the Selous Scouts had so hardened his will and his drive to survive that nothing could blunt it. I read him wrong. I was too young to appreciate how much those hard years and the even harder ensuing years of governing our disparate young nation had worn him down.

In the luxury of an old age to sit and reflect I allow myself sadness for my heroic father and for the overweening ambition that accounts for both the unlikely success of our revolution against Ian Smith and for the tragedy that led to my father's death.

I am happy that Oscar has written it as he has—and maybe as he still sees it—more love story than political. In my waning days I'm confident it will be the only love story—fact or fiction—in which I will be a major player. Other accounts may find me worth attention. But not for another love story. Though I am grateful to have been able to play what I hope was a helpful role in the world, I am equally grateful to Oscar. Only his persistence could have softened my single focus enough so I, too, could have a love story as part of my story.

My European and African friends had warned me I would find American boys entertaining but puzzling, a curious mixture of naïve and predatory. Unless you were on your guard, they counseled, you could be fooled into thinking their seeming innocence was authentic, beguiling. Until you discovered—usually painfully—it was a pose. A tactic.

Women around the world painted a portrait of American men in those days as an impulsive, largely unconscious breeder who viewed gender relationships as a Manichean struggle between male sexual appetite and female conniving, playing against that manic sex drive as a means to control men.

Such a male vision, of dominance as the prevailing human drive. And the myth adopted by many western leaders, most male, especially Americans.

American boys in those days were conditioned from an early age to keep their instruments of power—whether nuclear weapon or penis—lightly holstered. Many, especially those who rose to the top, never outgrew that.

Oscar largely resisted that male stereotype, but he was still an American male of his generation. At first it was as if he regarded our sex as a prize he didn't deserve. I found that puzzling until I came to understand that was how he understood his place in the world. *Invited by grace*, is how he put it, heavily shaped by his father whose influence he thought—mistakenly—he had left long behind. As his sense of undeserving began to give way he relaxed more and became a bed partner with animal energy. I could see a whole new world opening to him. He had a voracious appetite for living life, and eventually he trusted me—and himself—enough to give it full rein. That combination, passionate and sensitive—unlike African men, with plenty of the first and too little of the second—drew me to him and finally led me to trust him.

And love him.

I don't know that he ever was able to fully digest how deep that trust of him went in me. He could never fully shake the Yankee Puritan suspicion of his own motives, and that made him hang back, assuming he had no legitimate right to what he wanted.

His romantic illusion that I would become so absorbed by our love that it would eclipse everything else in my life was very American and very male. I know that's why he kept trying to maneuver me into telling him I loved him, to say the actual words. He believed that if I did that it would break through my determination to stay with my vocation.

Truth is, I did love him. He had a stronger hold on me that any man before or since. I was sorry I never felt I could tell him that in the words he wanted so much to hear. I feared if I did it would only stir up false hope.

This word *vocation*—from Latin, *vocare*, to call—is not much heard anymore. It refers to the idea that we have a purpose, and we turn away from it at the peril of our very soul.

In this post-religious world this can seem quaint. Almost no one any longer believes in a soul or a god who calls us like this. But it isn't necessary to believe in God to believe you have a purpose. I did, from an early age.

Oscar was brought up in a religious household but he never had this sense. Except—he kept insisting—about me. Likely one difference between American and Zimbabwean was that I regarded a purely personal vocation as narcissistic. I think he sometimes envied my vocation and maybe sometimes I envied his. But that difference meant he could never quite understand what he was asking of me.

How could he? His mother—a strong, successful woman—had designed her career so it left her free to provide dinner, maintain an orderly home, and warm his father's bed. To appearances she put his needs ahead of her own. Or she was clever enough to make it appear that way to Oscar and his father. When I saw how feared she was in the savage real estate world of New York City and learned the cost of their apartment and Oscar's school tuitions, I understood that she was—beneath that facade—an American Amazon. She was one of the few women who ever intimidated me. I knew she read me with dead-on accuracy. She understood that I would break the heart of her son, whom she protected like a feral female.

Oscar never knew what it cost his mother to organize her life for him and his father. And she meant him not to.

He assumed I could do the same for him—if only I would. He believed my willingness was the measure of how much I loved him. He saw a woman putting her men first as being built into the natural order.

Though I truly *did* (still do) love Oscar I never seriously considered giving up my vocation for him. I think Oscar saw why after his first few months in Zimbabwe. Perhaps it would have seemed unmanly, un-American, not to keep working to wear the woman down, make his agenda hers.

Am I being too hard on American men of those days? Perhaps.

As my father had feared, Wharton did shake some of my clarity about our nation's agenda. He was right that our history and culture steered us toward a collectivist, socialist government model.

But not only were the Wharton professors persuasive about the dynamic energy the so-called free market unleashed, but the reality was that the IMF was dominated by people with that view. And we desperately needed that loan.

Underlying all the Wharton courses was the old Reagan ethic: negotiate, compromise, disarm, but always verify. As fellow MBA students put it, "Never give a sucker an even break." To American power brokers, shaped by their business and law schools, suckers were whomever was on the other side of the table. In those days the Darwinian eat-or-be-eaten was a piece of American business ethic was still imbedded deep in western prejudice.

Wharton and Oscar's efforts to wean me from my life plan were valuable tutors when I found myself again and again in the eye of storms that threatened to scuttle the progress we were making inch by inch. Though I was fortunate to enjoy strong support—even from the Ndebele western part of the country—the old rivalries didn't just disappear. And when I faced a determined rival, who believed he could wear down a woman with his persistence, I picture Oscar coming around for another try. I finally learned that arguing my case fell on deaf ears.

What made the point was a silent stare. *You would turn away from love this powerful, for any reason?* he would ask, again, as if such a thing had never really seemed a serious possibility before.Once I had my say, I simply sat in stony silence, staring at Oscar. It worked with my political rivals as well.

Not to pretend to you that I felt confident holding my ground. Odd historical circumstance left me the first woman president among those old African chiefs. I had watched men playing cards, negotiating treaties, how they will bluff even under the most brittle circumstances. As the stakes grow breathtakingly higher they begin to regard it is a game of chicken, a test of their manhood. Who will swerve first?

Those men had not dealt with enough women in tight spots to know that women are likely to get to their bedrock, final position more quickly than men. And stay with it.

I have kept an editor's print of Oscar's story in my satchel. When I was up to my eyeballs with the cynicism, the lying, the posturing,—the necessities required for governing a troubled nation and presenting a good face to the IMF—I would sometimes let his book fall open to any page.

And for a moment I would relax, remembering those lovely days with that thoroughly decent American man.

It was reassuring to remember there had been another dimension to my life. Despite what the dark events in Zimbabwe required of me, I *had* lived for a moment in the light. Oscar remains my hedge against self-recrimination.

Oscar's altogether admirable effort to tell this story these decades later (With his pants zipped!) is sweet. It's so like Oscar, and those days. I treasure the leather-bound special edition of the book Oscar had made for me and so movingly inscribed. It is a welcome reminder—despite the horror of my father's end—of a time and a man I now look back on with the deepest pleasure and gratitude.

I like to think it all came out as it should have. Having met Allison a few times I'm sure she was a better life companion for him than I could ever have been.

I wonder about Oscar's understanding of the changing place of women? Allison didn't quite put her life on hold the way Oscar's mother had. She was every inch her own woman. But she made compromises for him and their children I never could have.

I watched my father's patriotism narrow into obsession. That narrowness—perhaps required initially—eventually left him and Zimbabwe vulnerable. The Americans and British scorned him as he became captive to the trappings of high office the British colonialists had enjoyed; the great houses, bullet-proof Mercedes (at least it wasn't a Rolls), ermine academic hood, throne. ***See,*** they said, ***he's no reformer, just a typical African despot. He doesn't care about his impoverished people. He only wants to feather his own nest.***

Those hypocrites were half correct. My father did love the perks of high office. As I did, no doubt more than was healthy.

But all that was not merely feeding his personal appetites. It also signaled our people (and Father himself) that we had finally wrested the royal prerogatives from our former masters. Now *we* had them.

Despite his seemingly impenetrable shell, his ruthlessness in dealing with his political enemies and his unwillingness to listen to anyone about moderating his programs—taking the big, prosperous white farms and pressuring white businesses to become majority owned by Africans—he *did* feel the sting of international opinion. Ironically, the harsh criticism from England (and worst of all being snubbed by the Royal Family) weighed on him maybe the most. He hid that from everyone but me. Me, and finally, oddly enough, Oscar. Ironic how much he came to trust Oscar—from the American ruling class—more than he trusted his closest Zimbabwe colleagues.

And though he felt he must not show it publicly for fear of looking weak, he lost sleep many nights over the desperate poverty of our people. Mostly forgotten now is that before things went sour he instituted universal education for Zimbabwe (girls as well as boys) and by the mid-eighties we had the highest literacy rate in southern Africa.

Looking back, I suppose most would say his confiscation of the white farms and businesses was a terrible mistake. If you measure it by its economic impact—as the western world measured everything then—there's no denying it destroyed the old economy and gave comfort to his enemies' accusations that he was interested only in his own power and cared nothing for our poorest people or the rule of law.

But he believed that so long as all the most productive farms and wealthiest businesses were in the hands of the old Rhodesians, the revolution was incomplete. He saw too late that letting his own cronies—who had no ability or interest in farming or business sense—seize the farms and businesses was going to result in disaster. In the beginning it was his way of ensuring their political support. When he finally saw where it was leading, his pride prevented him from backtracking.

He and I argued—sometimes angrily—over many a dinner about this. By and large I have come around to his view. Despite the terrible economic consequences, I think he did what had to be done. Given our cruel colonial past, there was no way the catastrophic events that turned our country into an international pariah could have been avoided. Perhaps it could have been done less violently. But it had to be done. I was the only person who knew how much he suffered over that. And when I could no longer bear those painful dinner arguments I turned to Oscar. I learned later, to my surprise, that Dad talked with Oscar about it too.

It was occupying Father's chair, through the most painful circumstance of my life, that led me to understand his decisions in ways I wish I'd never had to.

I am so grateful that our country seems to be continuing her gradual return to prosperity.

Oscar! Once a year or so I would hear from him on that spy phone they gave him back then. I would have thought he'd have returned that little phone. The blue green screen would light up and a text message appear:

Those guys in Zimbabwe may have doubted you could pull it off, Maudie, but I never did. You are that lioness watching the warrior males duke it out as if they were fighting for the throne. While you watch from the throne from which you will never be unseated.

Hang tough, Babe. I'll be rooting for you.

More than all the support and encouragement I received from world leaders, more than all the hyped media coverage lionizing me, those text messages from Oscar gave me heart. I never responded. I had disrupted his life enough. And knowing Oscar, he might have interpreted anything from me as wish to rekindle our love affair. I can't say that wasn't a tempting thought. But he was happily married to that wonderful Allison and I was up to my eyeballs in trouble.

By the time I was able to extricate myself from the seats of power, I was so ready to disappear.

Thanks to cyber communication I was able to come to this lovely farm in eastern Zimbabwe. It is a farm my father's family confiscated from Ian Smith's clan, people he had hated since colonial days. From this happy place I was able to carry on the remainder of my term as president of Zimbabwe, now long behind me. I expect to live out my days here where, I hasten to add, black Zimbabweans are growing and processing the finest tobacco in the world. So people can die of lung cancer rather than radiation poisoning.

Many of the same issues remain that my father and I both faced as leaders of a small, rural, agricultural country, mired in generations of tribal conflict and sorely lacking in capital development. Gradually a few western business men (and women), and even some young farmers, have emigrated here and have mostly been welcomed.

Our people are beginning to catch up to the production levels of the old white farmers. I get a perverse pleasure in the growing prosperity of the people working my tobacco farm. I tell them we export our product to China where smoking is still part of the culture, and where there are too many people.

The way my rise to power was portrayed appealed to people and helped wipe our slate clean with most of the world that had condemned my father's heavy handedness. I was not above using my new reputation for savvy and toughness—not entirely deserved, but neither entirely undeserved—to negotiate business deals that finally gave Zimbabwe a shot at a decent future. Amazing how a little prosperity can push generations of tribal and ethnic bitterness into the background. Had not Cecil Rhodes carved boundaries that suited his interests, Shona and Ndebele would have never considered themselves fellow countrymen. Now they conduct business together in pin-stripe suits in high-rise offices in Harare and Bulawayo.

I no longer watch the CNN reruns of those terrifying moments when it looked as the wheels might come off in Zimbabwe.

I prefer watching the brilliant African sunset over the fields from my veranda.

And I occasionally pull out that rabbit-eared leather volume that Oscar sent me—the one you just read.

Oscar's story, what a story!

*   *   *

OSCAR'S BOOK

Maudie still gets quite a lot of press, even all these years after she stepped down from being president of Zimbabwe. I read that she's become something of a recluse on a tobacco farm near the Mozambique border. It's a farm her father confiscated from Ian Smith's heirs during those chaotic days. The Economist says it has become as productive as it was when the white farmer ran it. If you knew Maudie, you'd have expected it to be. The Economist ran a photo of her with the story. She looks old. And beautiful.

I wonder if she ever thinks about me?